P9-CDS-825

Reserved for Murder

Also available by Victoria Gilbert

The Booklover's B&B Mystery
Booked for Death

The Blue Ridge Library Mysteries
A Deadly Edition
Bound for Murder
Past Due for Murder
Shelved Under Murder
A Murder for the Books

Mirror of Immortality Series
Scepter of Fire
Crown of Ice

Reserved for Murder

A BOOKLOVER'S B&B MYSTERY

Victoria Gilbert

NEW YORK

This is a work of fiction. All of the names, characters, organizations, places, and events portrayed in this novel are either products of the author's imagination or are used fictitiously. Any resemblance to real or actual events, locales, or persons, living or dead, is entirely coincidental.

Published in the United States by Crooked Lane Books, an imprint of The Quick Brown Fox & Company LLC.

Crooked Lane Books and its logo are trademarks of The Quick Brown Fox & Company LLC.

Library of Congress Catalog-in-Publication data available upon request.

ISBN (hardcover): 978-1-64385-590-5
ISBN (ebook): 978-1-64385-591-2

Cover illustration by Ben Perini

Printed in the United States.

www.crookedlanebooks.com

Crooked Lane Books
34 West 27th St., 10th Floor
New York, NY 10001

First Edition: June 2021

10 9 8 7 6 5 4 3 2 1

Dedicated, with sincere gratitude,
to my readers

"Ah, how good it is to be among
people who are reading."
–Rainer Maria Rilke

Chapter One

When your neighbor is a retired spy, it's easy to imagine innumerable dangers haunting the house next door.

This was one reason why the sight of the stranger in Ellen Montgomery's garden startled me into dropping my garden shears. Scooping up the clippers and shoving them into the pocket of my loose cotton slacks, I scurried under the shade of an oak tree and glanced at my watch. It was four o'clock in the afternoon, a time that, combined with his attire, made the unknown man's appearance in Ellen's garden particularly odd. Ellen tended to reserve her afternoons for reading or naps, not visitors. The stranger's nylon shorts, worn running shoes, and damp T-shirt, coupled with the perspiration glistening on his arms, led me to believe he'd just returned from a jog. That also wasn't a typical activity for Ellen's usual guests.

I tapped my foot against one of the old tree's exposed roots as I contemplated this unusual situation. If I hadn't known better, I'd have assumed the stranger was staying at Ellen's elegant three-story Victorian home. Which would've been a first. While she hosted numerous luncheons and dinner parties, Ellen never allowed anyone to stay overnight.

"Comes from my need to be cautious most of my life, I suppose," she'd told me when I'd once questioned this behavior. "I don't like other people lurking about when I'm sleeping." Which made sense considering the precautions she'd had to take in the past, when her career as a film and TV location scout had served as a cover for more clandestine activities.

All of which made the sight of a random visitor in her garden both intriguing and concerning. I narrowed my eyes as I examined the stranger. On the surface there was certainly nothing exceptional about the man. His height, build, and facial features were undistinguished. In fact, the only distinctive thing about him was his curly light brown hair, which was gilded with highlights by the sun.

I bet his hair was blond when he was a child, I thought, as the stranger casually sipped from his reusable plastic water bottle. He never glanced my way. That was probably for the best, since I was blatantly staring at him over the fence that separated Ellen's garden from mine.

Dabbing the perspiration from my upper lip with a crumpled tissue, I considered strolling over and introducing myself. But a voice in my head cautioned me against this. Ellen undoubtedly still had secrets she needed to keep.

I picked up my basket of cut flowers and exited the garden, determined not to glance toward the stranger again. But as I unlatched the garden gate, a prickling sensation danced over my forearms, and I turned my head slightly to catch the man staring at me. His eyes were hidden behind dark sunglasses, but I could tell from the set of his mouth and jaw that he was examining me as intently as I had previously studied him.

Keep walking, I thought. *Ellen will introduce him if he's someone she actually wants you to know.*

Which, considering her past, might not be the case.

I was so absorbed by these thoughts that I almost walked into one of my guests, who was crossing the flagstone patio that separated the garden from the back entrance to Chapters, the literary-themed B and B I'd inherited from my great-aunt, Isabella Harrington.

"What a lovely backyard." A tall, curvaceous woman slipped off the large sunglasses that masked her face and offered me a smile. "Hello, I'm Amanda Nobel. Your housekeeper, who just signed us in, told me I could find you outside."

I studied the woman for a moment, admiring the casual elegance of her turquoise silk blouse and white linen slacks. Amanda Nobel, bestselling author of a book series that had been turned into a hit television show, possessed a shining mane of blonde hair and skin highlighted by a light tan. She was every bit as beautiful as her promotional photos.

No photoshop needed. I held out my hand. "Welcome. I'm sorry I wasn't inside to greet you when you arrived. I'm afraid I lost track of time. I was just cutting a few flowers for the house." I set down my basket and held out my hand. "I'm your hostess, Charlotte Reed, but feel free to just call me Charlotte. We don't stand on ceremony here."

Although her bio claimed Amanda Nobel was thirty-eight, she could easily pass for a woman in her late twenties. *Unlike me,* I thought, my smile tightening as I recalled a recent glance in the mirror and the subsequent glimpse of wrinkles fanning out from the corners of my eyes.

Instead of shaking my hand, Amanda Nobel clasped it for a moment. "Nice to meet you, Charlotte, and do call me Amanda. Ms. Nobel sounds like you're addressing my mother." Her golden lashes fluttered over sky-blue eyes. "I'm so grateful to you for providing a place for me to relax. A little break from my book tour is just what I need. It's been nonstop travel, jaunting from city to city, for a solid month." She stared past me, obviously taking in the garden. "And I can see why you'd lose track of time out here. It's lovely."

I motioned toward the picket fence. "Of course, you're welcome to enjoy the garden while you're staying at Chapters. There are some benches shaded by the trees in the back, which makes it a little cooler than the patio. That can be especially helpful in this July heat." As my gaze swept over the area, I noticed that the stranger had disappeared, probably back inside Ellen's house. "I hope Alicia got you comfortably settled?"

"Oh yes, she even helped carry the luggage up to our rooms. Which are wonderful. All those books!" Amanda tilted her head and looked me over. "I must also thank you for putting me in the suite with the mystery books and décor. Most people would've chosen the romance-themed suite for me, just because of my novels. Frankly, I appreciate something different."

"I assumed you would've already read a lot of the romance titles," I replied. "Besides, you're here to get away from your regular life, right?"

"Absolutely." Amanda pursed her perfectly tinted lips. "I also appreciate being able to arrive before the other guests. It's nice to be settled in before I have to greet any fans."

"I thought that might be the case, so I told them check-in was a little later." I glanced at my watch. "They should be arriving any time now, so if you want to enjoy the garden before they show up, please do. I'm afraid I must leave you, though. I need to take these flowers inside."

"Trust me, I don't mind a little time on my own. I rarely have that when I'm on tour." A pained expression tightened Amanda's face. "Seriously, I'm so thankful to you for agreeing to my terms. I know it's inconvenient to keep my identity a secret, but you see, my fans . . ."

"Love you," said a man crossing the patio to join us. "You should be grateful for that," he added, shooting Amanda a sharp look.

"I am, of course." A shadow flitted over Amanda's lovely face. "It's just . . . Well, sometimes their enthusiasm is a little wearing."

"We're happy to offer you a brief respite." I extended a hand to the man, who I assumed was the publicity and marketing manager running Amanda's book tour. "Mr. Lott? Welcome to Chapters."

"Please, call me Tony," the man said, his hazel eyes assessing me as he gave my hand a quick shake.

I realized I'd probably betrayed my surprise and adjusted my expression. Tony Lott, who was clutching a paperback book in one hand, was bald and stocky. Shorter than either me or his boss, he didn't match the mental image I'd created from speaking to him on the phone.

You know what happens when you make assumptions. The truth was, Tony Lott looked nothing like my stereotyped image of a publisher's representative. When he'd told me he was a publicist and marketing manager over the phone, I'd imaged a tall, reedy fellow in tweeds, not a body-builder whose muscular arms bulged against the gleaming white sleeves of his polo shirt. Instead of the expected pressed trousers and dress shoes, he was wearing olive cargo shorts with sandals.

"Have we arrived before the fans?" The gaze Tony swept over me was as dismissive as it was haughty.

So maybe not entirely unlike the mental image I formed based on our phone conversations . . .

"Yes, I told them check-in was a little later," I said.

"That was thoughtful, don't you agree, Tony?" Amanda tossed her wavy hair behind her shoulders. "I know I appreciate the chance to rest and freshen up before I have to entertain anyone."

Tony cast Amanda a look of exasperation. "You're not really required to entertain them, you know. I realize you'd prefer to escape all your fans this week, except during tomorrow's scheduled event, but at least only three are staying here. And they've all sworn to keep your presence in town a secret."

Amanda frowned. "I'm not sure they will though."

Turning to me, Tony offered a smile that didn't quite reach his eyes. "As I mentioned on the phone, the three fans who'll be staying here won a contest sponsored by my employer, Amanda's publisher. They get to spend some one-on-one time with their favorite author, as well as enjoy a vacation in Beaufort, all expenses paid. But to protect Amanda's privacy, they were required to keep her lodging arrangements a secret from the public. Well, mainly from her fans. No comments or photos on social media and that sort of thing. Of course, Amanda won't be locked in the B and B while she's here, but we don't want her more rabid fans stalking her every move."

Amanda tapped her sunglasses against one palm. "That's just it. I'm not convinced they'll honor that promise."

"They signed a contract. Which includes penalties if they share your whereabouts on social media or fan sites," Tony said.

Amanda cast me an apologetic smile. "I guess that's not a benefit for you, in terms of publicity, is it, Charlotte? I'm doing the meet-and-greet here, sponsored by your friend Julie Rivera's bookstore, but I do hope to otherwise remain incognito. Most of my fans who'll show up tomorrow will think I just came into Beaufort for the day. That's the only event listed on my official appearance calendar and my publisher's website. Which suits my plans, but doesn't really give Chapters much exposure. However, I'm happy to write a testimonial you can use once I'm gone."

"That will be all the promotion I need," I said.

"Oh, I almost forgot—I have a little gift for you." Tony handed me the paperback. "It's an ARC, an advanced reader copy of Amanda's upcoming book. Signed, of course."

"Thank you very much." As I offered both Tony and Amanda a smile, I observed Amanda's pained expression and wondered why she didn't appear pleased.

Tony didn't seem to notice. He laid a hand on Amanda's arm. "Can we head inside now? Don't forget we have a few business matters to discuss. I prefer to do that in the comfort of air conditioning."

"Oh, very well." Amanda spat out the words as she yanked her arm free of Tony's grip. She turned to address me, softening her tone. "I suppose I must save the garden exploration for another time. See you later, Charlotte."

As I nodded and smiled at both of my guests, I noticed that the smile Tony Lott flashed in response was about as warm as the Bogue Sound in January.

I waited until Amanda and Tony had entered Chapters before I tucked the paperback under my arm and picked up my basket of flowers. Sympathizing with Amanda's desire for peace and quiet, I longed to stay outside for a few more minutes myself, but knew I needed to head into the B and B, especially since we were expecting three more guests shortly. I couldn't dump all the check-ins on Alicia. *Not if I want to look forward to a pleasant evening,* I thought, with a wry smile.

But before I could cross the patio to reach the back-porch door, I was stopped by a cheerful "hello" accompanied by a series of sharp yips.

I turned to see Ellen, who'd obviously just returned from taking her Yorkshire terrier, Shandy, for a walk. "Hey there, good to see you," I said, as I crossed to the gate that led into her backyard. "I know it's been a while since we had a good chat, and we definitely need to catch up. But unfortunately, I can't really talk right now."

"I know. You have guests showing up today." Ellen pushed her wide-brimmed straw hat away from her face, allowing it to dangle from its scarlet ribbons. A spry seventy-six-year-old whose blue eyes shone with intelligence, she mirrored her vibrant personality in her dramatic fashion sense, evidenced by the fuchsia dye streaking her white hair. "Amanda Nobel and some of her fans, if I'm not mistaken."

"How did you . . ." I shook my head. "Never mind. I should've known you'd uncover that little secret."

Ellen's eyes twinkled. "I have my ways. But I promise to stay mum about her visit, especially since I suspect she wants to remain incognito. Or at least that's what I deduced from her website. She has no public events scheduled, except for that 'meet the author' party Julie is throwing here tomorrow, even though I know you've planned some private gatherings, like our book club's discussion Monday evening." Ellen leaned down to scoop up a restless Shandy, who was straining against his leash. She cradled him against her breast before casting me a skeptical smile. "I can understand not wanting to tell the whole world where she's staying for the week, but I'd think it would be tough to keep that information quiet with some of her fans also staying at Chapters."

I set down my flower basket and adjusted the paperback, which was slipping out from under my armpit. "They apparently had to sign nondisclosure agreements. Can you imagine?"

"No, but then, I'm not famous. Not that I blame the woman for wanting to hide out for a few days. I imagine it can be exhausting to be 'on' all the time." Ellen absently stroked Shandy's silky fur as she looked me over. "Have you read her books?"

"I hadn't," I admitted. "I actually just finished the first in the series, and only because I thought I should know a little more about her work before co-hosting the author meet-and-greet."

"And?"

"And it's not my thing, but I can see why others really love the books." I snapped a dead bloom off of one of the climbing roses that draped the fence. "Very much a romance, with this eighteenth-century pirate who's mysteriously sent back and forth through time. Of course, he eventually meets a modern woman and they fall in love." I shrugged. "I mean, there's more to it than that. Lots of swashbuckling adventure and a villain who's also able to travel through time, but that's the gist."

"Sounds like a good beach read," Ellen said.

"Definitely perfect for that. And it is written pretty well. The English teacher in me can't fault Ms. Nobel on her writing."

Ellen glanced at her watch. "Well, as you say, you need to get to work. And I'd better go inside and get this pup some water." She hesitated a moment, her hand resting on the latch, before pushing her backyard gate open. "I'm hosting company this week as well. Family, which is not quite as demanding as your visitors will be, I expect." She closed the gate and unhooked his leash to set Shandy down in the grass before turning to face me again.

"Oh?" As I dead-headed another rose blossom, I examined her expression for any trace of guile. As usual, it was impossible to determine if she was telling the truth, which I suppose was a skill she'd perfected working for U.S. intelligence.

"Yes, his name is Gavin Howard. My first cousin's boy. Of course, he's not really a boy. He's in his early forties, like you. But when you're as old as I am, that seems young."

"You've never mentioned anything about your relatives before," I said, hoping my voice didn't betray my surprise. A family connection might explain Ellen allowing someone to stay at her house, despite claims that she hated such intrusions. But I couldn't shake the feeling that something was not quite right with this scenario. Given the tension deepening the lines that bracketed Ellen's mouth, and her former protestations about any overnight visitors, it still felt off.

But, I reminded myself, *you only moved to Beaufort a couple of years ago. Perhaps Ellen hosting overnight visitors is simply a rare occurrence, not an impossible one. You shouldn't read too much into it.*

I shifted the paperback ARC under my other arm and picked up my flower basket. "You'll have to introduce me. I'm curious to meet any relative of yours."

Ellen arched her pale brows. "To see if they're just as eccentric?"

I smiled. "No, just as interesting. But don't let me keep you. Or Shandy," I added. The terrier stared at me, his tongue lolling from the side of his mouth as he audibly panted. "He does look a little parched. Anyway, I should check on some last-minute details before the rest of my guests arrive."

"See you later, then," Ellen said, giving me a little wave before striding toward her back door, Shandy trotting at her heels.

Before heading inside myself, I surveyed the newly swept patio and my picket-fence-enclosed cottage garden. Everything looked clean and tidy and ready for company. *Close enough for government work anyway,* I thought, as I strolled toward Chapters's back porch.

Ironic, given Ellen's former occupation.

I allowed the flower basket to swing from my forearm as I climbed the few concrete steps that led to the porch's screened door, still mulling over my elderly neighbor's past.

Ellen might have been a government employee, but I doubted she'd ever followed the maxim of doing the minimum, as that old adage implied. *She couldn't have been nonchalant or sloppy in her work,* I thought, smiling grimly as I pushed open the door. *Not if she wanted to escape unfortunate consequences.*

Chapter Two

I finished the flower arrangements just in time to grab a shower and change into a pair of black linen slacks and a white silk top, attire I felt was more appropriate for greeting guests. Of course, Amanda and Tony had met me in my gardening clothes, but I figured that was a trade-off for allowing them to arrive early.

After welcoming the other guests—three women ranging in age from late twenties to early forties who were so busy chatting that they barely acknowledged me—I decided to check on the preparations for the evening's cocktail party.

"Is that you, Charlotte?" called out Alicia Simpson, Chapters's live-in housekeeper and cook.

"Yes, just settled the other guests in their rooms," I replied, allowing my gaze to wander as I entered my expansive kitchen.

Although the original portion of Chapters had been built as a private home in the early eighteenth century, it had been extensively renovated over the years, including a nineteenth-century addition that housed extra bedrooms, bathrooms, and a kitchen. Upgrading the kitchen to a professional standard was the last major renovation, done just before the death of my great-aunt Isabella Harrington. Fortunately, Isabella, who'd bequeathed the bed-and-breakfast to me three years ago, had made sure the new kitchen retained the historic style of the original home. White cabinets, some sporting mullioned glass fronts, were fitted with black iron hardware that wouldn't have looked out of place in a Revolutionary War–era home. The ceiling soared up to twelve feet, allowing tall windows to be inset into one pearl-gray wall. On a bright day, the light spilling through the windows danced across the white subway tile, dark gray soapstone counters, and stainless-steel appliances. Off to one side, French doors led to a large pantry that housed metal shelving, a standing freezer, and our commercial-grade dishwasher.

Alicia turned away from one of the counters to face me. "Guess those are the fans, then? I greeted the early birds, but I expect you know that, since I saw you chatting with them outside."

"Thanks again for doing that. I really wanted to create a fresh arrangement for tonight's cocktail party, and I'm afraid time got away from me." I examined Alicia, surprised to observe a bright glint in her dark eyes. It seemed she was interested in this particular group of guests, which wasn't always the case. Sometimes I thought she'd prefer to have Chapters to herself, although that was obviously not financially possible.

A short, plump woman in her early sixties, Alicia had worked for my great-aunt for many years before I had inherited Chapters. Pete and Sandy Nelson, who owned the Dancing Dolphin café in Beaufort, always claimed I'd inherited Alicia along with the B and B. I suppose that was true, in a way, although it wasn't a sentiment I liked to repeat out loud. Although I admitted that Alicia was integral to the success of Chapters, she was a person, not some object my great-aunt could pass down, as she had the extensive collection of books that filled Chapters's library and guest rooms.

"Almost done with the hors d'oeuvres." Alicia waved a paring knife in the direction of several colorful platters of food. "Tried to add in a little more flair than usual. It's not often we host such a famous author."

"I appreciate the extra effort. It is rather a coup for Chapters," I said, as Alicia laid down her knife and wiped her hands on the apron covering her black cotton dress. "We have Julie to thank for that, you know. She orchestrated all the arrangements once Ms. Nobel agreed to participate in an event hosted by Bookwaves."

"All I can say is it's a nice change. Amanda Nobel is someone I'd actually like to talk to." Alicia's dark brown eyes narrowed. "Although it's strange she'd allow those fans to stay here too, since she wants to keep her presence in Beaufort a secret. Seems like that's a perfect recipe for the news spilling out to everyone and their cousins."

"Tony Lott, the man managing the tour, said these fans had won some sort of contest put on by the publisher. Getting to stay at the same B and B as their idol was their prize. And it's not like we have to keep Ms. Nobel's presence an absolute secret. We just don't want to broadcast that she's staying here for a week, especially to her fans who are attending the event tomorrow." I examined Alicia with interest. "You seem more than usually pleased that Ms. Nobel is staying at Chapters. Have you read her books?"

Alicia tucked a couple of silver-streaked black curls up under the band of her hairnet. "Well, sure. Hasn't everyone?"

"Not me. I just finished the first one, and that was mainly so I'd have some context when I talked to her."

Alicia snorted. "What? Not highbrow enough for you? I know you were an English teacher before coming to Beaufort, but I didn't realize you were that picky about books."

"I'm not." Hearing the sharp edge to my tone, I offered Alicia an apologetic smile. "It's just that I never got around to reading her books when they first came out. Now there are so many, and they're each so long . . . Honestly, I just haven't felt like I had the time to commit to the series."

"I like them. Good escape from real life, if you know what I mean. Who doesn't enjoy an exciting tale about a time-traveling pirate, especially one as hot as that Adrian character? But, to be perfectly honest"—Alicia cast me a knowing look—"I like the TV show better."

"Because you can actually watch the sexy pirate in action?" I asked, with a lift of my eyebrows. I'd only seen snippets of the popular series but had to admit that the cast was exceptionally good-looking, especially the actor who played the time-traveling pirate, Adrian Ashford.

"Doesn't hurt," Alicia said, before turning back to the cutting board and vigorously slicing a green pepper. "But don't worry. I've followed orders. Not even a whisper to anyone that Amanda Nobel is staying at Chapters. Not that my family and friends are the type to stalk an author, but I know how word can get around."

"Thank you. It was her only special request. Apparently, she's in the middle of a grueling nationwide book tour. She's looking for somewhere quiet to rest for a week between engagements."

"Beaufort is pretty laid back, but I expect her fans will pack that event tomorrow."

"Which is fine, since that's part of her public tour schedule. It's just this week's other events that are limited to our guests and the local book club. It's also why I asked Damian to help with the food prep for the reception," I said, not surprised when Alicia's lips visibly tightened. She wasn't particularly fond of the young freelance chef I sometimes hired for special events. "But tomorrow's meet-and-greet is on Ms. Nobel's appearance calendar, so she expects people to show up. That's different than telling everyone she's actually staying in Beaufort for the week, rather than just driving in for one special event."

"I reckon." Alicia's knife expertly dissected a red pepper. "Must be quite an achievement for Julie Rivera, getting Amanda Nobel to do anything associated with her little shop."

I nodded, remembering how ecstatic Julie had been when Amanda Nobel had agreed to appear at an event sponsored by an indie bookstore in a small town. Even though Julie had applied to be part of the nationwide tour, she'd never expected to be chosen. "She thinks it may have something to do with the fact that Ms. Nobel's series is based around a pirate, and Beaufort does have a strong connection to pirate history." I shrugged. "It was actually Julie who suggested that Ms. Nobel and the others stay at Chapters. Since we didn't have any other events scheduled for this week, it worked out." I tapped my temple with one finger. "And I did think to ask a little more than usual for the rooms, especially since we agreed to keep Ms. Nobel's location under wraps."

Alicia glanced over her shoulder. "Smart thinking. See, you're learning."

Not able to come up with an appropriate response to that jibe, I simply made a noncommittal noise before heading into the pantry.

* * *

After ensuring that the wine, beer, and liquor supplies were in order for the cocktail party, I wandered back out into the hall, thinking I should look over the set-up in the front parlor, which functioned as a music room as well as a space for indoor receptions.

But before I could reach the parlor, voices drew me to the library.

The room, its walls covered with cabinets and shelves, held the largest portion of Isabella's extensive book collection. I often led book discussions or related events there, but while it was a large library for a personal home, the space couldn't accommodate a crowd. Which was why Saturday's event was being held outside—the author talk and question and answer segment on the front lawn, and the reception on the back patio.

As I stepped into the library, I noticed that three of the library chairs had been pulled around to form a semicircular seating arrangement on the Persian rug that covered the middle of the floor. With their focus on their own conversation, the three seated women didn't notice me. I tugged down the hem of my blouse as I paused in the doorway, examining them.

They were a study in contrasts. The oldest of the group, Lisette Bradford, was the forty-year-old head of a major Amanda Nobel fan club. Or so she'd informed me when she'd checked in. Tall and thin, Lisette wore her light brown hair in a pixie cut that accentuated the hollows of her face. Her glasses, with their round lenses and vivid purple frames, added to this effect.

The other two women were both younger. Harper Gregg, who was in her late twenties, had the slender but muscular build of a gymnast, black hair that spilled like a silky veil to her waist, and light eyes. Thirty-something Molly Zeleski was Harper's opposite—her figure was all soft curves, her eyes a vibrant brown, and her frizzy blonde hair cut in a shoulder-length bob.

"Well, you know Tony isn't really Amanda's choice for a companion," Molly said, her blonde curls bouncing as she tossed her head. "He works for her publisher in publicity or something and was assigned to manage the tour."

"You mean, to manage Amanda," Lisette said, with a lift of her penciled eyebrows.

Molly grimaced. "That's not very nice."

"Accurate, though. He has his work cut out for him. Amanda isn't always the easiest person to be around, from what I've seen," Lisette said.

"You've met her in person before?" Harper gripped the wooden arms of her chair.

"Of course, as part of the . . ." Lisette paused, cutting off whatever she'd started to say. "At events. As the head of her biggest fan club, that's to be expected." Lisette's knowing smile and smug tone were grating, even to me.

The other two women shared a look, betraying that they were as unified in their dislike for Lisette Bradford as they were in their love for Amanda Nobel's books.

I cleared my throat, loudly. "Hello there. I hope you found your rooms to be satisfactory."

"Oh, hello, Ms. Reed. And yes, definitely." Harper Gregg slid around in her chair to look at me. "I love the décor in the Romance Suite, and of course all those books on the shelves are a great bonus."

"Please, call me Charlotte. And I hope you don't mind that you have to share with Ms. Zeleski. We only have so many rooms, and of course Ms. Nobel and Mr. Lott had to have separate accommodations. There is the carriage house, but I prefer to rent that out to more long-term guests."

"It's fine," Harper said, with a wave of her slender hand. "I plan to use the room mainly for sleeping anyway. Too many other things I want to do during the day." She met my inquisitive gaze with a smile. "You can call me Harper, by the way."

Molly jumped up and circled around to stand behind her chair. "I actually live in Morehead City, which is just a hop and a skip over the bridge from here. So if there's a real problem"—she cast a glance at Harper—"I could just sleep at home and drive in each day."

Harper combed her fingers through her silky dark hair. "Don't be silly. Part of our prize was getting free lodging. Honestly, I don't mind sharing. Like I said, I'm not planning to hang out in the room much."

As I met her steady gaze, I couldn't help but notice Harper's eyes. Fringed by thick black lashes, they were an unusual shade of pale gray, so light they appeared almost colorless. "I thought it was best to give you two the Romance Suite, which is actually the largest of our guest rooms and has the extra bed."

"That seems incongruous for a romantic suite," Molly said, arching her pale eyebrows.

"Well, the reference is to the books shelved in the room, not that it's designed for honeymooners or anything like that. All of our rooms feature decorations and books that highlight specific genres. Ms. Nobel is in the Mystery Suite, and Mr. Todd has the Classics Room, and so on."

"Children's Room for me," Lisette said, waving her hand through the air. "Very quaint, although not exactly what I'd prefer."

Harper shot her a sharp glance. "Are the books in the rooms part of your great-aunt's original collection as well as the ones in here?"

"Most of them, and you're welcome to examine or read anything, although I do ask that you avoid the top shelves in the library. The rolling ladder is required to reach those, and I prefer that my guests not break any limbs. I'll pull any of them for you if you ask." I hoped my smile conveyed concern rather than a warning. The truth was, I kept the rarest books on the top shelves. Many were fragile, and a few were quite valuable. I preferred to retrieve those rather than allow my guests free access.

Molly gripped the back of her chair with one hand, her hazel eyes widening. "You said Amanda was already here, right? I can't wait to meet her. I've been a fan ever since she published *The Tides of Time* twelve years ago. I was still in college when it came out. I remember missing an important exam because I got so caught up in reading."

Harper nodded. "I was only sixteen. Still in high school, and not really a reader at that point. But then some of my friends introduced me to *Tides* and I became absolutely obsessed."

Lisette rose to her feet with a languid grace that made me wonder if she'd ever been trained as a dancer. "If you'll excuse me, I think I'll head to my room and freshen up before the cocktail party. I also need to check on some fan club business before tomorrow." She pushed her glasses up to the bridge of her narrow nose. "And there's always the writing to manage, too."

"That's seven," Molly muttered, giving me a wink when I cast her a confused look.

"Don't forget the cocktail party starts soon," I said, as Lisette strolled past me. "In the parlor, which is the adjacent room, closer to the front door. We hope to see you then, Ms. Bradford."

"Lisette," she called over her shoulder as she sailed out of the room.

"She just has to mention her own writing at every opportunity, doesn't she?" Molly flopped down in the chair next to Harper. "I kept a count and that was the seventh time just this afternoon."

"Does she write?" I asked, genuinely curious.

Harper shrugged. "She's put out a lot of fan fiction based on Amanda's books."

"It's pretty popular," Molly said. "Although there has been some controversy . . ."

"Let's not bore Ms. Reed—I mean Charlotte—with that." Harper pressed both her hands forward against the air, as if stopping a reversing vehicle. She looked up at me, her pale eyes shadowed by her dark lashes. "It's an old story and, anyway, you know how it is with fandoms. Lots of opinions and egos. And some people just like to stir up trouble."

"I don't, really," I said, with a rueful smile. "I've never really gotten involved with that sort of thing."

Molly bounced up out of her chair again. "What—you've never been a fan of a band or movie star or anything?"

"No. I like many things, and appreciate talent, but . . ." Meeting Molly's intense stare, I instinctively straightened to my full height. "I've never been what I'd consider a true fan. Not enough to join any groups, anyway."

Molly looked me up and down. "Wow, I can't imagine."

"Everyone's different," Harper said mildly. She stood and strolled over to stand beside Molly. "Some people aren't joiners."

"I just don't know what I'd do without the other Amanda Nobel fans." Molly bounced on the balls of her feet. "I mean, I have to share my admiration and love somehow, you know? Otherwise I think I'd just bust."

"It's great you have a way to do that, Molly," I said, not bothering to hide the smile twitching my lips. "I'd hate to see anyone explode, especially here at Chapters."

Molly hesitated for only a moment before offering me a grin. "Yeah, too nice a place for that sort of mess."

An image of another mess, from the year before, flashed through my mind. "I hope so."

Molly shared a conspiratorial look with Harper. "Let's just pray that Lisette's ex-husband doesn't find out she's here. That could be a disaster."

"What do you mean?" I asked, as the hairs stood up on my arms. After the events of the previous summer, the last thing I needed was a marital dispute playing out at Chapters.

Harper laid a hand on Molly's arm. "Don't worry, I'm sure Billy will stay away."

"Billy who?" I asked.

"William Bradford, Lisette's ex-husband. He's a stalker." Molly's fake shiver didn't mitigate the glee in her eyes.

Harper gave Molly's arm a little shake. "Don't over-dramatize, Molly. Honestly, we only know this from stuff Lisette's shared in our online fan group. Who knows how reliable that information is?" She offered me a tight smile. "Don't be too concerned, Charlotte. Lisette likes to be the center of attention, so she probably blew everything out of proportion."

"Okay, but if he shows up here tomorrow, will one of you promise to point him out to me?" I frowned. "That is, if you know what he looks like."

"I do. Looked him up when Lisette was going on and on about his antics. I'll be glad to identify him if he decides to crash the event," Molly said. "And honestly, Harper's right. All we know is what Lisette posted online. It may or may not be true. You know how that goes."

"If you mean how tricky the internet can be, I do. I used to teach high school students. The things some of them would post on social media . . ." I shook my head.

"Trust me, fandoms can be worse." Molly pulled free of Harper's grip on her arm. "Please don't worry too much, Charlotte. I'm sure this will turn out to be a wonderful week, with no problems whatsoever."

I kept a smile plastered on my face until Molly and Harper had left the library, determined not to display the concern their comments about Lisette's ex had raised in my mind.

But as soon as I reached the parlor, I pulled my cell phone from my pocket and called Detective Amber Johnson, my contact at the Beaufort Police Department.

If there was any chance a disgruntled ex-spouse was going to show up at any event held at Chapters, I wanted to make sure the police knew about the possibility ahead of time.

Chapter Three

I spent late Saturday morning alternating between helping Alicia and Damian prepare food and assisting Julie and Scott with setting up chairs on the front lawn and the patio.

"Thank heavens we have good weather." Julie glanced over at me as we straightened a row of folding chairs. "I know you had a contingency plan to hold the event inside, but I think that would've been problematic with the crowd we're expecting." As she adjusted the placement of one chair, her pink scoop-neck top rumpled up, exposing a narrow expanse of her toned midriff. Something her boyfriend, Scott Kepler, seemed to appreciate, if his admiring gaze was any indication.

I smiled, pleased that my friend had found happiness with the charming author. Although Scott, at forty-six, was ten years older than Julie, they were a good match. Julie even got along with his preteen daughter, Abby. Scott lived across the state, in Asheville, North Carolina, but he spent a considerable amount of time in Beaufort due to his interest in the history of pirates and boating in the area.

More and more time these days, I thought with a smile. Julie had experienced some unpleasant romantic affairs in the past. It was nice to see her finally involved in a positive relationship.

"I'm sure Charlotte is grateful not to have everyone tramping through her house." Scott shoved back the damp lock of silver-threaded auburn hair that had fallen into his eyes. "It's already hot, though, and I expect this afternoon is going to be blistering. I hope your guests are prepared for that."

"It's July in North Carolina," Julie said, flipping her long black braid behind one shoulder. "They should know to dress accordingly."

I frowned, considering the implications of this. "Hopefully no one will pass out or anything. Maybe I should've provided some fans."

Julie's dark brown eyes sparkled with good humor. "Never fear—your savvy local bookseller already thought of that. I had some of those basic cardboard fans made, with the Bookwaves logo and info printed on them, of course."

"As a smart entrepreneur would." Scott threw one arm around Julie's shoulders. "She's a clever one, this girl," he added, as he pulled her close to his side.

"Absolutely," I said.

"But rather sticky right now." Julie wrinkled her nose as she slipped free of Scott's embrace. "I'm afraid you don't exactly smell like a rose, either, my love."

Scott pulled his elastic features into a comical mask as he flapped his arms. "That's just my manly aroma."

"Uh-huh." Julie arched her brows. "Well, mister manly, I suggest that we run home and take showers before we greet Ms. Nobel and the other guests." She glanced at her Wonder Woman wristwatch. "We just have time if we leave right now. If that's okay with you, Charlotte."

"Of course. I need to do the same. Anyway, I think everything's ready, or as ready as it can be. Of course, we'll have to drape the author table and carry out the boxes with the copies of Amanda's books, but we should probably do that at the last minute."

"Right. I expect some of the fans will show up early, and I don't want anyone lifting a free copy," Julie said.

I surveyed Chapters's front lawn. The covered front porch served as a backdrop for the event, its white railings draped with author banners featuring Amanda's photo and pictures of all her books. We'd arranged the white folding chairs I'd rented from a party supply store to face the author table, which was placed at the foot of the front steps. I wasn't convinced that we had enough seating to accommodate all the fans, but as Julie had said, there was still room for others to spill out into the rest of the yard and onto the sidewalk. Ellen had even offered the use of her front yard if more space was needed.

Julie's words broke through my musing. "One more thing. I need to remember to bring my change box. Remind me, would you, Scott? I've got my phone set up to do debit and credit sales, but I know some people like to pay cash."

"Sure thing," Scott said. "If you'll remind me that we need to stop by Roger's house when we head back here. I promised him a ride, remember?"

I wiped a bead of sweat from my upper lip, thankful the magnolia and maple that flanked either side of the front lawn offered a little shade. "Roger? Is that someone I should know?"

"Roger Warren," Julie said. "He's a friend of Scott's."

"A colleague, really." Scott cast me a smile. "One of my former professors, to be exact. And one of the main reasons I was drawn to Beaufort when I decided to write a nonfiction book about pirates. He's an expert on the history of this area."

"He's a cool guy. A local, although I don't think he mingles much with anyone except for other history buffs," Julie said. "I had to twist his arm to get him to do a signing at Bookwaves a few years ago. He said no one would be interested in his scholarly writing, but we actually had a pretty big crowd."

Scott shook his head. "Roger always downplays his achievements. I don't know why. He retired from teaching but still writes articles that are crucial to understanding the history of the area."

"I wonder if Ellen knows him," Julie said, with a glance over at my neighbor's house. "I bet she does, since I think they're around the same age. How old is she, anyway? I mean, she's so vibrant and active, it's hard to guess."

"Seventy-six, I believe," I said.

"Roger's a little younger. Late sixties." Scott nudged Julie's arm with his elbow. "So don't go matchmaking, sweetheart."

Julie shrugged. "Who cares about a little age gap, especially at that age? But no, I wasn't planning on trying to hook them up. I just thought they'd enjoy talking to one another, if they haven't already met."

"That's true. Roger enjoys chatting with intelligent women. Which is why he likes you," Scott leaned in to give Julie a kiss on the cheek.

"Thanks, but I doubt I'm on Ellen's level." Julie's smile faded. "And of course I'm glad Roger agreed to attend, but"—she shot me a concerned glance—"I admit I'm a little worried too. I don't know what his reaction will be to Amanda Nobel's books. You know what a stickler he is for historical accuracy, Scott. I'm afraid he might challenge Amanda over some of her details. She doesn't exactly cling too closely to the facts."

Scott waved his hand through the air. "I wouldn't be too concerned. Roger may come off a little pompous sometimes, but he's a gentleman. He isn't going to be rude, especially not to a lady."

"I know, but . . ." Julie bit her lower lip "Oh well, I suppose it'll be fine. It's too late to change anything now, anyway."

"Speaking of late"—Scott tapped his watch—"we'd better get a move on, or that's what we're going to be. And I don't think you want that, since you're the host and interviewer."

"I certainly don't." Julie cast me a bright smile. "You feel good about everything, Charlotte? We'll be back as soon as we can, I promise."

"I think we're all set. Just remember those fans. I'm sure they'll be appreciated."

As soon as Julie and Scott headed back to Julie's apartment to shower and change clothes, I went inside to also grab a shower. After blow drying my short hair and applying a light touch of makeup, I slipped into one of my few dresses—a simple jade-green silk sheath that I wore with silver and peridot jewelry—before heading into the kitchen.

I found Damian in the pantry, collecting bottles of wine and liquor to fill several steel-mesh baskets.

"Working alone? Where's Alicia?"

Damian held up a blue bottle of vodka. "After we finished prepping the food, she decided she'd better shower and change before any guests show up. I plan to run home and do the same but first wanted to pull stuff together to have it ready to carry out later."

"Anything we need? Extra ice or garnishes or anything?"

"No." Damian placed the bottle in the basket close to his feet and straightened to his full height. Although I wasn't short, he was considerably taller. He gazed down at me with a smile. "Everything's all set. You did a great job with the shopping, as usual."

"I make lists," I said, with an answering smile. "Habit. I think it comes from being a teacher all those years."

"It works." Damian flipped a couple of his black dreadlocks behind his shoulders. "I know I look like a mess right now, but don't worry—I plan to pull the dreads back and change into something classier before I man the bar."

"I never worry about that. You always look professional on the job." I gave him a wink. "No matter what Alicia says."

"Alicia's old school. Kind of like my mama. Neither one of them approve of my hair. But you know"—Damian shrugged—"life's too short to worry about stuff like that."

"That's certainly true," I said, my expression sobering. An image of my late husband, Brent, flashed through my mind. He'd died unexpectedly, and much too young.

"Anyway, I think we're all set for this afternoon." Damian carried the basket to one side of the pantry and set it beside the others. "I'll just leave these here until closer to the reception." Adjusting one of the rows of bottles, he glanced over at me, his dark eyes full of curiosity. "I actually know one of your guests. Surprised me to see her staying here, especially since she lives so close."

"You mean Molly Zeleski?" I asked, remembering that she lived in Morehead City.

"Yeah. I knew her as Molly Dent, but I'm sure it's the same person. She looks pretty much the same, even after ten years. She went to my high school."

"Did you know her well?"

"Not really. She was a senior when I was just a seventh-grader." Damian wiped his fingers with the white dish towel he'd tucked in the pocket of his faded jeans. "It was a religious school."

I lifted my eyebrows. "Really?

Damian grinned. "Bet it seems unlikely, knowing me, but my mama is a strong Christian woman. She wanted all us kids to get the 'right teachings,' as she used to say. With my brother and sister, it worked—he's a Baptist minister, and she's a private duty nurse. But with me . . ." He lifted his hands. "I rebelled and ran wild, until I discovered cooking and got my head straight."

"It was a private school, I assume?"

"Yeah. It was a decent place," Damian said, "but pretty small. Nothing like the public schools where you taught, I bet. All the grades were jammed together in one building, so I'd see Molly around, but more than that"—Damian twisted the towel between his hands—"I heard about the trouble she got into."

"Oh?" I leaned against one of our steel pantry racks and studied him, noting the concern in his eyes. "Trouble like typical teenage antics or something more?"

"More. She had a real bad temper, at least back then. The hair-trigger kind. She'd be all fine and cheerful, but someone would say or do something that ticked her off and bam!"—Damian snapped the twisted towel through the air—"just like that, she'd go off on them."

I frowned, tapping my fingers against one of the perforated metal shelves. "She was aggressive?"

"Yeah, I guess you could say that." Damian tossed the towel over one shoulder. "That's why I was kinda concerned when I saw she was staying here. I know people can change, and I'm the last person who has any right to complain about a bad temper, but when I saw her it brought back memories. And not pleasant ones."

"Did she ever attack you?" I asked, stepping away from the shelf to face him directly. If someone had harmed one of my staff, even if the altercation was in the past, I wanted to know. While Damian did have a short fuse, he had never, to my knowledge, physically attacked another person.

"No, nothing like that. We don't have any real history." Damian looked down at his hands, which were now clasped tightly at his waist. "She called me a name once or twice, but that was it."

"I see," I said, considering what that name had likely been. "Well, if she says anything like that to you while you're working this event, or any time this week, you let me know right away. I'm not going to put up with that sort of thing at Chapters."

"Thanks, but I imagine she'll be on her best behavior, what with her idol staying here too." Damian lifted his head and looked me in the eye. "And I don't need you to save me from anything. I was fighting that battle long before I met you. I know how to take care of myself."

"I'm sure you do. I just want to assure you that I'll back you up."

Damian's lips twitched in a slight smile. "I know. Wouldn't work here otherwise. But I'd better get a move on if I want to run to my apartment and back in time for your party."

"Okay. See you later. And," I added, as his walked past me, "thanks for alerting me about Molly. Like you said, she may be a completely different person now, but it's probably a good thing that I know to keep an eye on her. We don't want any problems like we had last year."

"We sure don't," Damian said as he left the pantry.

I waited until I heard the back-porch door slam before I wandered out of the pantry and into the kitchen. Examining the covered platters that lined the center island, I considered the information Damian had shared about Molly Zeleski.

There's really no reason to worry, I told myself, as I tucked a loose piece of plastic wrap under one of the ceramic platters. *Just because someone was a hothead in the past doesn't mean they'll pull any shenanigans now. Besides, what are the chances that something so drastic could happen, two years in a row?*

Chapter Four

I was glad Julie had thought to provide fans for our guests. Despite the shade offered by the front yard trees, by the time we reached the second portion of our author event, the afternoon heat had slicked the inside of my elbows and soaked the back neckline of my dress. As Amanda talked about her road to publication, I stood at the edge of the lawn, blinking the sweat from my eyes while I tried to focus. It wasn't easy—I was at the back of the crowd, and the heat made everything even a few yards away appear to shimmer.

The crowd didn't seem to mind. While I waved my fan emblazoned with the Bookwaves logo so furiously that the cardboard pulled away from the wooden stick, the guests appeared oblivious to any discomfort. They were so attuned to Amanda Nobel's every word that many of them had dropped their own fans to the ground or into their laps.

After Amanda spoke about the inspiration for her books, Julie jumped in with a series of interview questions before opening things up to questions from the audience.

"Quite a crowd."

I turned to the tall, thin, older woman who'd moved close to my side. "Hello, Fee. Are you an Amanda Nobel fan?"

"Oh my, yes. I just love her books," Ophelia Sandburg said, as she adjusted the yellow sash decorating the waist of her daisy-patterned cotton dress. "But I'm also here for Julie. She's a book club friend, after all. And I do like to support Bookwaves. Having an independent bookstore in town is so important."

"Very true. I'm delighted to see Julie get so much publicity for the store. Hopefully that will translate into future sales."

"I'm sure she'll sell a good many books today, at least." As Ophelia shaded her eyes with one hand, her violet nail polish shone in sharp contrast to her fire-engine-red dyed hair. "Is that Scott in the front row? I can only see the back of his head, but that auburn hair is pretty distinctive."

"Of course it is," said the short, stocky woman who'd bustled up beside Ophelia.

"Hello, Bernie," I said, with a nod of welcome.

Bernadette Sandburg looked like she was dressed for a tennis match rather than an afternoon tea, in a white polo shirt and blue plaid Bermuda shorts. "Would you take a gander at all those slack-jawed faces. Never seen such a bunch of obsessed fans since I attended that Beatles concert back in the day."

"I imagine they think Amanda is just as much of a rock star," I said.

Bernadette ran her fingers through her hair, which, while cut short like Ophelia's, retained its natural steel-gray color. "Don't see the attraction myself. I expect it's that TV show that's actually made her so famous. I mean, the books are all right, if you like that sort of thing . . ."

"Now Bernie, I know you mean *if you like romance,*" Ophelia lifted her sharp chin. "Because the books are very romantic." She batted her pale lashes over her blue eyes. "Absolutely swoony."

"Not to me, they aren't," Bernadette said. "It's so typical. The antihero falls for some gal and changes his ways due to 'twu love' and all that sort of rot."

I smiled. The way Bernadette said "love"—drawing out the word while squinching up her face—reflected some of my feelings about the books, or at least the one I'd read. While I thought the writing was good, and the character and plot development were strong, the use of too many typical tropes had the overall effect of making the book feel clichéd. At least, in my opinion.

"Hello there," said a cheery voice.

I turned to the speaker. "Oh hi, Sandy. Hi, Pete."

Like the Sandburg sisters, the couple who'd joined our little group at the edge of the lawn were members of the local book club that Julie and I hosted at Chapters once a month. Pete and Sandy Nelson, a long-married couple in their fifties, ran a popular local café serving breakfast and lunch.

"Sorry we're late. Had to close up after the lunch rush." Pete eyed my fan with interest. "Hey, where can we grab a couple of those? It's sweltering, even in the shade."

"Julie was handing them out earlier," I said. "I believe she has a few more in a box up at the table."

Pete wiped perspiration from his brow. "Don't think I want to try to navigate this crowd to get one, so I guess that's out." He glanced down at his petite wife. "Perhaps you could slip through that maze of chairs better than my chunky self."

"I think we should wait until the question and answer portion is over," Sandy said. "I wouldn't want to cause a commotion while Ms. Nobel is speaking."

"Are you coming to the special book club meeting Monday night?" Pete asked the Sandburg sisters.

"Of course. Even if I'm not really a fan, I'm interested in talking with Ms. Nobel in a quieter setting," Bernadette said. "And I know Fee wouldn't miss it."

Ophelia fluttered her hands. "Not for the world."

"We'll plan to attend too," Sandy said. "Even if Pete hasn't read the books."

Pete pressed one palm against the Dancing Dolphin logo on his T-shirt. "I feel wounded, dear. Besides, I watch the TV series. I think that counts."

"The show does veer away from the books, although not as badly as some." Sandy patted her husband's arm. "I do try to keep Pete filled in on all the changes."

Her husband groaned. "Yeah, there I am watching an exciting episode, and Sandy's in the other chair, rattling on about how 'they didn't do that in the book.'"

"Uh-oh." Bernadette held up one hand to silence our humorous convo. "Isn't that Roger Warren grabbing the portable mic?"

"Looks like it," Ophelia said.

I focused my gaze on a man of average height and build, with a full head of white hair that was cut long enough to straggle over the collar of his pale-blue shirt. I then gasped as he cleared his throat before asking, in a clear, precisely annunciated voice, why Amanda hadn't bothered to do any research before writing her book series.

Tony, who'd been hovering on the front porch, his bald head gleaming from a sheen of perspiration, rushed down the steps in the silence that fell after this question. I tensed, ready to intervene if he or the fans decided to take action against the man who'd just insulted their idol.

But Amanda, in a watermelon-pink linen dress, remained cool as an icy sherbet. She motioned for Tony to step back, and hushed the crowd with a wave of her hand. "That's a legitimate question, mister . . .?"

"Roger Warren," her questioner said. "I'm an author as well, but I write nonfiction. My specialty is the colonial history of this area." As he turned to address the seated guests as well as Amanda, I noted his well-trimmed white beard and horn-rimmed glasses.

Very professorial, I thought, wondering if his appearance—from his tailored shirt, with the sleeves rolled up above his elbows, to his chino pants and tasseled leather loafers—had been chosen to evoke that response.

"Well, Mr. Warren, or is it Dr. Warren?" Amanda's gracious smile appeared almost beatific as she surveyed Roger. "I confess I didn't dig too deeply into the real-life history of the area, or of my pirates. I leave that sort of thing to actual scholars, like you."

"It's Dr. Warren, but never mind that." Roger flung out his hand as if sweeping such minor matters aside. "The problem is that many more people read your books than will ever read my historical tomes. And certainly, even more watch the television show based on your books. Unfortunately, they are likely to think that what you are presenting is the truth. Which it isn't, as you and I both know."

Murmurs rolled through the crowd like rumbling before a storm. After sharing a concerned look with my book club friends, I crossed to stand behind the last row of folding chairs.

"Of course it isn't, Dr. Warren. I'm writing fiction. Romantic fiction at that." Amanda's tone was smooth as cream. She sat back in her chair. "As in those classic adventure films, like *The Sea Hawk*, or *The Adventures of Robin Hood*. No one expects them to depict actual historical events with any great accuracy."

"But those are examples from the past, when there was less emphasis on depicting the truth in historical accounts, even fictional ones." Roger Warren held up his hands in a *mea culpa* gesture. "I'm not trying to stir up trouble. I'm simply genuinely interested in why any author writing today would not include more accurate research in their work. There's plenty out there, even if you only peruse the internet. It seems like sheer laziness to not make any attempt at accuracy, at least in my humble opinion."

Amanda's smile tightened as Julie rose to her feet and said something about "moving on."

I caught Julie's eye and pointed my finger to my chest and then toward the table, trying to indicate that I'd be happy to step forward. But before I could do anything, Scott leapt to his feet.

"I have to concur with my esteemed colleague," he said, nodding at Roger before turning to face Julie and Amanda. "You had a great opportunity, Ms. Nobel. I realize maybe you just had fun writing your first book, and probably hadn't thought about the necessity of doing a lot of research. I also understand that you got your book deal surprisingly quickly, so maybe it was all a big rush, and if your editors never questioned you"—Scott shrugged—"why would you think anything needed to be changed? But surely there's been time to reflect on this while writing the following books in the series, especially since scholars have called out all the factual errors."

Julie's dark brows drew together as she leveled a furious glare at her boyfriend. "As I suggested before, can we please move on? I think we've beaten this subject to death."

If Scott heard the anger vibrating in Julie's voice, he gave no indication. "I just think it would be nice for Ms. Nobel to address Dr. Warren's concerns, rather than dismissing them as irrelevant," he said as he sat back down.

"Trust me, I'm not doing that," Amanda said. "I simply don't see the problem. I write a certain type of fiction, one that's obviously not intended to educate anyone," she added, shooting Tony what I felt was an enigmatic glance. She focused back on the crowd of fans. "I just hope it entertains."

Several in the crowd shouted, "It does!" while others chimed in with, "We love you, Amanda!"

In a few swift strides, Tony crossed to stand behind Amanda's chair. "Of course we all know how beloved Ms. Nobel's work is. That's why we're here, right?"

The exclamations of love and approval rose to a low roar. I surveyed the excited crowd before my gaze landed on Amanda's face.

She looks tired, I thought, *or even beaten down. Which is odd, with everyone cheering for her . . .*

My musing was cut short by Julie's announcement that the Q and A session was over. She swept back the few loose tendrils of dark hair that had escaped her low bun and waved her mic toward the rows of chairs. "Anyone who wants signed copies of Amanda's books, please line up in the center aisle. Wrap around to the sides of the chair rows, if necessary, but let's keep this to one line." As the guests scrambled to their feet, Julie raised her voice to add, "After the signing, or if you aren't interested in books, please assemble on the patio at the back of the house, where we'll be hosting the reception."

Julie placed the microphone down with careful deliberation, before stepping around the table and marching over to Scott, who'd remained seated. "So are you going to help me lug those book boxes off the porch, or would you rather stew in your own superiority," I heard her say when I reached them.

Scott leaned back in his chair and stretched out his long legs before looking up to meet Julie's blistering gaze. "I'm guessing you're not too happy with me right now." His brown eyes widened in puppy-dog innocence.

"Good guess, Nostradamus," Julie replied, crossing her arms over her chest.

"I suppose I tapped the hornet's nest a little too hard," said Roger Warren, as he joined us. "By the way, Scott, it appears that both you and I will soon be sorry for our insolence." He waved one hand in the direction of the fans lining up for signed books. "Or so I've been told by a few of the other guests."

Julie looked him over with a sniff of disapproval. "Whatever it is, you can't say you haven't earned it. But enough of that." As she dropped her arms, she made a brushing motion with her hands. "I have to go sell some books." She stalked off; her head held high.

Roger offered Scott an apologetic smile. "Didn't mean to get you into trouble with your ladylove."

"It's okay. We'll work it out," Scott said, as he rose to his feet. "Sorry, Charlotte. I know you put in a lot of work to make this event succeed."

"As did Julie," I said, not bothering to temper the frostiness in my tone. "Anyway, you'd better go help with the books if you don't want to compound your troubles."

As Scott strode off to join Julie on the porch, I turned to Roger Warren. "We haven't met before, Dr. Warren. I'm Charlotte Reed, the owner of Chapters."

"Nice to meet you. And please call me Roger," he replied, extending his hand.

I gripped his fingers for a moment before giving them a quick shake. "Well, Roger, you do have a way of making yourself known."

"But not liked?" Roger raised his bushy white eyebrows. "I'm afraid my professorial inclinations got the better of me. And, to be honest, it does rankle, seeing someone lionized for writing appallingly ridiculous fiction when scholars and writers of authentic research are so roundly ignored."

I studied his intelligent face for a moment as I considered these words. It seemed there was some animosity buried beneath Roger Warren's calm façade. Perhaps a long-standing grudge against those who'd made fortunes off of a subject he'd spent decades studying, without reaping the same fame or financial reward. "I can see where that would be frustrating," I said. "But isn't that way it always goes? Society doesn't always reward the best and brightest, or the most dedicated."

"How well I know it." Roger cast me a rueful smile. "But perhaps I should head around back and grab a drink before this crowd fills up the patio. I'm sensing quite a few daggers aimed at my back, to be honest," he added, with a little head bob toward the fans lined up to meet Amanda.

"At least it's way past the Ides of March," I replied, with an answering smile. "Don't worry, we've hidden all the real knives. We learned our lesson last year."

"Ah yes, the murder. But, you know, knives aren't the only weapons easily obtained. In this century as well as in the past. Just ask any real pirate who, despite Ms. Nobel's rather romantic and sanitized depiction, is someone to be feared."

As Roger turned away, I caught a glint in his eyes that made me shiver, despite the heat of the afternoon. Gripping my upper arms with both hands, I allowed my gaze to drift, taking in the tightly packed line of fans waiting for their chance to meet Amanda. Some clutched their own copies of her books; others pulled out credit cards as they approached the table, now piled high with brightly colored paperbacks and more subdued hardback editions of Amanda's series.

As my gaze wandered, I noticed a man, half-hidden behind the magnolia tree. He appeared out of place, in his sleeveless shirt and baggy shorts, and he was staring at something with the intensity of a predator stalking its next meal.

Not something—someone. Lisette Bradford, oblivious to the man's gaze, continued her conversation with Harper and Molly, her sharp voice raised and her hands gesticulating wildly.

I bet the three of them are plotting revenge against Roger and Scott for dissing their idol, I thought, as I strode across the yard, dodging scattered chairs. But that wasn't what concerned me. I was worried about a stranger who appeared to be stalking one of my guests.

"Hey there," I called out, as I approached the man. "Are you here as a guest? Because if not, you need to move along."

Lisette and the two other women spun around at the sound of my voice, while the stranger jumped to one side before bolting. He took off down the street like the police were on his heels.

When I turned back to face my three guests, Lisette's face was white as paper. She gripped her upper arms as Harper stepped closer to me.

"That was him," she said, her voice hollow. "That was the man we warned you about—Lisette's ex-husband, Billy Bradford." She lowered her head, veiling her eyes beneath the fall of her dark hair. "Not to be overly dramatic, but I'd alert the police if I were you, Charlotte."

I glanced at Lisette. "Is that what you want?"

She bobbed her head. "Please. Even though we're divorced, he just won't leave me alone."

"Don't worry, I have a contact in the police department. I'll let them know about the situation right away." I offered Lisette my most comforting hostess smile. "Why don't you three head on back to the reception area. Ask Damian to make you his special Chapters cocktail. It's sweet, but has a kick," I added, with a more authentic smile. "I'll make sure our unwelcome visitor doesn't bother you again."

The women nodded before hurrying off. As soon as they disappeared around the side of the house, I pulled out my cell phone and called Detective Johnson.

I didn't know if William "Billy" Bradford was just annoying, or truly dangerous, but I wasn't taking any chances. I'd had to deal with one deadly incident at Chapters the previous summer. I had no intention of allowing something like that to happen again.

Not if there was any way I could prevent it.

Chapter Five

Despite the controversy stirred up during the question and answer session, the reception seemed to go off without a hitch. Of course, most of the fans spent their time circling around Amanda like moths flocking to a porch light, but with Tony's help, she seemed able to keep the more ardent admirers from monopolizing her time.

It was curious, though, how assiduously Amanda ignored Lisette, who appeared to have recovered from her concern about her ex and now seemed determined to insert herself into all of Amanda's conversations. With Tony's assistance, Amanda was able to circumvent Lisette's constant intrusions, but I could tell the author was getting frustrated. The situation intrigued me. I would've thought Amanda would grant the head of one of her major fan clubs at least a modicum of attention, but that didn't appear to be the case. Instead, she seemed to be actively avoiding Lisette.

Not that I blamed her, when I overheard Lisette whine to Tony that he was just being vindictive. Another thing I found curious, to be honest. His response also caught my attention.

"You wouldn't even be here if you hadn't forced my hand," he told Lisette, in a tone that vibrated with anger.

I tucked away these observations on my guests, determined to keep an eye on Tony as well as Lisette and Amanda. There was something going on between the three of them that set off alarm bells in my mind.

The last guest left the premises around five, followed by the guest of honor and my other lodgers. Tony had apparently arranged a private dining room in a local upscale restaurant so that Molly, Lisette, and Harper could dine with Amanda without being bedeviled by other fans.

"This was all set up ahead of time. Part of the perks of winning the contest," Tony had informed me, when I'd asked if perhaps Amanda would prefer to dine without any fans at all.

I'd given him a raised eyebrow, but bit my tongue before expressing my thoughts. Amanda had appeared utterly exhausted, which hadn't surprised me, given the events of the day. I'd thought he might put consideration for her welfare over additional promotional activities, but if Molly was right, Tony's loyalties lay with Amanda's publisher and the success of her books, rather than with her as an individual.

They're the ones paying him, after all, I thought.

After assisting with the breakdown and stacking of the rental chairs, Scott also headed out, claiming he was meeting Roger for dinner at a restaurant in Morehead City. He invited Julie to join them, but she responded with a swift refusal.

"I hope you and Scott can patch up your little misunderstanding," I told her, as she helped Alicia, Damian, and me clean up the patio.

Julie tossed a plastic cup into the recycle bin. "It'll be fine. I just needed to put him on notice about his superior attitude toward genre fiction. Especially when it interferes with my promotional events."

"I guess it's hard for a dedicated scholar to see other writers profiting from books when they play fast and loose with the facts," I said.

Julie pulled the pins from her bun and shook out her long hair. "I do understand his frustration. Roger's too. But Amanda Nobel isn't really their competition. She isn't even claiming to write historically accurate works. She's just trying to entertain her readers, not educate them."

I met her leveled gaze with a smile. "I know. It *is* a different thing. I just think that all her millions might rankle, given what both men write. Let's face it—they've spent years researching and fact-checking to create their books, but don't make a tenth of what she does. That has to sting a bit."

"But Scott doesn't really need the money. You know his dad left him plenty. Not that he doesn't work hard, but I don't see why another author making boatloads off what is basically a romantic fantasy should bother him."

I tied up the garbage bag I was holding. "It's more than money, though. There's also the fame aspect. I assume Scott's told you that he doesn't want to write fiction because he doesn't feel he can ever compete with his late father, who was one of the few authors who was a household name. But I'm sure that doesn't mean he wouldn't like a little more recognition."

"I suppose." Julie trailed me over to one of the garbage bins. "And maybe that's the thing that took me by surprise. I never expected Scott to chase after fame."

"I think we all want to be noticed, though, don't we?" I tossed my bag of trash and wiped my hands on the paper towel I'd stuffed in my pocket. "Although, take it from me—fame isn't all it's cracked up to be."

Julie shot me a side-eyed glance as we crossed the patio to join Alicia and Damian at the bar. "That's right, escaping that sort of attention is one reason you decided to move here, isn't it?"

I nodded, acknowledging that, although many people sought fame, I'd run from it.

I'd realized this truth about myself four years earlier, when my husband Brent had saved a schoolroom full of children and become a hero. Tragically, his bravery had cost him his life, leaving me a widow at the age of thirty-nine.

Although I'd approved of all the honors posthumously bestowed on Brent, I wasn't thrilled when his lingering fame had transferred to me. Not only was it a constant reminder of my loss; I also felt my own identity had been overshadowed. I'd been turned into a symbol of Brent's sacrifice, and it seemed no one in my town could see me as anything beyond that. So, a little over two years ago, with the help of my inheritance from my great-aunt, I'd made a major life change. I gave up my high school teaching career and moved to Beaufort, North Carolina, to take over Chapters.

"All done," Alicia said, when Julie and I reached the tall counter we used as the patio's bar. "If there isn't anything else, I'd like to head inside and put my feet up."

"Looks good to me." I pointed toward the baskets she and Damian had filled with bottles and barware. "If you'll just take what you can carry when you go in, I'll cart the rest in later."

"No need," Damian said. "If Alicia will help, we can get everything in a couple of trips."

Alicia tugged up one drooping strap of her crisp white apron. "Sure thing. A lot of the bottles are empty, so it's a lighter load now."

"Okay, well, I'll just leave it to the experts then," I said, before offering both of them a warm smile. "Thanks for all your assistance today. I know it was a lot of extra work."

Damian shrugged. "That's why you pay us."

"Oh right, speaking of that . . ." I turned to Julie. "Can I get you a sandwich or something, or do you want to head home? I'll understand if you're ready to leave. I need to grab my checkbook so I can pay Damian, and then I'm going to go inside and crash."

"Thanks, I think I'll head home," Julie said, before thanking Damian and Alicia for their help with the event.

"Need a hand with those boxes or anything?" Damian asked her.

"No, Scott loaded all the extra stuff into my car before he left." She flashed me a smile. "See—no real problem. The whole thing will blow over by morning."

"Good to know," I said, before giving her a hug. "I'm glad everything went so well. A few minor issues are to be expected. Heaven knows we always have a couple during our special events."

"Ain't that the truth," Alicia muttered.

I waited until Julie had driven off before running inside to grab my checkbook and write out a payment for Damian's services. By the time I finished, he and Alicia had already brought all the baskets inside.

"Just leave it," I told Alicia, when she started to pull out items to set in the sink. "You deserve to take a break. I know you've been on your feet practically all day. I'll take care of this later."

Alicia shot me a speculative look before thanking me and leaving the kitchen.

I handed Damian his check and told him he was free to take off as well. "Really, I can handle unloading the baskets and all that. I think I'll just take a short break before I do, though, so let me follow you back outside."

After Damian headed home to his apartment, which was located above the garage of a house only a few blocks away, I decided to take a stroll through the garden.

It was my favorite time of day, especially in the summer. The days were filled with light late into the evening, while some of the heat had dissipated. I wandered the garden, finally pausing next to a hydrangea whose pom-pom flower clusters were as blue as the sky above me.

"Charlotte, so glad to catch you without a multitude nearby," a voice called out.

I glanced across the fence to meet Ellen's bright smile and wave. Her houseguest stood behind her, his hair glinting in the sun.

Shandy yipped and bounced up against the posts as I approached the fence. "Hi, Ellen. I hope our event today wasn't too disruptive."

Ellen brushed this aside with a wave of her hand. "Not at all. Of course, no one was here to be bothered. I was attending a garden club talk in New Bern, and Gavin had to pursue some mysterious mission at the county archives." The look she shot the man standing next to her was as brittle as it was bright.

There's something going on here too, I thought. *Something more complicated than a visiting relative.*

"It was research." Gavin Howard's voice, although pleasant, didn't give away his background. He sounded like a professional newscaster—I couldn't place an accent of any kind.

His gaze swept over me. "Hello, I'm Gavin Howard, and you must be Charlotte Reed. Ellen's mentioned you several times. I'm glad we could finally meet." He popped off his sunglasses, revealing light brown eyes tinged with amber.

"Hi, I'm glad to meet you as well. Ellen said you're a cousin?" I allowed this question to hang in the air as I studied both their faces.

Ellen's smile had tightened into a thin line, and her eyes glittered like blue gems. She didn't look happy. *More tense than anything,* I thought. It was odd. Very little seemed to unnerve Ellen Montgomery.

On the other hand, Gavin Howard appeared completely at ease. He casually glanced at his watch. "Charlotte, I hope we'll have a chance to chat sometime soon, but I'm afraid I must head back inside. I'm expecting an important phone call." He flashed me a cool smile. "One that requires privacy."

I noticed Ellen stiffen at these words. Gavin sauntered back into the house. I started to say something, but Shandy, racing in circles until Gavin reached the door, barked so loudly that I was forced to remain silent. I waited until the little dog bounded back across the garden and plopped down at Ellen's feet before speaking again.

"Your cousin, you said?" I asked, with a lift of my eyebrows.

Ellen's right eyelid visibly twitched. "First cousin's boy. Haven't seen him in ages."

"I understand," I said, although I didn't. I suspected that Ellen was no more related to Gavin than I was, but decided to keep that suspicion to myself. "Well, you were fortunate to miss all the chaos earlier. We had quite a turnout for the Amanda Nobel event."

"I'm not surprised. She is famous." Ellen dropped her taut shoulders and relaxed her expression. "And I didn't miss everything. When I got home, I brought Shandy out into the garden to relieve himself and overhead something I found rather odd."

I brushed the velvety petals of one of my climbing roses with one finger. "Oh? What was that?"

"A couple of young women swearing vengeance on Scott Kepler and his friend, Roger Warren." Ellen wrinkled her nose. "Well, I say young. They were probably between thirty and forty, but of course, that seems young to me."

"Really?" I absently yanked a couple of petals off the rose.

"Yes, I was quite surprised. I can't imagine Scott or Roger doing anything that would evoke such fury. Still, one of the women—a tall, thin creature with short hair and glasses—said she planned to encourage everyone in some fan club to go on sites and one-star both the men's books." Ellen fanned her face with one hand. "A rather cruel thing to do to an author, I thought."

"It certainly would be." I considered how this might affect Scott in particular. His history of the pirates who'd operated around Beaufort and the rest of the North Carolina coast had just been published. I didn't know if Roger Warren had any recent releases, but if Lisette rallied Amanda's fans to discredit either man's books . . . I shook my head. "I hope no one else heard that."

"Unfortunately, the men in question did. While the women were speaking, Scott and Roger walked up and tried to apologize. Well, these gals were having none of that. The tall one told the men that they shouldn't be surprised to see their books slide down into dumpster ratings on several review sites."

"Ouch," I said. "What did Scott and Roger do after hearing that?"

"Just backed away, I think." Ellen smoothed her silver bob with one hand. "The truth is, I wasn't in a position to see everything, because I was lurking behind that lilac over there. And yes, I know eavesdropping is frowned upon, but I was intrigued."

"Curiosity killed your commitment to good manners?"

"Exactly." Ellen cast me a roguish smile. "Admit it, you'd do the same."

I grinned. "I'm sure I would. But I do hope nothing unpleasant arises due to that little confrontation today," I added, my tone sobering. "Just for context, both Roger and Scott challenged Amanda Nobel about her research, or lack thereof, during the Q and A portion of today's event."

"That does clarify the situation," Ellen said. "Hopefully, all the one-star talk was just blowing off steam. Roger and Scott would have a right to be angry, otherwise."

"I hope so too." I tipped my head and examined Ellen for a moment. "Speaking of research, what sort of research is this cousin of yours doing? Is that the reason he's staying in Beaufort?"

Ellen shook her head. "I shouldn't have encouraged you to become a sleuth."

Which, of course, didn't answer my question. I eyed my neighbor, curious about her evasiveness. I could've pressed her, but decided against it. I knew she had secrets; some of which she probably wasn't allowed to divulge. I had to respect her boundaries if I wanted to remain her friend and confidant.

"I hope to talk to Gavin some other time, when he doesn't have to run off to answer important phone calls."

"You may be waiting a while," Ellen said dryly. "Come, Shandy, let's go back inside. I imagine Charlotte's tired of talking after all the hustle and bustle today."

I was tired, but not of talking. Not if it would explain Ellen's obvious uneasiness around her houseguest. But that conversation could wait. Looking forward to a cold glass of wine and a light supper, I simply wished Ellen a good evening before she and the Yorkie trotted back into her house.

I was relaxing in the front parlor a few hours later, reviewing Amanda's first novel, *The Tides of Time,* so I could create some discussion questions for our book club meeting on Monday evening. As I worked, several times I heard the front door open and close with a creak. Each time, I looked up to see which of my guests had returned.

Over the course of the evening I spotted Amanda, Tony, Molly, and Harper. None of them announced their return, preferring to slip in unnoticed and rush up the stairs to their respective rooms. Nor did they all return at the same time, which I found a little odd, since they had all gone out to dinner together. But perhaps they'd split up after the meal.

When the clock chimed eleven, and Lisette still hadn't returned, I rose to my feet with a sigh. We didn't lock the door until everyone had returned from their evening pursuits, or at eleven, whichever came first. Anyone arriving later had to ring the bell for admittance. I didn't encourage this, but since it happened fairly infrequently, I put up with it. As Alicia had informed me when I first took over Chapters, strictly enforcing a curfew could be viewed as inhospitable.

But it was annoying to know that either Alicia or I would have to answer the doorbell and let Lisette in whenever she decided to return. I padded over to the front door and locked it before climbing the stairs and knocking on the door to Alicia's suite. "Lisette Bradford isn't back," I told Alicia when she cracked open the door. "But don't worry—I'll take care of it tonight." I pressed my copy of *Tides of Time* to my breast. "I still need to do a little more work before the book club meeting on Monday, anyway."

That wasn't strictly true—I had completed writing down all my discussion questions. But it was enough to mollify Alicia, who wished me goodnight with relief stamped on her face.

I went back downstairs and headed to my own bedroom. It was at the back of the house, but Great-Aunt Isabella had rigged the doorbell to ring in that room as well as in the hall. The bedroom bell was amplified, resounding like the chimes in a church tower, so there wasn't any way I'd miss Lisette's return.

Which was why, when I sat up in bed, startled by the jangling of the landline phone, and glanced at the digital clock on my nightstand, I was shocked. It was three o'clock in the morning, far past the time I would've expected any guest to return to Chapters.

The voice on the other end of the line surprised me as well.

"Hello, Ms. Reed, I hate to bother you," said Detective Amber Johnson, "but I'm afraid I have bad news."

"What do you mean?" I asked, rubbing my eyes with my fist. My thoughts careened from one possibility to another. Had Julie been hurt, somehow? Or had Damian been struck by a car on his walk home and the accident just now discovered? I jumped out of bed and paced over to my window, which overlooked the quiet back patio and garden. There'd also been that interloper earlier—Lisette's ex-husband. Perhaps he'd caused more trouble.

Detective Johnson's next words confirmed my fears.

"It's about Lisette Bradford. You told me earlier that her ex-husband, William, or Billy, as I believe he's called, was spotted stalking Lisette at your author event."

"Has he shown up somewhere else?"

"That's the problem, we aren't sure. We don't know where he is, and we'd really like to."

"I haven't seen him since then," I said, squinting to peer out into my backyard, just to make sure. "Has he done something else?"

"We aren't certain, but we do need to talk to him. You see, just a little while ago"—Detective Johnson took an audible breath—"we pulled Lisette Bradford's body out of the water near the Beaufort docks."

I gripped the window frame for support. "She's dead?"

"Sadly, yes."

"Maybe it was an accident?" I asked, hoping against hope that this was true. I'd had enough of murder for one lifetime.

"I'm afraid not. Although it may not have been what killed her, there's obvious trauma to the temple that's not consistent with her falling and hitting her head on something. We'll know more later, but my suspicion is that she was dead before she was tossed in the water." Detective Johnson cleared her throat. "It's why I wanted to alert you, as well as inform you about her death."

"Because Billy Bradford is still out there, somewhere?"

"Yes, and it seems, from talking to people who overheard conversations at the restaurant where Ms. Bradford dined tonight, that he isn't our only viable suspect."

"Do I need to worry about my guests, then?"

"I don't think there's any immediate danger. But I'd definitely keep your eyes and ears open and stay on your guard."

I stared at the phone receiver for a moment before speaking again. "Thank you for informing me. I'll bear that in mind."

Detective Johnson's stern tone softened. "Please do. Because I'm afraid that it's quite possible that once again you might have a murderer sleeping beneath your roof."

Chapter Six

Needless to say, I didn't fall back asleep after that news. Instead, I headed into the kitchen to scrub things down that didn't actually need cleaning.

After exhausting myself to dull my anxiety, I showered and changed before helping Alicia serve breakfast to our guests. Not that many of them showed up for the meal—Amanda asked for coffee before disappearing back upstairs, and Molly and Harper didn't even make an appearance. Tony was the only one who actually sat in the dining room, but he only wanted a couple of slices of toast along with his coffee.

"Guess they must've heard the news from somewhere," Alicia said, as she wrapped up a plate of uneaten cinnamon rolls.

"I suppose." I poured some coffee into a white ceramic mug before tipping the percolator into the sink to dispose of the rest. "Have you noticed any odd behavior from our guests, by the way?"

"Odder than usual? Can't say I have." Alicia tapped her blunt fingernails against the counter. "So what—is this group of guests part of the investigation now? They were all out together last night, but surely that doesn't automatically make them suspects."

"It was just something Detective Johnson said. I wanted to warn you . . ."

Alicia huffed as she shoved the cinnamon rolls into a bread box. "To watch my back? As if I haven't spent a lifetime doing that."

"It's a little different when murder is involved." I frowned as I realized how little I knew about Alicia's life before Chapters. *Because you never asked,* I thought, flushing with embarrassment. Perhaps I *had* treated her more like something I'd inherited along with the house than a person with her own, independent life. At least, more than I liked to admit.

"Well, I'll keep my eyes and ears open. You can depend upon that," Alicia said.

I stirred some cream into my coffee. "Probably a good idea."

Alicia didn't respond, choosing to busy herself with cleaning off the counters I'd already scrubbed earlier. I took my mug and strolled into the library to sit and ponder the few facts I had concerning this latest murder. Surrounded by the thoughts of so many minds more brilliant than mine, I hoped I could sort out some of my confusion.

It seemed someone else had the same idea. I discovered Harper slumped in one of the leather armchairs, a book lying open on her lap. But she was staring blankly at the shelves on the far wall instead of reading.

"Sorry to bother you," I said, pausing in the center of room. "I can leave if you'd rather be alone."

"No, it's fine." Harper motioned toward the chair facing hers. "Please, have a seat. I was just trying to take advantage of some of your fascinating books, but I'm afraid my mind doesn't seem capable of comprehending written words right now."

"I understand the feeling." I sat down, cradling my mug between my hands, and studied Harper's face, which was pale but composed. "I know it must have been a shock to hear the news about Lisette. Did you know her well?"

Harper shook her head. "Not really. We were mainly acquainted through online interactions. I was active in the fan club she managed, but we only met in person a couple of times, at some signings, or a few conventions where Amanda was a featured guest."

"But you were aware that her ex-husband was a problem?"

Harper closed the book in her lap and rested her hands on the cover. "Definitely. And he was lurking around yesterday, as you saw."

"I suppose he is the most likely suspect. The police are actually looking for him as we speak."

Harper lowered her gaze onto the book in her lap. "I imagine they have him at the top of their list, but there were tons of Amanda Nobel fans at the event yesterday, and I bet a lot them stayed in the area overnight."

I eyed her with interest over the rim of my mug. "But why would any of them want to harm Lisette Bradford?"

As Harper dipped her head, her dark hair fell forward, veiling her face. "That's the thing; some of them might have a motive. You wouldn't know this, but there was a pretty vicious online feud in the fandom a few years ago."

I sipped my coffee and considered this information before speaking. "In the fan club run by Lisette?"

"It started there." Harper straightened, tossing her hair behind her shoulders. "Like Molly and I mentioned before, Lisette wrote a lot of fan fiction based on the *Tides* series. She often promoted it in the club."

"It wasn't good?" I asked, curious about the segue.

"It was actually pretty decent. The thing was, she didn't simply draw on Amanda's characters and themes and use them as a jumping off point for her own work, she was adept at copying Amanda's writing style. A lot of fans enjoyed reading her stuff." Harper shrugged. "It filled their need for more content in between the release of the actual Amanda Nobel novels."

"Was Amanda unhappy about it? I know some authors disapprove of fan fiction, while others don't mind."

"She seemed okay with it, from what I could tell." Harper drummed her fingers against the book cover. "Maybe she was flattered, or maybe she didn't even realize it existed, I don't know. But I never heard her condemn fan fiction in general, or Lisette's works in particular."

"This fan infighting wasn't about that, then?"

"Not precisely." Harper cleared her throat. "I kind of hate to even bring it up, but if someone who was here yesterday was still angry . . ."

"You think it's possible one of them killed Lisette? But why? What did Lisette do, or not do, as part of this fan war?"

"She was accused of plagiarism," Harper said, meeting my intent gaze with a lift of her chin. "Stealing from another fan fiction author, to be precise."

I sat back in my chair. "And did she?"

Harper stood and carried the book she was holding to one of the library shelves. "Hard to say, or prove, anyway. The person she supposedly stole from used an invented name, as did most of the people in the group. That writer disappeared completely once most of the fans rallied behind Lisette. I heard they wiped their stories from all the fan fiction sites, and since no one knew their real name, they really couldn't be traced." Harper turned to face me. "At least not by anyone I talked to."

"I don't quite follow," I said. "Were there people supporting the supposedly plagiarized author, who were shut down by those backing Lisette?"

"Basically yes." Harper leaned against the cabinet that sat beneath the ceiling-high range of shelves. "The thing was, this fan fiction writer only posted one or two stories, while Lisette had dozens. So when a reader accused Lisette of lifting the concept and even passages from someone else's story, that other author didn't have the readership to rally behind them. Lisette did."

"And you think this fan fiction author or one of their supporters might still hold a grudge."

"It's possible. Lisette and her followers even turned the tables, saying the other writer had stolen from *her*." Harper rolled her shoulders. "Things got pretty ugly. It drove numerous people out of the group and caused a lot of hard feelings that spilled over into other Amanda Nobel fan clubs. Or so I'm told. I have to confess that I didn't join Lisette's group until after all this went down. But I heard rumors and checked it out online. There's still discussion and documentation available on various sites if you look hard enough."

"So you didn't experience this directly." I sighed. "You should still talk to the police, but if all your info is secondhand . . ."

"I know. They might not take it as seriously. That's what I've been debating ever since I heard the news about Lisette. But"—Harper fixed me with an intense stare—"don't you think it's worth mentioning, given the fact that so many fans were in the area yesterday? Any one of them might been involved in that online drama, which could've led to a fight with Lisette."

"An argument that led to a murder?"

"Right. I'm not suggesting that someone came here specifically to kill Lisette. At least not if it was one of the fans. Now, Billy Bradford is another thing entirely. From what I could tell, Lisette was really afraid of him."

I took a long swallow of my coffee as I filed away all the information Harper had shared. One thing was certain—there was more than one person who might've had it in for Lisette Bradford. *But don't forget Detective Johnson's warning about your own guests,* I told myself.

Which was why I didn't question Harper about the dinner she'd shared with Amanda and the others the previous night. Instead. I rose to my feet, clutching my now empty mug to my chest. "I definitely think you should tell the authorities what you just told me. As you said, there were other people who might have a motive to kill Lisette, and some of them could've been in Beaufort yesterday."

Harper flashed a sad smile. "Thanks. That was what I needed help deciding. I mean, that's why I brought it up with you. I wasn't sure if I should mention all that fan club stuff to the police, but since you seem to think it might help . . ." She lifted her hands. "Guess I will."

"I think that's a good move. Now, if you'll excuse me, I'm going to see if there's anything I can do for the other guests." I turned and crossed the library, pausing at the door to add, "I hope the rest of your day goes much better."

"Pretty much guaranteed to, isn't it?" Harper said as I left the room.

I wandered into the pantry and deposited my mug in our commercial dishwasher. Spying no other guests, I decided to head outside. I was sure the police would arrive any minute to question me as well as Alicia and our guests, and I wanted to enjoy a little fresh air before facing that ordeal.

As I paused on the edge of the patio, I heard Ellen call my name.

"Charlotte," she said, waving me over to the gate that led into her back yard and garden, "Come talk to me."

"Wouldn't mind picking your brain, actually," I replied, as I jogged over to join her.

"I was so sorry to hear about the death of your guest," Ellen said, as she ushered me into her yard.

"Murder, it seems." I glanced around, surprised to see no evidence of Shandy.

"Really?" Ellen arched her brows. "They know this already?"

"Apparently she sustained a blow to the head before she was dumped in the water. At least according to Detective Johnson."

"Oh dear, another murder on your doorstep." Ellen led the way into her garden. "Here, have a seat," she added, motioning toward a white wooden bench.

"At least it didn't happen at Chapters, but since it involves one of my guests . . ." I sighed heavily as I sat down.

"Very unfortunate." Ellen pulled off her straw hat and dropped it in her lap as she sat beside me. "I understand the woman was the primary one vowing vengeance on Scott and Roger too."

I shot her a sharp glance. "You don't think one of them would kill her over such a thing?"

"I don't," Ellen said, fanning herself with her hat, "but I'm afraid the police might."

I clasped my hands in my lap. "Only if you talk to them."

"Which I must, of course. And I'm sure you'll feel compelled to confess the same. Right?" She side-eyed me.

"I wish I'd never heard you say anything about it," I replied. "But there are other suspects. More likely ones, such as the disgruntled ex-husband who showed up uninvited."

"I heard the police were looking for him." Ellen stopped fanning and placed the hat back in her lap before shifting on the bench to look me in the eye. "Are there more? Come now, we're a sleuthing team. You must tell me."

"Detective Johnson mentioned something about diners overhearing an odd conversation between Amanda and her entourage when they were at a restaurant last night."

Ellen stretched her legs, shaking out the folds in her loose navy and red sail-patterned pants. "All your current guests are on the list? It's like déjà vu."

"Unfortunately," I said, thinking back on the events of the previous summer. "I don't know all the particulars, but it seems Amanda, Tony, Molly, and Harper must be added to our suspect list."

"Along with . . . what was his name? Billy something?"

"William Bradford, who apparently goes by Billy. Lisette's ex."

"Ah, yes." Ellen's garnet-painted toenails sparkled as she wiggled her feet in her open-toed canvas sandals. "That's seven possible suspects then—Scott, Roger, Billy Bradford, Amanda, Tony, Harper, and Molly."

"You can't really suspect Scott." I squinched up my nose in distaste.

"He has a motive," Ellen said. "Not sure about his opportunity, though. If he was with Julie and she can vouch for him, perhaps we should let him off the hook."

"That won't help." I leaned back against the bench and stared up at the cloudless sky. "He wasn't with Julie, at least not the entire evening. She stayed at Chapters for a while after he left. She also mentioned that Scott and Roger were going out to dinner together, so I don't know. Maybe he came home early and she can clear him due to the time of death, but maybe not."

"Someone would have seen him dining with Roger, perhaps?"

"That's possible. I hope that's the case. But honestly, the whole thing is more complicated than you know. There were more than seven people who possibly had motive or opportunity in this case." I took a deep breath before detailing the information that Harper had shared about a serious conflict in the Amanda Nobel fandom.

"That does muddy the waters," Ellen said, when I'd concluded my story. "From what you've told me, it could've been any one in that large group gathered at Chapters yesterday.

"Sadly, yes. Of course, I'll let the authorities know about that possibility, as I'm sure Harper will. Not that it will be particularly helpful to their case. We do have the names of all the registered attendees, but it's a long list, and most of them have probably already left the area."

"The police will have plenty of investigating to do, that's for sure." Ellen gave me a wink. "Which is why they shouldn't mind if we help them out. Unofficially, of course."

"But what can we really do?" I asked absently, my attention diverted by the monarch butterfly flitting through Ellen's bed of fringe-petaled crimson bee balm.

"Well, Julie has some contacts in the book world. Perhaps she could find out more about Ms. Nobel and Mr. Lott. Any rumors of problems with Lisette or her fan club, I mean."

"That's true. And I did overhear an interaction between Tony and Lisette that indicated some animosity between them." I turned my head to look at Ellen. "I could check into that fan war Harper mentioned. She said there was still info about it, if one dug deep enough. I know enough about researching online to turn that stuff up, if it exists."

"Good. As for me, I have several contacts in town who can help me check out Roger Warren's background. I can certainly find out if he's the type to retaliate if someone attacks him professionally."

"Sounds like a plan." I gnawed on the inside of my cheek for a moment. "I think we can leave Billy Bradford to the police. They're already on his trail."

"A reasonable assumption. Now, as for Scott . . ." Glancing over my shoulder, Ellen broke off her sentence. "Oh, hello Gavin. Back so soon?"

"Shandy decided he'd had enough." Gavin Howard, holding tightly to the end of the Yorkie's leash, stepped around to face us. "Hello, Charlotte. Nice to see you again."

"Hi," I said, pasting on a smile. Even if I hadn't already decided to fall silent, Ellen's swift look had warned me against continuing our previous conversation. "So you're the dog walker now?"

"Apparently." Gavin bent down and unhooked Shandy's leash from his harness. "Go on then, you rascal. Run amok like you've been wanting to do all along."

Shandy happily followed this suggestion, dashing off to run circles around the garden beds.

"Thank you for taking him along on your walk," Ellen said.

Gavin ran his hand through his hair, pushing a few drooping curls off his damp forehead. "No problem. I needed to check out the boat anyway."

"Gavin has a cabin cruiser moored at the Beaufort docks." Ellen's tone was conversational, but her eyes seemed wary. "Not sure why he didn't want to bunk there, but I suppose one occasionally gets tired of living on the water."

"I couldn't pass up the opportunity to enjoy your hospitality, Ellen," Gavin said, his tone much lighter than his expression. "Besides, as I told you, it was a better base for the work I needed to do while I was here."

"And what work is that, Mr. Howard?" I asked, fixing him with an inquiring stare.

"Historical research," he replied, meeting my gaze without faltering. "And please, it's Gavin, not Mr. Howard."

I could feel Ellen stiffen beside me. "Well, Gavin, I must be going," I said, as I stood to face him. "I suppose you heard about the murder of someone who was lodging at Chapters?"

"I saw all the activity down near the docks," he replied, his eyes narrowing. "I had to navigate the police perimeter, although it fortunately didn't prevent access to my boat."

I looked him over, realizing there was an unusual air of intensity about this man—a certain coiled energy, and a glint in his eyes that reminded me of an animal constantly on guard against danger.

I squared my shoulders as I shook such foolish thoughts from my mind. "Thankfully it didn't happen at my house. But I'm sure the police will be along any minute now to question me as well as my staff and guests, since we were acquainted with the victim."

Gavin inclined his head. "My sympathies. Interrogations are never fun."

"You sound like you know that from experience." I circled around him to reach the garden gate.

Instead of answering, Gavin laid a hand on my arm. "Take care," he said, before lifting his fingers and stepping back.

"Thank you," I replied as I strode past, calling, "See you later, Ellen," over my shoulder.

"You should be careful," I heard Ellen say before I walked out of earshot.

I didn't think she was speaking to me.

Chapter Seven

After giving my statement to the police when they stopped by to question everyone at Chapters, I decided to walk to Julie's shop. Located in an older, two-story wooden building next to the boardwalk that skirted the docks, Bookwaves was a small store, with an expansive picture window that Julie decorated in keeping with the seasons or holidays.

In fact, as I approached the bright blue front door, I noticed Julie reworking her window display. She was changing it from a red, white, and blue salute to the Fourth of July to something aqua and indigo and sparkly.

Apparently glimpsing my wave through the window, Julie stepped away from her half-finished display to greet me at the door. "Hi there. Looking for a book or for a chat?"

"The latter," I said, breathing in the lovely scent of new books that filled the shop. "Although you know whenever I step foot in a bookstore, I'll probably end up buying something."

"Not that I mind."

"What's it going to be this time?" I asked, motioning toward the display.

"A celebration of mermaids and other fanciful tales related to the sea." Julie wiped her fingers over her Bookwaves apron, dusting some glitter from her fingers. "Highlighting children's books, mostly. I wanted to evoke something light and fun, and a lot of young adult or adult titles that feature mermaids tend to be pretty dark these days."

"I've noticed that too," I said, glancing at the table where Julie had piled colorful stacks of picture and chapter books. "Anyway, I just wanted to stop by and see how you were doing. I know the police have probably questioned you as well as Scott about this latest murder."

"Not me, not yet, although I got a call that someone would be by later today." Julie fiddled with the rubber band tying off her long braid. "They asked Scott to come into the station, which is where he is now."

I studied her face for any signs of concern. Finding none, I decided to ask some blunt questions. "Scott went to dinner without you last night, didn't he?"

"He was supposed to meet Roger at a restaurant in Morehead City. The cool one we went to once, in the old house, a few blocks back from the waterfront. Remember that?"

"Oh right, the one that had great cocktails along with good food."

"Exactly. Anyway, Scott went there to meet Roger. But apparently"—Julie snapped the rubber band so hard that it broke—"Roger never showed."

"Really? Did he call or text?"

"Nope. At least not until much later." Julie used her fingers to unravel the plait, fanning her hair over her shoulders. "Scott got back around ten. He'd run into someone else he knew and ended up joining their party for dinner. I was upstairs in the apartment by the time he returned, of course. I closed down shop at seven, like I usually do on summer Saturdays. I was by myself at that point, because I sent Dayna home early."

"I'm guessing Dayna covered for you yesterday."

"Thank goodness she was able to work most of the day." Julie combed her fingers through her hair. "Anyway, I was upstairs, reading, when I heard Scott come in. He was pretty upset over Roger's disappearing act, even after Roger finally called around eleven with some bogus reason why he didn't show. I mean, maybe it wasn't bogus, but Scott sure felt it was a lame excuse."

"So no one's sure where Roger was all evening?"

"I don't know about that, but what he told Scott didn't really sound believable. Something about his car battery dying and he had to get someone from his auto service to replace it." Julie shrugged. "Maybe that's true, but it doesn't really clarify why he didn't call to explain the situation to Scott earlier."

"No," I said, my mind processing this information about another suspect in Lisette's murder. "It certainly doesn't."

"Fortunately, there are several people at the restaurant, the staff as well as Scott's other friend and his guests, who can vouch for Scott's whereabouts during the time that Lisette was probably killed."

"That is good," I said, striking his name from my mental list. "I guess Scott's telling the authorities about the weird situation involving Roger Warren? I bet he hates having to do that."

"He was definitely upset about it. But you know Scott—he isn't one to lie."

"True. He's always struck me as an honest person."

Julie absently shuffled a few of the books on the table. "He is. Even when it's difficult, like today. I know he doesn't want to cast any suspicion on Roger, but he has to tell the police what really happened."

"Of course he does. I'm just glad he has a solid alibi." I held up my hands as Julie shot me a sharp look. "Not that I ever really suspected him. But it's great that he's been quickly cleared, so neither he nor you have to worry about that anymore."

"That's definitely a relief." Julie picked up a thin paperback and fanned her face. "What about the rest of your guests. How are they handling things?"

"Honestly, I'm not sure. Most of them have stayed hidden away in their rooms today." I considered what I'd heard from Detective Johnson and Harper. Since they'd both shared information willingly, I didn't think it would hurt to fill Julie in on the problematic restaurant conversation, what little I knew about it, as well as the fan club dispute.

"Wow," she said, when I'd finished speaking. "I wonder what those other restaurant goers overheard to put Amanda and the rest of that crew on the police radar?"

"I don't know, but it must've been an argument of some kind. Maybe even threats?" I started as the bell attached to Julie's front door jangled. "You have a customer. I should get out of the way."

"No need to rush off, but I guess we should watch what we say." Julie looked over my shoulder, flashing a professional smile. "Hello there. Can I help you find something?"

"Just browsing," said the woman.

"Okay, let me know if you have any questions," Julie said brightly, before turning her focus back on me. "I tell you what—I have some contacts in the publishing world, from back when I was interning and thinking I might want to become an agent. Maybe I could pick their brains and see if there are any rumors concerning Amanda or Tony or anyone related to Lisette's online group. I mean, if there was a fan war, a few of my friends might've heard something, if only because it was tied to a big name like Amanda."

"That would be interesting. Thanks." I gave Julie's arm a pat. "I'm just glad Scott is out of it."

"Me too. Except for giving evidence against his friend." Julie made a face but adjusted her expression when the customer asked about books written by authors from the area. "We have quite a few. Fiction and nonfiction," she said, as she bustled toward the woman.

I mouthed a goodbye before I left Julie with her customer.

Outside, I strolled over to the railing that separated the boardwalk from the boat slips and harbor. Planters that straddled the wooden top were filled with a vivid mixture of summer flowers and greenery, while masts rose like slender trees from the decks of gleaming sailboats. Of course, there were regular powerboats too, and even a handful of yachts whose size and elegance told a tale of wealth. A few of these were so massive that they loomed over the more modest vessels like whales dwarfing a school of fish.

One of the smaller cabin cruisers, while well-maintained, harkened back to an earlier era. It had a white-painted wooden hull, varnished wood decking and cabin, and gleaming chrome fittings. I shaded my eyes as I admired this vintage craft, then dropped my hand in surprise when I recognized the figure cleaning the windows on the covered portion of the deck.

It was Gavin Howard. He moved like an experienced sailor, and looked the part too, in a brilliant white shirt and khaki shorts, with a navy canvas cap pulled down low over his forehead. I opened my mouth to call out a greeting but shut it again when I remembered how tense Ellen seemed around this man.

There is something strange going on there, I thought, turning aside before he could catch a glimpse of me. I hurried home, staying on Front Street until the shops and restaurants were replaced with stately old homes. Some of the larger ones facing the water had once been boarding houses for sailors, but were now pricey private homes.

I turned up one of the side streets that led away from the waterfront. Before I reached the turn onto Ann Street, I passed by the charming home owned by Bernadette and Ophelia Sandburg. It was a one-story bungalow with white clapboard siding and a covered porch. Aqua-blue shutters framed the tall windows that flanked the cobalt-blue front door, and white wicker chairs and tables, along with planters overflowing with flowers, filled the wide front porch. Not seeing either of the sisters in the yard or on the porch, I didn't stop. I would've chatted with them, just to be hospitable, but was secretly glad I could head directly to Chapters. I needed to know what was going on with my guests, especially after the police interviews.

Still, after turning on Ann Street and walking a few blocks, I paused in front of Ellen's house. A quick glance over at Chapters showed no signs of police vehicles, so I assumed the authorities had already left. I decided I had time to check in with Ellen before I returned home.

After ringing her doorbell, I allowed my gaze to sweep over her front porch. The fans mounted in the beadboard ceiling spun lazily, barely stirring the fronds of the ferns hanging from purple enameled chains. With its white porch swing and brightly painted Adirondack chairs, the porch was a perfect setting. I was sure most people would imagine a Southern lady of a certain age gracefully lounging there, sipping sweet tea without a care in the world.

They probably wouldn't imagine that the same lady had once directed dangerous intelligence operations. But then, Ellen's long-term cover had been her work as a location scout for film and television projects. I smiled. She did know how to use settings to create the proper atmosphere.

"Charlotte, how nice to see you," Ellen said, holding Shandy back with one foot as she opened the front door. "Do come in. I'm all alone right now and would welcome the company."

"I know. I saw Gavin on his boat down at the waterfront. It looked like he was preoccupied and not likely to head back here any time soon, which is one reason I decided to stop by."

"So we could speak in confidence? Good thinking." Ellen lifted Shandy up in her arms before ushering me inside. "Let's sit in the parlor. It's cooler in there."

I followed her into the adjacent room. She set a squirming Shandy down and smiled as he bounded off to jump up on the bench placed in front of a window. "He likes to keep an eye on things," she said, before sitting in a wood-framed upholstered armchair. "Especially everything happening outside."

Like her fashion, Ellen's décor was a blend of casual and modern styles, but unlike the vivid colors she preferred in her clothing, her furniture was a mix of muted tones accented by pale wood. This simple background set off vivid paintings and other works of art. Traveling the world in her role as a location scout, Ellen had amassed an eclectic collection of art pieces—everything from Indian wall hangings to Asian ceramics and German cuckoo clocks. Somehow it all blended with the Victorian features she'd retained in her home, including wainscoting, deep moldings, and hardwood floors.

"By the way, you can take Scott off your suspect list. He has a solid alibi, with witnesses, or so Julie tells me," I said as I sank into a suede-upholstered chair. "Unlike Roger Warren, unfortunately."

"Good for Scott, not so great for Roger."

"I find it hard to believe that a distinguished scholar would kill someone over bad reviews. Still . . ." I took a deep breath. I'd wanted to keep Ellen up-to-date on the investigation, but that wasn't the real point of my visit. "I just have to ask—is Gavin Howard really your cousin? The sleuth in me is saying 'no,' if only because of the way you act around him. You're not exactly the warm and welcoming hostess I would have expected."

Ellen surveyed me for a moment, approval shining in her blue eyes. "Very good deduction. You're right to question me on that."

"So what is he, and why is he here? Can I ask that?"

"You can, and I'll tell you, even though I probably shouldn't." She tipped her head to study me more intently. "But I trust you, and his reason for coming to Beaufort touches on something, or should I say, *someone,* related to you."

I slid forward and rested my chin on my entwined fingers. "Isabella? But how in the world does she come into it? It's been a few years since she passed away, and she wasn't active in intelligence activities for a while before that, if what you've told me is true."

"It is, but"—Ellen lifted her hands—"there are always repercussions from the sort of work we did. Things that echo, even over decades."

I stretched out my legs over the neutral toned geometric rug covering the parlor's polished floors. "Such as?"

"Such as the reason Gavin is here. And yes, you have guessed correctly—he is a colleague, not a cousin."

"An agent?" I raised my eyebrows. Gavin Howard lacked the flash that matched my image of a secret agent. *But then,* I thought, *Ellen doesn't fit the mold either. And while Great-Aunt Isabella was a charmer, I never would've pegged her as a spy.*

"Exactly. I didn't know him personally before he showed up here the other day, but I'd heard of him."

"Even though you've been retired for so many years?"

Ellen waved her hand. "There's retired and *retired*. You never really leave my former career. Not entirely."

"He's here digging into Isabella's past, then. Looking into some things she was involved in long ago?"

Ellen shifted in her chair. "A specific operation I believe. And he isn't only interested in Isabella. Me too. I was her handler for many years, you know."

I straightened, dropping my hands onto the arms of my chair. "Is he trying to implicate you? I mean, I'm guessing this is an operation that went wrong in some way."

"It didn't go wrong, not if it's related to what I think it is. It did what it was intended to do, so it went right, but"—Ellen's lips twisted—"perhaps in a very wrong way."

I tightened my grip, digging my short nails into the soft arms of the chair. "Now I'm thoroughly confused."

"I'm sorry. I really can't say more. I don't have all the facts about why Gavin was sent here, to be honest. The main thing is that you need to be careful around him. He isn't the man he'd like the world to think he is."

"I'd already figured that out." I loosened my grip. "Maybe I do have a bit more super sleuth qualities than I thought."

"Just like I've always told you." Ellen stood and crossed to the bench where Shandy was perched, his front paws up on the windowsill and his nose pressed against the glass. "It's good that you have a second sense about such things," she added, as I swiveled in my chair to look at her. "Especially if you want to continue to be my friend."

"Of course I do. We're sleuthing partners, after all."

Ellen shot me a humorless smile. "Yes, but this is a little different than just discussing crimes over tea. Or even helping the police now and then. Someone like Gavin Howard, and the people behind him . . ."

I stood to face her. "We confronted a killer together, remember?"

"I'm not questioning your bravery or your resolve. It's just that I don't want to drag you any deeper into these matters than I already have."

"What do you want me to do? Avoid Gavin, or try to get information out of him?"

Ellen's snort of derision made Shandy bark in response. "You won't be able to do that, not unless he allows it. But no, you don't need to avoid him. That might look peculiar. It would be better if you just treat him with casual friendliness. Act like you believe he's my cousin. Definitely don't let him know you're aware of his deception. And"—Ellen's eyes narrowed—"don't invite him into Chapters. He has no business snooping around in Isabella's old home."

"I think I can manage that," I said, rubbing down the hair that had risen on my arms. "But if I do hear, or even overhear, him say anything I think you should know, I'll definitely share it with you."

"I'd appreciate that," Ellen said, as she absently stroked Shandy's silky back. "Now, I should let you get back to your guests. I saw the police cruiser leave earlier, so I imagine they've all been questioned."

"Along with me." I crossed to the parlor door, but turned before heading into the hall. "This operation that Great-Aunt Isabella was involved in—she wouldn't have documented it in that journal I found and gave you by any chance? I know you recently passed it along to some experts to see if they could break her secret code."

Ellen's pained expression told me all I needed to know, but all she said was, "Good afternoon, Charlotte. I hope we can find a chance to speak again sometime soon."

Chapter Eight

On Monday morning I stepped out of the dining room after breakfast and was greeted by Molly at the front door with her suitcase.

"I'm checking out," she said. "Since I live in Morehead City, the Beaufort police said I could go, as long as I stay close to home for a while. In case they need to question me again or anything."

I looked her over, noting the dark circles under her eyes. "I'm sorry for the circumstances. I know this tragedy has spoiled a special event you were looking forward to."

"Yeah, not much of a prize after all, was it?" Molly squinched up her face. "But at least I got to spend some one-on-one time with Amanda before everything went south. And, if Amanda stays on and you're still holding some of the events this week . . ."

"You're welcome to come back for the book club discussion tonight if you wish. That's not open to the public, so it will be a select group. As Tony told you, we're trying to keep the information about these additional events limited. But of course, as a contest winner, you're allowed to attend everything. There's still the small tea party I arranged for Friday afternoon and the cocktail party that night," I said, acknowledging that Amanda's publisher had already paid for Molly's stay. "And, I tell you what—since you're losing out on several days lodging with us, why don't I give you a voucher that you could use for another visit? We host many book-related events throughout the year, and since you live so close . . ."

Molly cut me off with a wave of her hand. "That's very nice, but while I don't mind popping in for a few events while Amanda is around, I don't know if I'll ever feel like actually staying here again." She grabbed her suitcase and opened the front door. "Too many bad associations. I know Lisette wasn't killed here, but still . . ." She rolled her shoulders in a dramatic shudder.

"I understand, but the offer stands if you ever change your mind."

Molly bobbed her head before rushing out onto the porch. It seemed she couldn't leave Chapters fast enough.

A little odd, I thought, as I walked back to my bedroom. *Sure, she knew Lisette from the fan club and her brief time here, but they didn't appear to be friends. Her reaction seems excessive. Of course, if she killed Lisette . . .*

I couldn't really imagine Molly killing anyone, even if she had a bad temper, but I'd been wrong before. She *was* part of the fan club.

With breakfast done and an hour or so at my disposal before I needed to help Alicia with some cleaning, I decided do a little internet sleuthing. Harper's mention of serious conflicts in the Amanda Nobel fandom, along with Molly's speedy departure, had sparked an idea in my mind. Perhaps Molly had been deeply involved in the fan war herself. Maybe that was why she had seemed so antagonistic toward Lisette, and so anxious to leave Chapters.

I cast a glance at the ARC of Amanda's latest book before I pulled out my laptop and settled down on my bed. *Maybe I should give that to Harper or Molly,* I thought, as I leaned back on the pillows I'd stacked against the headboard of my iron-framed bed. *Especially since I'd have to read eleven other books to catch up before I read this new one.* I dug my bare toes into the ridges of my white chenille bedspread. My bedroom, with its coral-painted walls set off by crisp white curtains and glossy white trim, still bore the imprint of Great-Aunt Isabella's decorating. My only additions had been photos taken with Brent during our vacations. I'd also hung one of my favorite pictures of Brent in a prominent spot. It was a photo that captured all of his charm and vitality and, I had to admit, sometimes spurred me to talk to him when I was alone in my room.

"What do you think?" I asked the portrait. "Am I entertaining another murderer at Chapters, or is the killer someone from the outside?"

Or someone who just left, I thought, as I scrolled through the results of my first search. Molly Zeleski's name popped up almost immediately. I zeroed in on one promising article from a fan blog, where they identified her as one of the major players in an incident involving Lisette Bradford's Amanda Nobel fan club.

Apparently, she'd participated online using the handle "MerryMolly." Reading through the timeline of events associated with the fan war, I was shocked by the vitriol MerryMolly had spewed in post after highlighted post.

She was no fan of Lisette, that was for sure. In fact, she'd led the charge against one of Lisette's most popular pieces of fan fiction, claiming it was a plagiarized version of another writer's work. Molly was supported by several other members of the fan club, but strangely, the author who'd supposedly been victimized—someone who wrote under the pseudonym "Amethyst Angel"—was silent. Although Molly referenced her repeatedly, Amethyst Angel's fan fiction was posted on other sites, and she never popped up on the fan club to defend herself. Apparently, she wasn't even a member of Lisette's online community.

Which made me wonder if Molly and Amethyst Angel were one and the same person.

I surfed through several analyses of the incident on other blogs and websites before calling Ellen to share what I'd learned about the online conflict.

"You think it's possible that Molly was actually the author of the story that Lisette was accused of stealing?" she asked when I'd recited all the facts I'd gleaned from various sites.

"It isn't uncommon for people to have more than one online persona," I replied. "Especially for distinctively different sites. If Molly wrote the story she claims Lisette stole, wouldn't that be a good reason to hate her?"

"But enough to murder her?" A tapping sound told me that Ellen was drumming her fingers against the phone receiver. "I suppose there are some who would kill over such a thing, but I think someone would need to be an extremely volatile, perhaps even unstable, person to do that."

"Molly certainly seemed to dislike Lisette, and she does appear to have a short temper, but I don't know if I'd call her unstable. Not that I know her well, or anything, but she didn't come across that way on short acquaintance."

"Did Lisette profit off the fan fiction?"

"I don't think so. It was on a free site and her website, from what I could tell."

"Which means she didn't actually steal any income from this Amethyst Angel person." Ellen cleared her throat. "Would bragging rights over a popular story really have spurred anyone, including Molly, to kill Lisette?"

"Hard to say, isn't it? People can commit murder for strange reasons."

"Very true, but then you also said there were other members of the fan club who were equally vicious in their attacks on Lisette. Some of them could've been in attendance at Saturday's event, couldn't they?"

I stared at my blank laptop screen for a moment before closing the computer with a sigh. "Absolutely. Which doesn't really narrow the field of suspects."

"It will give the police something else to go on, though. I assume you plan to tell them about what you discovered online."

"Of course. I already shared what Harper Gregg told me about a fan war, and this confirms that story."

"Good." Ellen exhaled an audible breath. "This Harper person—wasn't she a member of the fan club too?"

"She is now. But she told me she didn't join until after the plagiarism controversy went down."

"I'm sure the authorities will check to make sure that's true."

"I would hope so." I ran my hand over the smooth surface of my laptop. "Of course, we can't forget Lisette's ex, who's still apparently on the run."

"And there's also Roger Warren, unfortunately," Ellen said. "I'm glad Scott was cleared. I'd hate to see him have to deal with all that scrutiny again."

"Julie's relieved, that's for sure. Not that she suspected him, of course. But having that hanging over one's head . . ."

"Ah yes, the looming shadow of suspicion," Ellen said, her tone oddly sharp. "Anyway, I should let you go. I'm sure you have a lot to manage right now."

"Not as much as you'd think," I said, surprised when Ellen just threw out a quick "goodbye" and hung up before I could respond any further.

Something is bothering her, I thought, as I left my bedroom. *I expect it's tied up with that business involving Gavin Howard. But with all the secrets she seems to juggle with aplomb, I wonder why his snooping has her so particularly concerned.*

Wandering into the kitchen, I was surprised to see Damian lounging against the island. It was unusual for him to stop in for a chat unrelated to work.

"Hi, Charlotte. How're you doing today?" he asked, hooking his thumbs through the belt loops of his egg yolk-yellow cotton shorts.

I could see why. The shorts, which hung off his slender frame, had slid down far enough to reveal the elastic band of his underwear.

Alicia side-eyed him. "They still make belts, you know."

Damian shot me a grin before meeting Alicia's disapproving gaze. "I know. But since I'm not working today, I thought I could play it more casual." He tucked his tropical-print shirt into his shorts. "There, maybe that will help."

Alicia sniffed. "A few extra meals might do more good. I swear, you aren't much of an advertisement for your food, skinny as you are."

"That's just genetics," Damian said. "You've seen my mama. She's the same—tall and thin."

"Like her grandpa," Alicia said. "He was originally from the low country down in South Carolina, as I recall."

Damian fiddled with one of his dreadlocks. "Yeah, we apparently have some Gullah heritage. Too bad he died before I was born. I never got to meet any of that part of the family."

"I bet you could find them if you tried," I said, thinking of all the genealogical information available at libraries as well as online.

"Never really gave it much thought." Damian hitched up his shorts. "But I've been pretty busy, just trying to survive. Not enough time or cash to just take off to visit distant relatives. Being a freelance chef . . . Well, you know how it goes. No steady income."

"I know, and I wish you could land a full-time job at one of the local restaurants," I said. "Although that wouldn't really be in my best interest, I suppose."

"I'd recommend someone else for Chapters if that happened." Damian frowned. "Even though it doesn't seem too likely."

Alicia, wiping her hands on a kitchen towel, turned to face Damian. "I reckon you didn't stop by to talk about your job prospects, so what brings you here this morning?"

Damian straightened to his full height. "That guest of yours. Molly Zeleski. Told you I knew her from school."

"I remember," I said. "But you said you didn't know her well, even if you did know she had a bad temper. Did you hear some additional news about her?"

"Not really anything new. Just remembered something else when I heard about that murder." Damian lowered his lashes over his eyes. "Felt like déjà vu, didn't it?"

I cast him a sympathetic smile. Like me, he'd been considered a suspect in another murder, last summer. "At least this one didn't happen at Chapters."

"There is that," Alicia said, pulling off her hairnet and shaking out her curly hair. "That girl took off this morning, by the way. Molly whatever, I mean."

"Really?" Damian's angular face expressed surprise. "The police didn't make her stay in town?"

"Well, she lives in Morehead, so I guess they figured that was close enough. I mean, they can still easily question her," Alicia said.

"Suppose that's true." Damian swept back his hair with one hand. "That kind of makes me stopping by pretty useless. I mainly wanted to warn you all about Molly, since she was staying here."

I crossed my arms over my chest. "Warn us? Why? You told me she got in some fights, but that was years ago."

"Yeah, but with this new murder, I reconsidered a few things. Things I didn't think were necessary, or appropriate, to mention before. The truth is, she has a reputation for getting . . . well, violent is the best way to say it, even though that sounds a bit too dramatic."

Alicia shared a quick raised-eyebrow look with me before returning her focus to Damian. "She beats people up or what?"

"She used to. Like I told Charlotte before, she had a bad temper when we were in school. Most of it was just verbal outbursts, but she got into physical fights too." Damian shrugged. "Understand, a lot of this comes from the rumor mill. I didn't witness the fights, so I don't know who started what. I do know she was suspended after one altercation, so it must've been pretty bad. My school didn't expel many people, or even suspend them. They mostly sent kids to in-school suspension."

"So she has, or at least had, a raging temper," I said, my mind drifting back to the information I'd uncovered online. Molly's verbal attacks on the fan club site had been fierce and filled with vitriol. If she had a history of physical violence as well . . .

"Sounds like we're well rid of her," Alicia said.

"Let's just say I'm glad she's not staying here anymore." Damian stepped away from the counter. "Think I'll be heading out then. I'm considering stopping by the police station to mention this to Detective Johnson or someone. What do you think?" he asked, glancing at me.

"I believe that would be a responsible thing to do," I said.

"I don't know." Damian traced the outline of a floor tile with the tip of one of his sandals. "It's all hearsay and rumors. Not sure I want to get someone in trouble over that."

Alicia pursed her lips. "Just tell them what you know. Can't hurt. I mean, as long as you aren't making stuff up."

"I'm not," Damian snapped, before holding up his hands. "Sorry, I just don't like being accused of things. Stuff I've never done, and wouldn't ever. Had enough of that in my life."

I was surprised to see Alicia's stern expression soften at these words. "I can imagine. All right, you go on then. Tell the police what you just told us, and let them sort it out."

"If it helps, I really don't think Detective Johnson would accuse anyone of anything without solid proof," I said.

"No, she's a good one," Damian said, before he turned and headed for the back door.

"And thanks," I called after him. "I appreciate you thinking of us and wanting to give us a warning."

Damian paused with his hand on the latch to the back door. "No problem," he said, shooting me a grin. "Wouldn't want anything to happen to my steadiest employer."

I laughed, but Alicia grabbed the kitchen towel and snapped it at him. "Go on, you," she said, as he left the kitchen. Dropping the towel onto the counter, she glanced at me. "You shouldn't encourage him."

"He's a good kid," I said. "I don't know why you're so hard on him."

"Tough love," she muttered, using her fingers to fluff out some of her silver-streaked dark hair.

"Anyway, I'm free to help with the cleaning, if you're ready to take that on."

Alicia looked me up and down. "Don't trouble yourself. I can handle it. We have one less guest, and the others are still holed up in their rooms, so I can't get to those yet anyway. I'm sure you can find something else that needs doing, especially with that book club meeting coming up tonight."

I slapped a hand to my forehead. "Goodness, I'd practically forgotten about it. How are we doing with snacks? Anything I need to pick up at the store?"

"Nope. We're well stocked from that do on Saturday. Lots of leftovers." She eyed me with a questioning expression in her brown eyes. "I suppose that's all right? I didn't think the locals would mind leftovers, but if Ms. Nobel needs something special . . ."

"I'm sure she won't care. She seems pretty easy to please, honestly."

"True enough. Certainly not what I expected." Alicia slipped the black net back over her hair. "Thought she'd be more demanding, famous as she is."

I left Alicia in the kitchen and headed back to my room, where I called Ellen again to share Damian's warning about Molly Zeleski.

"I think we should move her to the top of the list, just under Billy Bradford," I said.

"Good deduction. But don't forget Roger Warren. I meant to ask—did Julie and Scott ever find out why he never called earlier when he supposedly had car trouble?"

"No," I said, realizing that this was another clue. "And apparently neither she nor Scott have heard anything from him since Saturday."

"Which is a little odd, don't you think? It doesn't look good for him, especially since the people I contacted about his personality and behavior were not that reassuring. Apparently, he was quite a firebrand back in the day. He even got into legal trouble over threatening a colleague at a conference. Something to do with plagiarism, from what I heard. That was many years ago, but still . . ." Ellen's voice tapered off, as if she was distracted. "Hold on, Gavin's coming in. I don't really want to discuss any of this around him."

"Why? It isn't really connected to his snooping."

"I just don't want him to know that we're sleuthing on the side." Ellen sniffed. "Especially you."

I stared at my phone screen for a second before the realization struck. "Oh, I see. You want him to think I'm clueless, so maybe he'll spill some information about his secret mission around me?"

"Precisely. So"—Ellen raised her voice and added a sugary edge to her tone—"nice to talk to you, dear. Let's catch up later, okay?"

"Jolly good, Sherlock."

Chapter Nine

Everyone but the guest of honor and her entourage had assembled for the book club meeting Monday evening when Ellen appeared with Gavin in tow.

I widened my eyes as I cast her a glance. Maybe bringing Gavin along was just part of their cover for his real identity and activities, but it still surprised me. As Ellen introduced him to the others as her cousin, I busied myself rearranging the drinks and glasses on the linen-draped desk we used as a serving table in the library.

"Very nice to make your acquaintance," Bernadette Sandburg said, giving Gavin's hand a firm shake. "I don't believe I've met any of Ellen's relatives before."

And you still haven't, I thought, forcing a bright smile and asking, "Anyone want lemonade?"

To his credit, Gavin played the part to perfection, making polite but cryptic remarks about his work in "research" when questioned by Pete Nelson. "I'm mostly freelance," he said, after Sandy Nelson asked where he was employed.

Scott, who was eyeing Gavin with more than a little curiosity, nudged Julie with his elbow. "Another freelancer. We should form a club."

Julie took a sip of her white wine as she studied Gavin. "I'm glad you've been able to carve out a career for yourself in research. I imagine it's difficult."

Gavin nodded. "It is. But I'm not an author, which I think is perhaps a more precarious occupation. I collect data and other such boring information."

Ellen cleared her throat. "Anyway, I hope you all don't mind that I brought Gavin along tonight. I just hated to leave him alone, rattling around my big old house."

"No doubt," I said under my breath, a comment that earned me a warning glance from Ellen.

"And you must be Ophelia," Gavin said, as he clasped the taller Sandburg sister's hand. He kept hold of her fingers while he fixed her with a strangely intense stare.

"Why yes, I am." Ophelia cast a glance at Ellen. "Has your cousin been talking about me and my sister? I wouldn't have thought we'd be of much interest." She fluttered her eyelashes as she refocused on Gavin.

"I just gave him a quick rundown on the folks who'd be in attendance tonight," Ellen said, the sharp edge in her tone making Bernadette narrow her eyes as she looked from Gavin to Ellen and back again.

"How about we all take a seat and get this discussion underway? I'm sure Amanda and the others will show up momentarily," I said, crossing to one of the hard-backed chairs I'd pulled in from the dining room. "And don't forget—there are plenty of snacks and drinks. Just help yourself whenever you want anything."

"Please sit next to me, Gavin," Ophelia said, as she settled into one of the library's leather-upholstered chairs. "We get so few guests at our book club meetings. It's always nice to see a new face."

Gavin gallantly thanked her and chose a wooden chair placed beside her while Bernadette selected one of the other upholstered chairs.

Ellen hurried across the room and plunked down in the dining room chair on the other side of the leather armchair, almost knocking Pete out of the way. "Sorry," she told the plump café owner. "Didn't see you there."

Pete mumbled something about being hard to miss before ambling over to one of the folding chairs I'd used to complete a circle on the rug.

"We should leave this one for Amanda, don't you think?" Julie motioned to the library's remaining leather armchair. "And the seat beside it for Tony," she added, as she sat in a folding chair a few seats away.

"He does seem to want to monitor her every move," Scott said, sitting beside Julie.

"That makes sense, though. Isn't he her personal assistant?" Bernadette scooted so far back in her deep chair that her short legs didn't touch the floor.

"No. He's a marketing and publicity specialist who works for her publisher." Julie shrugged. "There might be some divided loyalties there."

Ophelia leaned across one arm of her chair to address Gavin. "Now, tell me, what do you think about this murder in Beaufort? It's the second in as many years, you know."

"So I've heard." Gavin's expression, while pleasant, gave no hint of his feelings on the matter.

"At least we aren't discussing a murder mystery book this time," Sandy said with a dramatic shudder. "That would be too spooky."

"I think it was that Billy Bradford character." Pete cast his wife an amused glance. "You know they always say that the husband, or in this case, the ex-husband, did it."

"I hope that's not a warning," Sandy replied, widening her eyes in mock horror.

Pete grabbed her hand and lifted it to his lips for a brief kiss. "Never, my love. How could I manage without you?"

"Not well, I imagine," Bernadette said dryly. "And as for this latest murder, my money is on Roger Warren."

"Now wait a minute." Scott slid to the edge of his chair as if preparing to jump to his feet, but sat back when Julie laid a hand on his arm.

"I overheard Ms. Bradford threaten to rally Amanda Nobel's fans to downgrade the review rating on his books on that Goodbooks site and elsewhere." Bernadette met Scott's perturbed gaze without faltering. "You must've heard it too, since you were standing right there."

"It's Goodreads," he said. "And yes, both Roger and I were threatened by Ms. Bradford, but you can't imagine either of us would kill someone over negative book ratings."

He shifted his elastic features from anger to amusement. "I'd have to become a serial killer if that were the case."

"Anyway, Scott's been cleared by the police," Julie said, her fingers tightening on his arm. "He was seen by several people in a restaurant during the time the murder likely occurred."

Bernadette raised her eyebrows. "And Roger?"

"Come on, Bernie," Ophelia said. "We've known Roger Warren for years. Even though he does have a temper, he's no more a killer than we are."

"Honestly, Fee, are you sure I haven't knocked off someone in the past?" Bernadette crossed her arms over her chest and flashed a wicked grin.

"I'm sure we'd never find out if you had," Ellen said. "But getting back to the discussion at hand, had any of you read Amanda Nobel's books before this?"

Sandy raised her hand and waved it above her head. "Me. I love the entire series."

"First for me," Pete said. "Sandy's been hounding me for years to try the first one, but it took this book club pick to convince me."

"I've read all the books too." Julie cast a questioning glance at Scott. "Even if I don't think Scott approves."

"It's not for me to approve or disapprove of your reading material," Scott said. "But this is the first one of her books I've tried." His lips twitched. "And I think you know my opinion."

"Everyone knows that." Ophelia offered him a smile before turning to Gavin. "What did you think? Was the research a little too weak for you as well?"

"I must confess I haven't read the book," Gavin said. "Ellen brought me along as a kindness. Just so I wouldn't be left at her house all alone."

Just so you wouldn't snoop through her things. Of course, I didn't voice this thought aloud, choosing to sneak a glance at Ellen's face instead. As I expected, her expression was as bland as milk.

"Hello, so glad you all decided to attend, especially after the terrible news about Ms. Bradford," Amanda Nobel said as she sailed into the room, trailed by Tony Lott.

"Is Molly coming?" I whispered to Harper, who slipped into the library behind Tony and then crossed the room to sit in a folding chair next to me.

Harper shook her head. "Got a text from her saying she couldn't make it."

"Too bad," I said, adding this information to my mental checklist of items casting Molly as a likely suspect.

"We're impressed that you were still willing to participate, Ms. Nobel." Sandy, her eyes bright with excitement, clasped her hands together at her breast. "It's such an honor to get to speak directly with any author, but especially you, because you're one of my all-time favorites."

"Why, thank you," Amanda said, glancing at me.

I realized I hadn't made any introductions and leapt to my feet.

"Please, call me Amanda," the author replied, after I rectified my failings as a hostess by introducing everyone else. "And feel free to ask me any questions. I really don't mind. I can even take criticism, if you want to share it." She flashed Scott a warm smile.

Color rising in his cheeks, Scott pressed a hand to his heart. "Forgive me for Saturday. I was defending my friend, Roger, and got carried away."

"No problem at all." Amanda's emerald and sapphire studded rings glittered as she waved her hand through the air. "I know my books aren't to everyone's taste. Heavens, sometimes even I don't like them," she added with a throaty laugh.

"Of course she's kidding." Tony rubbed his bald pate with one hand as he swept his gaze over the assembled group. "She loves all her books. How else could she write so many so quickly?"

"How indeed?" murmured Amanda, before straightening in her chair. "Seriously, I really do want to know what you all think. Be honest. And, again, ask me anything."

The conversation took off after that, with everyone freely offering their opinions, most of which were positive. I was impressed that even the few criticisms were met with gracious smiles from Amanda.

"What I really want to know," Sandy said, "is how you create the original idea. I just don't understand how you writers come up with all these amazing concepts. I couldn't do it."

Amanda settled back against the soft leather upholstery of her chair, allowing her gaze to wander over the shelves full of books that filled the library. "It is astonishing, isn't it? Books, I mean. All the books by so many authors. You'd think all the ideas would be used up, but somehow they're not." She turned to Sandy with a smile. "Actually, it was the reading I did when I was young. I loved all books but was particularly fond of the classic adventure novels. Especially the epic ones, like *The Count of Monte Cristo* or *The Scarlet Pimpernel*. I fell in love with all those gallant heroes who had to overcome such odds to achieve their happy endings."

"I can see that," Julie said. "I think that comes through in your own books."

"I hope so." Amanda gazed upward, as if seeking inspiration in the varnished beadboard ceiling. "I adore tales of intrigue and grand adventure. I guess I've always been entranced by the swashbuckling deeds of handsome but dangerous men."

"Oh, so am I!" Ophelia said, clapping her hands together.

Bernadette side-eyed her sister. "Maybe a little too much so in the past."

At these words, Gavin leaned back, lifting up the front legs of his chair. "Really, Ms. Sandburg? Sounds intriguing. Perhaps you should elaborate."

Ellen shot him a sharp look. "Getting back to Amanda's books, I'm sure we can all agree that Adrian is quite the heroic main character, even if he is a pirate by trade. What made you decide on that profession for your protagonist, Amanda?"

"I don't know. The mysterious enchantment of the sea, I suppose. And I expect I was influenced by the legend of the Flying Dutchman, in a way."

Julie held up one finger. "Ah, there it is. I knew I felt the hint of some other legend haunting the story, but couldn't quite place it."

"The cursed man redeemed by love," Scott said thoughtfully. "I see it now too."

"Yes, poor Adrian. Cast back and forth through time, continually separated from his beloved Katarina." Amanda's smile, while bright, appeared to me to be a little strained. "I must admit it's difficult to keep that seesaw in motion. All that back and forth—will they get their lasting happy ever after or not? It can be a bit tricky to maintain the balance."

"After twelve books, I guess so," Bernadette said. "That's a lot of will they or won't they. I suppose there'll be a thirteenth book?"

"Of course." Tony jumped in before Amanda could reply. "It's undergoing final proofing as we speak, and the ARCs are already available. Should be out early next year."

"Something to look forward to," Sandy said.

"Yet another book to add to my towering TBR." Julie gave Amanda a broad smile. "But I promise to bump it to the top of my list."

"Don't feel compelled to do that," Amanda said, ignoring an acrid glance from Tony. "I would hate for my book to displace many other, undoubtedly more worthy, titles."

"Not more worthy in my eyes." Julie grabbed one of Scott's hands and squeezed it. "Despite the love of my life being such a stickler for facts, there's nothing I like better than an exciting story, true or not. I love a great escape."

Amanda gazed down at her own hands, which were clasped tightly in her lap. "I'm glad my books can give you that."

"And will, for many more years to come," Tony said.

Sandy scooted to edge of her chair. "Okay, so what I really want to know now is how you deal with working with the people running the TV show. Do you get much say in it, or not?"

As the conversation veered off into a discussion of the perils and rewards of media adaptions, I allowed my gaze to wander over the colorful spines of the books that filled the library. My Great-Aunt Isabella, who'd built a personal collection that rivaled some small public libraries, probably would've loved Amanda Nobel's books. She was certainly no stranger to adventure. *Although, come to think of it, perhaps Amanda's books wouldn't offer a real escape to someone who was a spy,* I thought, a smile twitching my lips. *Maybe she preferred a heartfelt romance.* My smile faded. *Which was sadly not something she was likely to have experienced in her real life.*

Isabella, I'd recently learned, had worked as an agent for U.S. intelligence for much of her life, getting involved in a relationship with a Soviet spy named Paul Peters, whose upbringing in England had allowed him to successfully pose as a British academic. Based on things Ellen had said, as well as my own remembrances, I suspected that my great-aunt had never loved Peters and had just used the relationship to keep tabs on his activities and feed him disinformation. Whether she'd ever found love elsewhere, I didn't know, but it was clear that she hadn't been able to openly enjoy a true love, since she'd had to pretend to be loyal to Peters for years.

I glanced over at Ellen, idly wondering if she'd ever known any true, uncomplicated love of her own. She'd never spoken about such a thing, which didn't necessarily mean it hadn't happened. *But,* I realized, *I don't even know her preferences. She's never talked about anyone in that way, male or female.* I shook my head. I couldn't allow such fancies to distract me from my hosting duties. *Besides,* I thought, as I rose to my feet, *it's none of my business.*

"You've been talking for quite some time; you must be parched. Can I get you something to drink?" I asked Amanda as I crossed to the desk. "Or you, Tony? Or anyone else?"

"Water would be great," Amanda said.

Tony echoed her, adding, "And maybe it's time to wrap things up? It's been a difficult couple of days for Amanda. She's always so gracious with her fans, but I do like to make sure she doesn't become exhausted."

"I think I'm the best judge of that," Amanda's words cut sharp as razor blades, but she immediately adjusted her tone to offer me a pleasant *thanks* when I handed her a tumbler of ice water.

"We have taken advantage of a good deal of your time," Harper said as she stood to face Amanda. She glanced at me. "Maybe we should switch to a social hour?"

"I vote for that. Those snacks are definitely calling my name," Pete said, standing and offering a hand to pull Sandy to her feet.

"That sounds like a good idea," I agreed. "We can mingle and chat among ourselves while still giving everyone a chance to talk to Amanda one-on-one." I held up one hand. "After she gets a little break, I mean."

"Really, I'm fine," Amanda said. "And before everyone digs too deeply into the food, I would like to share an announcement about a new book."

Tony coughed and sputtered. "Sorry, just swallowed wrong," he said, when asked if he was okay.

Harper, balancing a plate of hors d'oeuvres on her lap, looked up and fixed an inquiring gaze on Amanda. "A new book that isn't in the *Tides* series?"

"That's right. Something completely different," Amanda said.

"Ooo, that sounds fabulous." Sandy paused with a bite-sized cucumber sandwich halfway between her plate and her mouth. "Another romantic saga, I hope."

"Well . . ." was all Amanda managed to say before Tony cut her off again.

"I don't think we should be discussing that yet, Mandy," he said, shooting her a side-eyed glare. "Might jeopardize things, you know."

Amanda took a long swallow of her water before replying. "If you say so. And please, for the hundredth time, don't call me that."

"Whatever you say." Tony stood and headed toward the desk holding the snacks and drinks. "Now, let me see—what can I get you?"

"Nothing," Amanda said, also rising to her feet. "I am perfectly capable of getting my own food. And anything else," she added, in a quiet tone I could hear only because she'd moved close to me.

After she placed a few hors d'oeuvres on her plate, Amanda wandered off to talk to Harper, Sandy, the Sandburg sisters, and Julie, while Pete tried his best to chat up Gavin, who replied with noncommittal answers that I could tell frustrated the congenial café owner.

"A man of mystery," Scott said, as he refilled Julie's wine glass before pouring a drink of his own.

"Which one?" I asked, motioning surreptitiously toward Tony, who was examining the bookshelves.

"Not him. Ellen's cousin. Looks like an accountant but, somehow, I don't think that's the sort of thing he does. Researcher, my . . ."

I cut him off with a swift slicing motion at my neck. "Hey, Ellen. Ready to read more of the *Tides* series now?"

"We'll see," she replied without looking at me.

Scott gave her a wink before carrying the wine glass over to Julie.

I glanced at Ellen out of the corner of my eye. Her gaze was still fixed on Gavin.

"Did you at least enjoy the discussion?" I asked, keeping my tone as innocent as possible.

"It was very illuminating. As was the entire evening," she said.

I took a sip from my own glass of wine. "That's good."

But I wasn't fooled. I didn't think she was referring to anything related to Amanda Nobel or her books.

Chapter Ten

After the book club meeting ended, I helped Alicia clean up the library and kitchen.

"They barely made a dent in the food," she said as she plopped one of the trays of hors d'oeuvres on top of the kitchen island. "We're going to be swimming in this stuff for days yet."

"I think they were too busy fangirling over Amanda," I replied with a smile. "Even the guys. Although not so much Scott, of course. And it's hard to tell with Gavin."

Alicia thrust her yellow latex gloves into the soapy water filling the sink and pulled out a pewter tray. "There it is. I knew there was one more." She rinsed the small platter and stacked it in the dish rack before turning to face me. "About that fellow . . ."

"Who, Gavin Howard?"

"Yeah, or whatever his name is." Alicia yanked off her gloves and flapped them through the air. "There's a reason I steered clear of the library tonight. The truth is, I've seen him here before."

I paused in my tidying to stare at her. "What? When?"

"A few years ago, not long before Isabella died." Alicia slapped one of the gloves against her bare palm. "Even though I admit he's something of an average Joe, I remember him all right. We didn't get too many visitors in those days, other than the paying guests, and he sure wasn't one of those."

"Did he say his name was Gavin Howard?"

Alicia shrugged. "Didn't introduce himself. Not to me, anyway." She tossed the gloves on the counter. "Truth is, I was out that morning. I always used to go to the farmers market once or twice a week, like you do now, because Isabella couldn't handle that task anymore. It was a week where we didn't have any guests. Sometime in November I think it was. Anyway, it was cold."

"He was here when you came back from the market?"

"Yep. I don't think he ever saw me, 'cause I slipped in through the back porch. I crept in pretty quietly, thinking Isabella might be napping. That's what she said she was going to do before I left, so I just assumed she'd be asleep in her bedroom."

I leaned my hip into the bullnose edge of the soapstone counter. "You didn't notice a strange car parked in the lot or out front?"

"No, I reckon he must have parked around the corner or something. So when I walked in and heard voices, I was shocked, and more than a little worried."

"I would guess so." I examined Alicia's face, noting the concern in her dark eyes. "How do you know it's the same man if you never met?"

"Because I saw him. I heard those voices, Isabella's and some man's, and I grabbed a kitchen knife . . ."

I raised my eyebrows but said nothing. I probably would've done the same.

". . . then sneaked down the hall to the parlor, where they were talking." Alicia met my intent gaze with a lift of her chin. "You know how that door has those fancy hinges, so there's a goodly gap between the door and the frame? Anyway, it allowed me to hang back against the wall and still peek into the room."

"And you saw the man now staying with Ellen?"

"Clear as a summer day," Alicia said in a triumphant tone.

"Did you hear what they were talking about?"

"Not really. I mean, I heard him say something about *protecting her friends* right before Isabella ordered him to leave the house." Alicia cast me a knowing look. "I scurried on back to the kitchen at that, because when Isabella issued a command, it was likely to be obeyed. Which it was, from the sound of footsteps on the floorboards and doors opening and slamming."

"What did you do next?"

"Waited a few minutes, then"—Alicia grimaced—"opened and closed the door to the back porch as loudly as I could, so anyone would think I'd just come inside. Don't get me wrong, I didn't like deceiving Isabella that way, but something told me I shouldn't let her know I'd seen that guy, or heard anything of their conversation." She pulled off her hairnet and crumpled it in one hand. "Which, as I said, I really didn't."

I snapped the lid down on the plastic container I'd been filling and carried it over to the refrigerator. Leaning back against the refrigerator door after closing it, I faced Alicia. "Thanks for telling me. I don't know what it means, but I think we should keep an eye on Mr. Howard, just to be safe."

"Couldn't agree more." Alicia snatched up the yellow plastic gloves and tucked them behind the dish rack. "Always seemed peculiar to me, and now that he's claiming to be Ellen's cousin, well, I just don't know. Why would any relative of Ellen's pop in to talk to Isabella when no one else was around, including Ellen?"

"That is strange," I said, my mind reeling from this new revelation. Gavin Howard definitely wasn't just any agent looking into something from the past. He'd actually interacted directly with my great-aunt at least once. "But Ellen is going along with the cousin story. Maybe there's a good reason?"

"I'd like to hear it, if there is." Alicia turned back to the sink. "Anyway, I just wanted you to know, in case Ellen was in trouble or something. You know there are younger men who like to scam old ladies, so I thought I should alert you. Two sets of eyes are better than one and all that."

"Agreed," I said, smothering the laugh that had bubbled up at the thought of any man, young or otherwise, duping Ellen Montgomery. "Unless you need me to do anything else, I'm off to bed. Well, to my room to read, anyway."

Alicia waved me off. "No problem. I'll be finished here in a minute and plan to head on up to bed myself after that."

I wished her a good evening before escaping to my room. After mulling over Alicia's comments about Gavin, it took a while for my mind to focus, and just as I found myself enjoying the world created by Mary Stewart in her classic romantic suspense novel, *Airs Above the Ground,* the jangle of my cell phone pulled me back to reality.

"Sorry to bother you so late again," Detective Johnson said, "but I felt it was important to give you a warning. Unfortunately, we haven't been able to bring him in for questioning yet, but William Bradford has been spotted in the area."

"Billy Bradford is still hanging around Beaufort?" I asked, with a glance at my bedroom windows. I'd need to make sure they were locked as soon as I got off the phone. *As well as check all the doors and windows in the rest of the house,* I thought, with a sigh.

"Yes, we've had some credible sightings. We're actively trying to track him down, of course, but I wanted to put you on notice in case he decides to return to Chapters. If you see or hear anything, please call me at this number, no matter the time."

"I will." I considered the information Damian and others had recently shared with me. "And if you have a minute, I'd like to inform you about some things I've discovered over the last couple of days."

"Thanks for that," Detective Johnson said, when I finished filling her in on what I'd learned. "We'd gotten some of the same info from Mr. Kepler and Mr. Carr, but hadn't received anything on that fan war yet."

"Harper Gregg didn't mention it?"

"Not to my knowledge. But we have another meeting with her scheduled for tomorrow. Perhaps she was waiting until then to share that information."

"It does open up the field of suspects, I'm afraid."

"Unfortunately. Especially since many of the fan club members could've been in Beaufort for your event, and who knows how many stayed over Saturday night." There was a brief pause before the detective spoke again. "I wonder if I could ask a favor?"

"Of course. As long as it doesn't require putting myself, or anyone else, in danger again."

"It shouldn't. I just remember how well you and Ms. Montgomery handled yourselves during that murder investigation last year, and wondered if perhaps you'd be willing to be of assistance again?"

I stared at my phone for a second before answering. The idea set off a frisson of excitement in me—which I wasn't sure was a good thing. "In what way?"

"Simply be my eyes and ears when you're around your current guests. Since Molly Zeleski has returned to her home, we're working with the Morehead City police to keep tabs on her, but I thought perhaps you and Ms. Montgomery could watch Ms. Nobel, Mr. Lott, and Ms. Gregg. Not that I want you to pump them for information, but if you were to overhear anything related to the case . . ."

"I'll l be happy to pass along any relevant information," I said, glad her request didn't involve anything more intrusive. While I wanted to help the police, I wasn't comfortable directly interrogating my guests. "And I can talk to Ellen about assisting with a few pertinent questions. I haven't canceled the tea party I planned for Friday afternoon yet. That is an intimate affair, only involving Ms. Nobel and the fans who were supposed to be staying at Chapters. I could invite Ellen to that event, as well as the cocktail party scheduled for later that day. Perhaps it will seem more natural if she asks some pertinent questions rather than me. I mean, she has the background to do it in a way that won't be perceived as odd."

"Which is why I mentioned her in the first place. She does have a unique set of skills. Even more than you probably know."

"Oh?" I wondered what Detective Johnson had been able to discover about my enigmatic neighbor. Undoubtedly, her law enforcement connections would've unearthed more than my feeble attempts at research, which so far had yielded nothing. But of course, she wasn't going to share classified information with me. "All right, I'll talk to Ellen tomorrow, and perhaps set up some sort of get-together where she could chat informally with my guests." *As long as Gavin Howard stays out of the picture,* I thought, but decided not to share that concern. Detective Johnson seemed to know too much about Ellen already. At least, more than I thought Ellen would be happy to share.

After Detective Johnson hung up, I debated calling Ellen immediately. But it was late, and there was nothing we could do at the moment. It would keep until tomorrow. For now, I needed to walk around Chapters to make sure the house was properly secured against Billy Bradford or any other intruder.

I made the rounds through the ground floor first, double-checking every door and window. With that task completed, I climbed the stairs to the second floor. Of course, I didn't think anyone could easily access the upper-level windows, but we did have a fire escape built against one side of the house. It was possible that a determined intruder could use those metal stairs to climb to the second floor, even if the final steps were a ladder pulled up so it didn't touch the ground.

As I made my way to the fire escape door at the end of the hall, raised voices stopped me in my tracks. They were coming from the Mystery Suite, where I'd placed Amanda Nobel.

I slipped closer to the suite and pressed my ear against the door. Yes, I was eavesdropping, but the loud voices, combined with Detective Johnson's request for surveillance, overcame my scruples. I'd already identified the voices as belonging to Amanda and Tony. Given their less than cordial relationship, clearly evidenced at the book club meeting, I was curious to discover the reason for their argument.

"That's the most ridiculous thing I've ever heard." Amanda's voice cracked on the final word.

"No more so than you accusing me of killing someone," Tony replied, his words staccato as bullets.

I clasped my hands together to stop their shaking. Amanda obviously believed that Tony had some motive to murder Lisette, but what?

"You have a reason. I don't," Amanda said.

Tony's laugh was as sharp as one of Shandy's barks. "Since when is jealously *not* a motive for murder?"

"You really think I'm jealous?" Amanda's peal of laughter was edged with mania. "Why would you think that? I agreed to the scheme without hesitation, remember?"

"But maybe you decided differently when you really saw it come to fruition," Tony said. "Maybe it rankled that you couldn't change your mind, when all was said and done."

"No, and no." The tapping of heels across the wooden floorboards alerted me that Amanda was approaching the door. "It's time for you to go, Tony. I'm too exhausted to have this discussion with you right now."

"Not exactly a discussion, more like an attack," he replied, before stomping toward the door.

I scooted away, hurrying down the hall to reach the fire exit before the Mystery Suite door flew open and Tony strode out.

I was prepared to offer up my excuse of checking the locks, but Tony didn't even glance in my direction. He simply marched to his adjacent room and entered, slamming the door behind him.

Amanda poked her head around the door to her suite. Catching sight of me at the end of the hall, she lifted her hand in greeting and replaced her angry frown with a smile. "Oh, hello, Charlotte. What brings you upstairs at this time of night?"

"Just checking the doors," I said, tapping the fire escape door for emphasis. Of course, for safety reasons, the guests had to be able to push open the door from the inside at all times, but an indicator on the door showed it was secured against anyone trying to enter from outside. "Can't be too careful these days."

"I doubt we really need to worry, but I appreciate your diligence," Amanda said, her blue eyes narrowing.

I plastered on a smile I hoped didn't look as false as it felt. "Well, good night, then," I said, walking closer to her room.

"Good night," she replied shortly before shutting her door in my face.

I stared at the plain oak door for a moment. *She suspects I heard something. I wonder why that seems to have upset her so? Perhaps because there* is *something to Tony's jealousy claim after all?*

Descending the stairs, I allowed my fingers to slide along the railing, worn to a satin finish by a multitude of hands over many years. *But what reason would Amanda Nobel, bestselling novelist with a popular television adaptation, have to feel envious of Lisette Bradford? Or, for that matter, what would've been Tony's motive to kill Lisette? Amanda seems to think there's something, and they did display a level of mutual animosity . . .*

I puzzled over these questions as I made my way back to my bedroom. Crossing to the window that looked out over the back yard, I caught a glimpse of movement.

Someone was walking across the back patio. Not really a crime, and not that unusual—I'd caught inquisitive tourists, hoping to get a better look at Chapters's enclosed garden, doing the same thing many times. But it was late for anyone to be wandering off the streets of Beaufort, especially in a residential area.

The figure looked male, but with a black hoodie and their back to me it was hard to be sure. I squinted as I peered out the window, hoping to get a better look. Finally, the visitor turned and took two steps toward the house, setting off the automatic floodlight on the back porch. The dark-clad stranger ducked their head. But I caught a glimpse of hair falling over a pale brow—light brown curls turned to gold by the wash of light.

It was Gavin Howard. There could be no mistake. Possessed by some inexplicable urge born out of fascination mixed with fury, I rapped the window glass with my knuckles.

Gavin jumped back, staring up at my window. The surprise on his face was immediately replaced by his typical calm expression. He lifted one hand and waved, as if loitering on my back patio late at night was nothing that should concern me.

I didn't wave in response, choosing to yank my white eyelet curtains across the window panes instead.

Gavin was investigating something connected to the past and my late great-aunt. Something that had ties to national security, despite the decades that separated Isabella's espionage work from current affairs. Like the conversation I'd overheard between Amanda Nobel and Tony Lott, it didn't make any sense. At least, not yet.

But I was determined to unravel both these mysteries, if I could. With or without Ellen's help. I might only be a

Watson, but like that fictional character, what I lacked in deductive brilliance, I made up for in sheer determination and persistence.

Besides, I thought, as I padded over to my bed, *you taught high school for years before taking over Chapters.*

If there was anything likely to toughen someone up and teach them how to play a long game, dealing with a classroom full of high-energy, hormonal, sometimes oppositional, teenagers was definitely it.

Chapter Eleven

The next morning all the guests left after breakfast to take advantage of the boat tour I'd arranged as part of their stay. I wasn't expecting them to continue to follow this agenda after everything that had happened, but once Amanda declared her intention to participate in the tour, the others followed her lead. Before they departed, Harper told me that she'd gotten a text from Molly, who was driving over to Beaufort to join them. I almost warned her to be extra careful around Molly, but closed my lips over the words just in time. Ellen and I might have placed Molly near the top of our suspect list, but that didn't mean that she was actually a danger to anyone.

While everyone was away, I stood at the sink, enjoying the solitude of the quiet house while mentally trying to pick apart the tangle of clues. My musing was broken by Alicia striding through the kitchen on her way outside.

"By the way, there's something I forgot to mention." Alicia paused at the door to the back porch. She had the day off, which was why I was cleaning up after a simple breakfast of her premade cinnamon rolls and other baked goods.

"What is it?" I asked, rinsing a glass platter before setting it in the dish rack.

"It's that Gavin Howard character again. He knocked on the back door while you were serving the guests in the dining room. I talked to him briefly on the porch."

"What did he want?" I yanked out the stopper to drain the soapy water in the sink.

"To speak with you, apparently. I told him you were busy and to return later this afternoon, because no one would be around this morning." She adjusted the strap of the large leather purse slung over her shoulder. "I hope I did right. I know the guests will be gone most of the day and figured you'd probably be out this morning, picking up things at the market."

"That was my plan." I dried my hands on a kitchen towel as I met her concerned gaze. "Don't worry, I won't let him in the house if I'm alone."

"Good idea. I'm having dinner with family, so I won't be back until late. Better not to let any strangers in, what with murderers running around." Alicia raised her hand in a quick goodbye before leaving the kitchen.

I finished cleaning up the kitchen as I considered my next move. Alicia's comments about Gavin had me questioning why he was interested in our schedules. Given Ellen's warning about Gavin probably wanting a chance to search Chapters, I couldn't discount the possibility that he might break in while he thought everyone was out of the house.

Looking to set a trap, I decided to keep to my plan and left in my car, as if going to the market. But I actually only drove around town for about ten minutes, then headed back to Chapters.

Parking on the street so I could quickly return to complete my errands, I slipped inside through the front door. As soon as I stepped into the hall, I stopped short. The faint sound of footsteps echoed through the otherwise silent house.

The noise was coming from upstairs. I pulled out my cell phone before setting my purse down on a side table. Clutching the phone, I slipped off my sandals and climbed the stairs as quietly as possible. I knew that there could be a simple answer to this unnerving occurrence. Perhaps one of the guests had changed their mind about the boat tour and returned to Chapters. But I had to make sure. I had to see if my trap had worked.

When I reached the second floor the footsteps thumped again—louder this time, and still over my head. Someone was in the attic.

The door to the attic stairs stood slightly ajar, which was another warning sign. I debated whether I should call the police. I always kept that door locked to prevent anyone from accessing the third floor, which was an unfinished attic filled with tripping hazards like old trunks and boxes. Lacking air conditioning and decent lighting, it wasn't a space I visited often, and I certainly didn't want any of my guests messing around up there.

But I suspected this was no guest. The one person who probably had the ability, and inclination, to not only pick the lock to one of the back doors but also jimmy the attic door was staying at Ellen's house, not mine.

I crept up the stairs, phone in hand, my finger hovering over the key that would instantly call 911. If my intruder was who I suspected, I wasn't afraid he'd harm me, but there was that little twinge of doubt. What if Billy Bradford had decided to hide out at Chapters so he could sneak down later and attack Amanda or any of Lisette's fan club acquaintances?

Before I reached the top of the steps, I leaned back against the rough wood of the stairwell wall and peered up, hoping to catch sight of the intruder without them seeing me. At first all I could see were shadows dancing over the timbered ceiling, but then I caught a glimpse of someone bending down to open a trunk. I could only see their back, but it was enough to tell me who was rummaging through my attic. The light brown, curly hair was a dead giveaway.

Just as I was about to call out Gavin's name, something silenced me—a pressure on my skin, as if someone had laid a hand on my shoulder. I snapped my mouth shut and delicately picked my way back down the stairs, almost expecting to see someone waiting on the second floor. But of course, no one was there.

I rubbed the spot where I could swear I'd felt the touch of fingers and considered my next move. Gavin apparently had been too engaged in his snooping to notice me, which meant I might be able to escape without him realizing I'd caught him in the act.

That gives you the advantage, I thought, as I slipped back down the stairs to the first floor. Even though I longed to confront Gavin over breaking into Chapters and rifling through my great-aunt's things, something told me that it was better to confer with Ellen first. She might want to use this knowledge as leverage against him.

I shook my head. It was certainly not a typical train of thought for me. I wasn't given to subterfuge. *It's almost like someone else is in your head right now,* I thought, as I stuck my bare feet back into my sandals and exited the house through the front door. I wasn't worried about leaving the house unlocked. I was sure Gavin would lock up behind him, if only to cover his tracks.

I was convinced he wasn't going to steal anything either, unless it was information related to Isabella's past activities. And frankly, I didn't really care about that. If some U.S. intelligence agency wanted to ferret out evidence of my great-aunt's past mistakes, they were welcome to it. She wasn't around to be harmed by such a thing, and surely, they wouldn't dare tarnish her reputation by announcing their clandestine operations to the world.

Although there's still Ellen, I thought, as I climbed into my car. Pausing for a moment before I drove away, I dialed her number on my cell phone.

She didn't answer, and I was leery of leaving a message about such a thing. I would check in with her when I returned from the market.

Hopefully her house guest would have fled my home by then.

* * *

Gavin was gone and all the doors were locked tight when I returned to Chapters about an hour later. I called Ellen but still got no answer, so I decided I'd better put away my groceries, which included several frozen items, before trying again. Just as I tossed the last package of frozen spinach into the freezer, my phone rang.

"Hey, glad I could catch you," said Julie. "I have some interesting news to share."

"Oh?" I locked the freezer and wandered into the kitchen. "What might that be?"

"Remember how I said I'd check with my publishing peeps about Amanda Nobel and Tony and all? Well, I just heard a couple of juicy rumors."

"Involving that fan war thing?" I asked, as I poured myself a glass of ice water.

"No, everyone thought that was old news. This is something that's churning through the rumor mill right now."

I sat down at the small café table in the kitchen where Alicia and I usually took our meals. "So it's not a secret?"

"I wouldn't say that. The person who told me this story said it's pretty hush-hush. I mean, there are rumors circulating and some chatter, but no one actually has any proof that it's true." Julie drew in a breath before continuing. "Anyway, that thirteenth book that Amanda mentioned? Apparently, there's talk that it's been ghostwritten. The scuttlebutt is that Amanda created the outline and checked over the final draft, but someone else wrote the bulk of the manuscript. And guess who that someone might be—none other than our murder victim, Lisette Bradford."

I leapt back to my feet. "Wait a minute. Are you saying that Lisette was hired to write a book in the *Tides* series?"

"Exactly. It's the next one coming out, book thirteen. My contact said Lisette had written a lot of fan fiction that was well-received, and she thought maybe that's why she was chosen as a ghostwriter."

"Is that typical?"

"No, not really. But it has been known to happen. Fan fiction turning into major deals, at least. Anyway, that's the first rumor I wanted to share."

"There's more?" I asked, my mind racing as I considered this new information in light of the argument I'd overheard between Amanda and Tony. Maybe Amanda did have a reason to be jealous of Lisette, after all. If she'd written the outline and approved the draft, she had to know what was going on, but perhaps she was forced into doing that . . .

"As for the other rumor, it has to do with Tony Lott. Apparently, there's a rumor that he had a fling with Lisette Bradford about a year or so ago. They met at fan-based events from time to time and supposedly hooked up. To be fair, this was after her divorce."

"Really?" I cleared my throat. "Well, that might explain their obvious dislike for one another, especially if it ended badly."

"Very badly, if the rumors are true. A few people observed an extremely ugly breakup at a conference not long ago. And apparently it was Lisette doing the dumping."

Which gives Tony Lott an even stronger motive for murder, I thought, before asking Julie for more information on the ghostwriting rumor.

"What I've already told you is all I really know. Like I said, it's just rumors. And no one associated with the publisher is going to confirm such a thing."

"If you think about it, Tony *has* been very careful when discussing book thirteen, I mean, the next *Tides* book." I thought back on his comments at the book club discussion. "He also cut Amanda off when she tried to talk about a new, and different, book. Something obviously not related to the *Tides* series."

"Probably because he wants the focus to remain on her successful series," Julie said. "It's a real cash cow for everyone involved. I'm sure he thinks that talking about something else, especially something new and unproven, isn't the best strategy."

"But if this ghostwriting rumor is out there, won't Amanda's fans find out about it?"

"Not necessarily. Maybe her mega-fans will hear something, but not the average reader, and definitely not the TV show audience. And I'm sure, like most of these publishing rumors, it will be contradicted by other powerful forces."

"Like Amanda's publisher or the producers of the TV show, no doubt."

"Honestly, ghostwriting happens all the time. Most people don't realize how much." Julie cleared her throat. "I do have an inside track, but it's not like I feel I can provide this information to anyone besides you."

"Don't worry, I'm not going to spread rumors, even if they are probably circulating widely already." I sighed. Just to be sure to protect Julie, and her unknown source, I'd have to consider some way to put Detective Johnson on this trail without being too obvious. Perhaps I could just suggest that her team look into any rumors about Amanda Nobel floating around in the murky seas of the publishing business.

I would tell Ellen, though. This information had to be included as part of our amateur investigation.

"Oh, by the way, Amanda is signing book stock for me later this afternoon. When she texted me she asked that I let you know, because she'd be returning from that boat tour you arranged a little later than the others."

"Okay," I said, wondering why Amanda hadn't mentioned this to me directly, rather than relaying a message through Julie. *Or why she thought she had to say anything about it,* I thought, after wishing Julie a good day and finishing our call. *I don't keep tabs on my guests during the day. Maybe she just wanted to be polite, keeping me apprised of her whereabouts so I wouldn't worry if the others returned without her.*

Or perhaps she was testing me—seeing if I'd be tempted to snoop through her suite if I thought she wouldn't return until much later? If she thought I'd overheard something significant in her argument with Tony, she might be worried about my next move and, as I had with Gavin, had figured out a way to set a trap to confirm her suspicions.

I pressed my palms against my temples. Now I was seeing conspiracies everywhere. I really had to get a grip.

One more failed attempt to reach Ellen by phone forced me to leave a cryptic message about needing to see her whenever she was free, before I decided to forget all this murder and espionage business for a while. Instead, I phoned my younger sister Melinda in New York.

"Hey, Mel, how's it going?"

"Fine." I could tell by Mel's suspicious tone that she was surprised by my call. "Anything wrong on your end?"

"Not, not really." I debated bringing up the murder but decided against it. I knew Mel had just completed a major costume design project for an off-Broadway show and was in the middle of talks for a new project. Not to mention the fact that her wife, Beatrice, had given birth to their first child only a few months before. "I just wanted to check in and see how you and Bea were doing, and what my niece is up to these days."

"A lot of sleeping and pooping and crying," Mel said before adding in a warmer tone, "and being totally adorable, of course."

"Of course. I can't wait to see her again. I bet she's changed a lot already."

"From when you saw her as a newborn? Absolutely. She still has that head of dark hair, though. Bea says she was the same as a baby." Mel must've held the phone away from her face because I heard her shout something but couldn't distinguish the words. "Sorry, I've got some of the team here to talk about our plans for the Shakespeare in the Park show I told you about—the Scottish play."

I grinned, remembering that theatre people thought it bad luck to say *Macbeth*. "Is that a definite thing, then?"

"On top of everything else." Mel sighed dramatically. "Of course, I'm not going to complain. Too much work is always better than none, especially in this business. And at least we can meet at the apartment, so I can stay with Irene."

"Is Bea back at work?"

"Not full-time, but yeah, she's at a meeting with a client today. Hold on, I'll be right there," Mel called out before lowering her voice again. "Sorry, the director sent over some notes and we're talking concepts today."

"I'll let you go then. I just wanted to check in and, well, hear a friendly voice, I guess."

"Seriously, is everything okay? You seem kind of off," Mel said, concern lacing her tone.

"Everything's fine. I mean, I'm dealing with guests as per usual. And it doesn't help that it's so hot here. I guess I'm just exhausted."

"Tell me about it." Mel sniffed. "Sorry, my allergies are going wild. Anyway, sorry I can't talk longer right now. I'll call you sometime soon, okay?"

"Sure," I said, tightening my fingers around the phone. For some reason, I didn't want to hang up. "Tell Bea hi and give Reenie a kiss for me."

"Will do," Mel said.

I stared at the phone for a moment, wondering why I felt suddenly bereft. Perhaps it was because my family was scattered across the country—Mel and Bea and Irene in New York, my older sister, Sophie, and her family in California, and my parents in Virginia.

Or perhaps, I thought as I pocketed the phone, *it's just the normalcy Mel represents. No murders or snooping spies, except on the stage. Where they belong.*

Chapter Twelve

Ellen returned my call around lunchtime, explaining that she'd been out buying groceries when I'd tried to phone her earlier.

"Gavin left this morning, saying he was going to be out on his boat most of the day, so I thought it was a good time to leave the house," Ellen said.

"Boat, huh? Well, maybe that's where he is now, but . . ." I took a deep breath before detailing my discovery of Gavin rummaging through the trunks and boxes in Chapters's attic.

I didn't have to see her face to know that Ellen was livid. Her voice shook with anger. "You would've been within your rights to call the police on him. Breaking and entering is still a crime, even for a government agent."

"True, but I thought it might be better to hold off and offer you some leverage over him. Maybe if you threaten him with my taking legal action, he'll actually tell you what he's up to." I drummed my fingers against the kitchen countertop. "One thing still confuses me—why do you have to allow him to stay at your house? I know he's digging into past operations that might've involved you as well as Isabella, but now that you're retired . . ."

"As I've mentioned before, no one really retires from my line of work. Not entirely." Ellen's sharp tone softened. "I was ordered to provide him with a base of operations. To refuse could've made things worse."

"It would have made it look like you had something to hide?"

"Yes. And I thought my willingness to help might mitigate any . . . negative information he digs up."

"Is there any?" I asked, before I could stop myself. "I mean, do you have any skeletons rattling around in closets I should know about?" I punctuated this question with a nervous laugh.

"Doesn't everyone?" Ellen sighed. "Anyway, I appreciate you thinking of me, but I still say you have every right to confront Gavin about breaking into your house. If he needed to search your attic, I'm sure you would've allowed it, if I vouched for his actual identity. At any rate, he could've asked."

"I don't know what he might've found this morning. Maybe you should query him about that. Catch him off guard by letting him know you're aware of his clandestine activities."

"I might just do that."

A fleeting shadow made me start and glance out one of the kitchen windows. It was just a bird flitting by, of course. *Your nerves are frayed as an old rope,* I thought, before deciding that I wanted to take a walk. Some fresh air would clear my head, and if I wandered down to Front Street, I knew the waterfront vista would calm me.

"Listen," I told Ellen. "I wonder if you could do me a tremendous favor?"

"Certainly, if it's within my power."

"I'd like to take a walk, but I don't want to leave the house locked up with no one here. Alicia's off today, and I'm afraid some of my guests might return from their boat excursion before I get back. Do you think you could come over and stay here while I'm out? You're welcome to bring Shandy along, if that's an issue."

"I'd be happy to do that, and Shandy will be fine in his crate for a few hours." Ellen's tone brightened. "I can spend some time in the library. I never get tired of perusing Isabella's books."

"Thanks so much. I really feel like I need a little break. Maybe I'll go and visit Julie at the shop or something."

"Excellent idea. Hold on, I'll take Shandy out and then pop over."

"You're a lifesaver," I said.

"It's really no bother. I wouldn't mind a little change of scenery myself," Ellen said, before hanging up.

While I waited for Ellen to arrive, I changed into a gauzy white cotton blouse and aqua-blue linen slacks. I also switched out my sandals for a pair of sturdy tennis shoes. I wanted to make sure I had the appropriate footwear for a hike.

When Ellen was safely ensconced in the library, and after I gained her promise to attend Friday's tea and cocktail parties as a secret interrogator, I headed out the front door, locking it behind me. She'd easily hear the doorbell if any guests returned before I did.

My feet carried me toward the water, which wasn't unusual. I found the waterfront soothing and visited it whenever I felt anxious or upset. Reaching the midway point on the boardwalk, I decided to stop by Bookwaves to see if Julie was available for a chat. I knew she often ran the shop by herself during part of the afternoon so that Dayna, her only full-time employee, could take a class at the local community college.

But as soon as I stepped inside Bookwaves, I realized Julie wasn't alone. *Of course,* I remembered, *Amanda promised to sign books today.*

"Sorry to interrupt," I raised my voice over the jangling of the bell that hung from the top of the front door.

Amanda looked up at me over a stack of hardback books. "Don't worry. I'm just signing stock for Julie to sell later."

Julie waved a sheet of stickers that read *autographed copy.* "Which is entirely too kind, especially when you're supposed to be on vacation."

"An author's work is never done," Amanda replied as she flexed the fingers holding her pen. "Besides when you sell books, I make money too. I'm happy to aid that process."

"As if anything extra is required. Your books will fly off the shelves regardless," Julie said, before turning to me. "Is there something you needed, Charlotte?"

"Just passing by." I pointed to my walking shoes. "Thought I'd get out of the house for some fresh air and exercise while my guests enjoyed a boat trip. Although I suppose they're already back in port, if Amanda is here."

Amanda completed her signature with a flourish and closed the book she was signing. "I think that's all of them. But perhaps you'd better check behind me, Julie. I sometimes miss one or two if there's a big stack."

"I'll do that. Meanwhile, please feel free to scope out the store. If there's anything you'd like, I'm happy to gift you a copy."

"I do want to peruse the shelves, but of course I'll happily pay." Amanda stood and stretched her arms above her head.

"I should move along," I told Julie, who was checking through the signed copies of Amanda's books. "I'm not really getting any exercise standing here, and besides, I need to head back to Chapters before too long." I met Amanda's curiously intent gaze with a smile. "Alicia has the day off, so my neighbor, Ellen, who you met last night, is holding down the fort. But I don't want to force her to cover for me for hours." I shrugged. "If you're here, the other guests might start showing up at Chapters soon, and someone needs to let them in."

"I doubt that," Amanda said as she examined some shelves. "Harper and Molly trotted off to explore the shops, and Tony claimed he was going to visit the Maritime Museum." She cast an amused glance over her shoulder. "Honestly, I suspect he's grabbing a drink at the tavern down the street. And making business calls. That's more his speed."

"I should still head home sooner rather than later. But definitely enjoy your chance to wander through a bookstore without being accosted by fans," I said to Amanda. "Talk to you soon," I told Julie before wishing them both a good afternoon.

I exited the store to the merry jingling of the bell. Staring at a boat pulling into a slip, I decided I wasn't quite ready to return to Chapters. I'd walk to the end of the boardwalk first.

Reaching the end of the wooden plank walkway, I walked a little farther, to a small park that featured a wooden gazebo overlooking the water. The open-sided, covered structure had brick flooring and bench seating along five of its six sides. It offered a lovely vantage spot, where one could gaze across Taylor's Creek to the nature preserves of Carrot Island and Bird Shoal.

My reverie was broken by a voice calling out my name.

"Charlotte, so glad I could catch up with you," Amanda said breathlessly. She motioned toward the gazebo. "Could we sit and talk for a moment?"

"I do need to get back to Chapters," I said, but something in Amanda's eyes made me add, "but sure, we can chat for a bit." Taking a seat that allowed me a view of the water, I waited until Amanda sat down on the bench beside me before asking her what was on her mind.

"You overheard Tony and me arguing the other night, didn't you?" She held up her hand to stop me when I opened my mouth to explain my presence in the hallway. "It's all right, I don't mind. I know you were just making sure the house was secured against any intruders."

I flashed her an apologetic smile. "I shouldn't have lingered, though."

Amanda waved off this comment as if it were one of the gnats buzzing around our heads. "Don't worry about that. We were loud enough to catch your attention. And that's not the reason I wanted to speak with you in private. The thing is"—she glanced around the gazebo and surrounding area—"I'm truly concerned that Tony had something to do with Lisette's death."

"He was accusing you." As I studied her elegant profile, I reminded myself that I didn't know Amanda well. As nice as she seemed, I had no way of proving her trustworthiness. She could be a practiced liar, for all I knew.

"As a deflection, I think." Amanda frowned. "A way to focus a spotlight of suspicion on me so he could remain in the shadows."

"He said you were jealous." I stared at a white skiff sailing like a feather over the water. "I think I know what that might be about." Turning back to Amanda, I pressed my palms against the weathered boards of the bench seat. "I recently heard a rumor that Lisette Bradford had ghostwritten your upcoming book."

"It's true." Amanda shifted, leaning her shoulder against one of the posts supporting the gazebo's roof. "She did write book thirteen."

"And you approved that?"

"Yes, because I just couldn't bring myself . . ." Amanda dug her fingernails into the wood of the post. "You have to understand my state of mind. I was so tired of writing the series when I would've needed to start that book. Perhaps if my publisher had allowed me to take a year or two off"—she tossed back her golden mane of hair—"but they didn't. I mean, it isn't their fault, really. There's a lot of pressure to pump out books on a regular basis. The fear is that if too much time elapses between releases, readers may become disillusioned with the author, or even abandon them and move on to the next bestseller." She met my gaze with a sad smile. "It's a tough business for publishers too. Not just authors."

"But why couldn't you write the book? Did you develop writer's block or something?" I asked.

"Not really. My problem wasn't with writing in general. It was with writing another one of those books." Amanda released her grip on the post and dropped her hands into her lap. "Please understand that I'm very grateful to my agent and editor and publisher. They've always been good to me. Their promotion and support are why my books are bestsellers and why there are extras like a TV show. I've made a lot of money off the *Tides* series, and I couldn't have done that without them. So when they asked for another book in the series, I didn't want to say no. I wanted them to have their share of the profit from a new book, sooner rather than later. I just knew I couldn't write it."

"Which is why you agreed to allow someone else to write it for you. Understandable." I brushed a dusting of sand from the hems of my slacks. "Did you know it would be Lisette Bradford?"

"No, definitely not, and I wouldn't have agreed if I had known. Anyway, I didn't get involved in that discussion.

I was required to create a general outline and jot down a few notes to guide whoever was writing the manuscript. After that, except for a final read-through of the draft, my work was done. Of course, I thought they'd hire an experienced ghostwriter; someone who'd done it many times before. A professional." Amanda grimaced. "Not someone like Lisette."

"Who chose her then?"

"The editorial team, of course. But I did hear a rumor that Tony suggested her. Which really wasn't any of his business, since he's in publicity, but I suppose he did have enough clout with the publisher to put forward her name for the applicant pool."

"Because of the fan fiction she'd written based on your books?"

"I see you know about that too." Amanda shot me a side-eyed glance. "You're quite the little amateur investigator, aren't you?"

"I have my sources," I said, keeping my tone light. "What I don't really understand is why Tony would choose Lisette, especially if she didn't have a professional writing résumé."

"I didn't understand it at first either, until I found out that he and Lisette had engaged in a brief affair. One that ended badly, I'm afraid." Amanda shook her head. "I heard she totally humiliated him, in public too. But apparently it was still going on when he suggested her name to the publisher. He shared some of her fan fiction with them as well, according to one of my sources at the publishing house. I hear they were particularly swayed by her most popular story." Amanda exhaled a gusty sigh. "I understand it was quite good. Not that I've read any of her fan fiction. As I've mentioned before, I don't read anything based on my own books. Too weird."

"But if Tony championed Lisette as the ghostwriter, why would he kill her? Surely that would be counterproductive."

Amanda pursed her lips. "My guess is that he only did that because they were involved in a relationship and he wanted to please her. Once she broke it off with him—*after* securing the ghostwriting deal—I imagine he felt used. Don't you?"

"I'm sure I would, especially since she did it in such an ugly fashion," I said, processing this new theory. If Tony had felt truly humiliated by Lisette, it was possible he'd planned to kill her as revenge. He had said something that suggested he was responsible for her being one of the contest winners. Or perhaps he'd simply confronted her after dinner and an argument had escalated. I tugged my fingers through a knot in my windblown hair. "Detective Johnson told me some restaurant patrons heard your group arguing on Saturday evening. Was Lisette antagonizing Tony or vice versa?"

Amanda shifted her gaze, staring out over the water rather than looking at me. "Yes, but only obliquely. I imagine she didn't want Harper and Molly to know what was going on."

"You don't think Molly and Harper were aware of the rumors?"

Amanda shook her head. "I don't believe so, although they may have become suspicious after the conversation Saturday night. But Tony had no doubts as to Lisette's intentions, and he was furious. He kept warning her to keep quiet or else. Which is why I think he's the one who killed her."

"Have you told the police anything about your suspicions?"

"Not yet." Amanda touched my shoulder. "It's really all secondhand information. I believe Tony did put forward Lisette's name as a possible ghostwriter because of their affair, and then was furious when he was publicly humiliated. But honestly, as much as I dislike Tony, I can also see how Lisette Bradford could drive someone to murder." Amanda clenched her fingers. "She was so manipulative and conniving . . ."

Curious about this comment, I shifted on the bench so I could see her face. "Oh? In what way?"

"I can't say too much. But early on, right after she started the fan club, I'm afraid I shared some confidences with her over email. Things I shouldn't have told anyone, especially not Lisette. But never mind that; I refuse to speak ill of the dead." Amanda once again averted her gaze, making me question whether she was telling me the whole story.

Tony had accused Amanda of being jealous, which didn't make much sense to me. But I had the strong sense that something else was going on. Like Tony, Amanda had tried to avoid Lisette at the meet-and-greet reception. There had to be a reason for her obvious dislike, even if it wasn't jealousy. Perhaps Lisette had stabbed her in the back in some way, like she had with Tony?

Although I liked Amanda, I had to remind myself that she could simply be trying to offload her own guilt onto Tony Lott. While she appeared sincere, I knew that was no guarantee of innocence. *Anyone can be bamboozled if the person doing the lying is good enough,* I thought, recalling a few instances where I'd been totally conned by a sweet demeanor or charming words from students or their parents.

"I think you'll feel better once you share your concerns with Detective Johnson or someone on her team," I said. "I appreciate you telling me, if your intent was to warn me to be careful around Tony . . ."

"It was," Amanda said in a rush.

"But I can't really do anything. I mean, I can talk to Detective Johnson, but my information will still be secondhand. Or even thirdhand, I guess. You're a much better source, so you should talk to the police, as soon as you can. That's my best advice."

Amanda slid a little farther away from me. "I will."

"Good. Now, tell me—what's this new book that Tony doesn't want you to talk about? I noticed how swiftly he cut you off, and that made me curious."

This change of topic seemed to relieve Amanda, who dropped her hunched shoulders and smiled. "Oh, that. It's just something I'm working on. Very different than the *Tides* series, which means it may never be published. But I don't really care about that at this point."

"A passion project?"

Joy illuminated Amanda's face. "Definitely. It's the book of my heart. Something that actually speaks to the truth of my own life."

"Swashbuckling, time-traveling pirates don't do that?" I asked with a little grin.

“No.” Amanda stood to face me. “I really can’t say any more about the new book. It’s not that I’m under the control of Tony Lott or my publisher or anyone else, I just don’t want to jinx it.”

I studied her serious expression. “I’ve heard other authors mention that. They don’t like discussing much about a new project before writing it. It’s like too much talk can turn it stale.”

“It’s true. I mentioned it the other night because I’m so excited about the idea, but I really shouldn’t do that in the future, with or without Tony present. It’s better to do some of the exploration and discovery before sharing all the details.” Amanda offered me a bright smile. “At least, for me.”

“I won’t press you on that, then.” I motioned toward the boardwalk, and its row of restaurants and shops. “Do you want to walk back with me?”

“I think I’ll stay here for a while,” Amanda said, shading her eyes as she looked out over the water. “It’s a good spot for contemplation.”

“It’s definitely that. Well, goodbye for now, then.” As I turned away, I heard a noise, almost like a little sob, but when I glanced back, Amanda was standing by the edge of the gazebo, looking perfectly composed.

Chapter Thirteen

Later, I called Ellen to thank her again for "babysitting" the B and B while I took my walk.

"It was no problem at all," she said. "As I mentioned when I left, I even found a few new books to read, so that was a bonus."

"You know you're welcome to borrow anything any time."

"I appreciate that." There was a pause before Ellen continued. "Is Alicia back yet? I wondered if you might pop over for a face-to-face chat. Only if you feel like it, of course. I know it's a little late."

"Is Gavin still out?" I asked, curious as to whether we could actually talk without any fear of him walking in on us.

"He's spending the night on the boat. Or so he says."

"Okay, I'll be right over."

I let Alicia know I could be reached at Ellen's house, in an emergency.

"I think I can handle most of those," she said, shooing me off. "Anyway, the guests are already holed up in their rooms, so I don't expect many demands this evening."

I gave her a little salute before grabbing my keys and dashing out the front door.

Ellen met me at her own front door with Shandy in her arms. “He’s more perturbed over visitors after dark,” she said, as she led the way into the parlor. “He’ll want to dash outside to investigate, and I don’t want him running out into the street, especially the way some people drive around here.”

“That’s the truth.” I settled in my favorite chair and waited until Ellen sat down with Shandy in her lap before asking about Gavin again.

“I did think it was peculiar. He hasn’t slept on his boat since he arrived.” Ellen absently stroked Shandy’s silky fur. “But I suspect he had some late-night meeting with someone in the area he didn’t want me to know about.”

“Who would that be? Don’t tell me there are more former spies skulking around Beaufort.”

“No, but there are people who knew Isabella.” Ellen gave Shandy a final pat before setting him on the floor. “Go along and eat your supper, you rascal,” she told him. “He refused it earlier,” she added, meeting my gaze. “He got overheated from our evening walk, I guess.”

Shandy yipped twice before trotting off into the hall. He was headed to the kitchen and his food bowl, no doubt.

“It is almost too hot for anyone to want food,” I said, tracing a circle in the suede fabric of the arm of my chair with my forefinger. “But that isn’t why you called me over. Was there something you wanted to tell me?”

Ellen drew in a deep breath. “Yes, I’m afraid so.”

I raised my eyebrows as I looked up at her. "Afraid?"

"It's something I suspected, and hoped wasn't true, but"—Ellen shrugged—"it's pretty much a sure thing now."

"Let me guess—you've discovered the reason Gavin is snooping around?"

"I have. At least, I think so." Ellen rose to her feet and crossed to a built-in mahogany shelving unit that filled one wall of the parlor. Picking up a Dresden figurine of a young girl holding a basket of flowers, she turned to face me. "It's linked to a situation in the distant past. Something I thought would never come to light."

"Some sort of intelligence operation that involved you and Isabella?"

Ellen nodded. "It was one of my first. Over fifty years ago now. I was only twenty-five at the time, and just assigned to be Isabella's handler, among my other duties."

"She would've been"—I calculated quickly—"in her early forties at the time, I guess."

"Just the age you are now," Ellen said, with a wry smile. "Still very much in her prime."

"Not sure I feel the same, but okay." I studied Ellen's face, noting the tension accenting her wrinkles. "She was still involved with Paul Peters at the time, I suppose."

"Yes, of course. As she was for most of her life."

I mulled this over, remembering that the majority of my great-aunt's espionage work had involved Peters, who was born in Russia but raised in England. He'd been the perfect "sleeper spy," educated to blend in with other academics and, hopefully, use his position as a gentleman and scholar to infiltrate both British and American upper-class society during the Cold War era. He thought he'd recruited Isabella as a spy, as well as his lover, while my great-aunt was actually working for U.S. intelligence. She'd not only kept tabs on his activities, preventing him from truly doing harm; she'd also fed him disinformation over the years. It was the reason Isabella had been given Chapters—then used as a private home and a setting for gatherings of the rich and powerful—as well as a healthy stipend to maintain her social butterfly façade. She hadn't converted Chapters into a B and B until after Paul Peters's death.

"The operation Gavin is researching was closely tied to Peters." Ellen held up the figurine and stared at it as if examining it for defects. "He introduced Isabella to a friend that summer; a younger man named Leo Evans. Or at least that's what he called himself at the time."

"Was he also a Russian asset?"

"He was Paul Peters's protégé, so, yes." Ellen examined the figurine a moment more before placing it back on the shelf. "We couldn't exactly use Isabella to charm any information out of Leo. For one thing, he thought she was an 'old lady,' despite the fact that she was still quite lovely and vibrant. But the main thing was that Leo knew of Paul's romantic involvement with Isabella. Leo was a smart guy and ambitious. He wasn't about to flirt with his mentor's lover."

"So, what? You stepped in to charm the info out of him instead?"

Ellen's peal of laughter reverberated throughout the parlor. "Heavens, no. I couldn't have pulled that off, not back then. I was quite the mousy little thing in my twenties. Besides, I never had any direct interactions with Paul Peters or any of his associates. I met with Isabella infrequently, and then only when we could be alone."

"You stayed behind the curtain." I rolled my eyes when I realized the appropriateness of my words.

"Not an iron one, but that's correct. I had to maintain my anonymity, or my other activities—the ones related to my location scout work—would've been compromised." Ellen leaned back against the wooden cabinet situated under the shelves. "To be perfectly frank, working with Isabella was a very small part of my duties. There wasn't that much to do by the time I was assigned as her handler. She'd already established a long-term relationship with Peters at that point, and was well integrated into her role. She had no trouble keeping tabs on him, or feeding him disinformation when necessary."

"But then this new guy showed up on the scene . . ." I mulled over Ellen's words, considering how a young protégé might've changed the situation.

"Exactly. We needed to monitor him as well. The fear back then was that he'd befriend or romance someone important to U.S. security." Ellen tucked a lock of fuchsia-streaked white hair behind her ear. "I think that was Peters's plan for Leo. He wanted Leo to make connections at Isabella's parties, primarily because her guests included people of significance in military or other government circles."

"I read about that when I researched her last year. She hosted lots of wealthy, high-society types too."

"The perfect hunting grounds for those seeking to uncover our secrets or influence policy," Ellen said. "It was the same with Paul Peters, which was why Isabella was assigned to watch him. But one thing different about Leo was that he was actually British, unlike Paul. He wasn't a sleeper agent; he was an actual British subject."

"Like the Cambridge Five?" I asked, remembering stories I'd read about the group of English spies operating from World War II into the Cold War era.

"Yes, although Leo was obviously recruited much later. He was only twenty-one in 1969, when Paul Peters first brought him into Isabella's orbit. And I think it was money, not ideology, that motivated him." Ellen strolled back to her armchair and sat down. "Anyway, Isabella was very suspicious of Leo. She felt he could end up being much more dangerous than his mentor. So she conferred with me. We came up with a plan to collect more information on his activities, at least while he was in Beaufort and attending Isabella's parties."

"Okay, but why would anyone dig into this old operation now? Isn't it ancient history at this point?"

"That's what I thought, until Gavin was sent here by my former bosses. When he asked certain questions . . ." Ellen drew her legs in close to the skirt of her chair. "The truth is, the problem isn't Leo, it's the person who helped Isabella and me track his movements and collect information on him."

"You recruited someone else?"

"In a way." Ellen leaned forward to grip her bent knees. "We didn't exactly recruit this individual, though. I guess it would be more accurate to say that we made use of them."

"I don't understand. You're saying the person didn't realize they were involved in espionage?"

"They didn't. Not then, not now. And I want to keep it that way."

"That's what you're afraid of? That this person will discover how you, and my great-aunt, once used them?"

Ellen slumped back in her chair. "I know it sounds self-serving, but it would be devastating. Not simply because of the deception that Isabella, under my watch, employed in the past, but also because it could change the way someone viewed a very important part of their life." Ellen lowered her lashes to shadow her eyes. "I honestly think the truth would break their heart."

I stood and paced from one end of the room to the other. "You must care about this person," I said, pausing in front of Ellen's chair. "Which means it's someone you still know. Someone who lives here in Beaufort."

"Good deductive reasoning, as usual." Ellen's smile was brittle as thin ice.

Someone who knew Isabella back in the sixties . . . I covered my gasp before dropping my hands and staring into Ellen's calm face. "One of the Sandburg sisters."

"Bingo." Ellen stood to face me.

"I doubt it was Bernadette, since she served as a military nurse during the Vietnam War. She was probably overseas in 1969."

"Another hit. To be honest, it suited our purposes that Bernie wasn't around to keep watch."

"And I doubt even Isabella could've fooled Bernadette for long. It had to be Ophelia."

"Yes, lovely Ophelia Sandburg, who was twenty-four, but rather sheltered. She'd attended college, majoring in home economics, and taught part-time at the local high school. But she still lived with her parents and, from what Isabella told me, hoped to meet a nice man who'd marry her and take her away from Beaufort."

"It seems she met a not-so-nice man." I crossed my arms over my chest. "Assuming you and Isabella used her to gather information about Leo Evans."

Ellen balanced her elbow on the arm of her chair and rested her chin on her hand. "We didn't initially plan to use Ophelia in that way. She just happened to attend one of Isabella's parties, where she met Leo. It was only after it became obvious that there was a mutual attraction between them that Isabella came up with the idea to encourage the relationship for operational purposes."

"She didn't think it dangerous to place Ophelia in that position?"

"She knew it was. I knew it too. I'm not proud of that, but at the time we thought the benefits outweighed the risks. Isabella was deeply concerned about the damage Leo might do to our country and I"—Ellen sat back and stared at me, her expression blank as unlined paper—"was ambitious."

I backed away, dropping down into the suede armchair. "What did you do? Pump Ophelia for information on her supposed boyfriend?"

"I didn't, and Isabella was a bit subtler than that. She simply befriended Ophelia, who she'd known only casually before." Ellen smiled grimly. "Trust me, if Isabella wanted to become your friend, it would happen. Ophelia was no match for her, and Bernadette wasn't around to question Isabella's sudden interest in her sister. Soon enough, Ophelia was eager to tell Isabella all her secrets and dreams, including her crush on a certain young Englishman."

"And I imagine Isabella encouraged him to visit when Ophelia would be around."

"Indeed." Ellen's gusty sigh sent Shandy, who'd appeared at the entrance to the parlor, scurrying back into the hall.

Or maybe he just senses the tension in the room, I thought, loosening my white-knuckled grip on the plush arms of my chair. "With Isabella playing the role of Ophelia's confidant, I suppose she was able to gather a great deal of information on Leo Evans? Clever." I shook out my tensed fingers. "Horrid, but clever."

"We thought so at the time, at least for a while. The problem was, Isabella was looking at the situation from her point of view. She just saw a harmless flirtation. I don't suppose she could even imagine Ophelia falling deeply in love in such a short time." Ellen lifted her hands. "Neither could I, to be honest. We believed it was a summer fling that would fade with the autumn leaves."

"But you were wrong about that." I didn't frame this as a question.

"Very much so, I'm afraid. And not just on Ophelia's part. I believe Leo Evans truly loved her too. He even asked Ophelia to marry him and move to England. But of course, it couldn't last." Ellen clutched her upper arms, as if she'd felt a sudden chill. "When Paul Peters and others above him found out, they bundled Leo off without so much as a goodbye. They saw Ophelia, with her sister in the armed forces and family connections to other military personnel, as the danger."

"Why? Wasn't his whole mission to gather information by charming or conning U.S. citizens?"

"True, but his feelings for Ophelia made him vulnerable to being turned. Even Paul Peters didn't go so far as to propose marriage to Isabella. Honestly, I think Paul hid his deeper feelings for Isabella from his superiors, which Leo failed to do." Ellen shrugged. "I suppose his handlers were afraid Leo could become a double agent or some such thing. Anyway, they forced him to return to England, which is where I suppose he stayed. I didn't keep up with him after he left Beaufort—not in my job description and none of my business, or so I was told. Even though I tried to find out more later, I couldn't. Leo seemed to have disappeared."

"But what about Ophelia? Paul Peters was around, still linked with Isabella, after that. Didn't he have to explain what had happened?" I stared down at the fingers I'd intertwined in my lap as I considered this tangled web of deception.

Ellen sighed. "Oh, he offered an explanation all right. He told Isabella and Ophelia that Leo had received news of a dire family emergency and had rushed back to England, planning to contact them when he arrived. Tragically, Paul claimed, the small plane Leo had chartered to carry him from London to his family home had crashed in a storm."

I jerked my head up. "He told Ophelia that Leo died?"

"Isabella knew this was a lie, but she didn't dare contradict Paul. She couldn't tell Ophelia the truth, no matter how devastated the poor girl was."

"It would have blown her cover."

"Right." Ellen met my gaze with a weary smile. "She couldn't risk it. Not for a young woman she'd only befriended to use as a pawn in a spy game."

I sat back in my chair, processing this information and reassessing my opinion of my great-aunt. Yes, she'd been caught between a rock and a hard place, but . . . "Who made the final decision about keeping Ophelia in the dark? Isabella or your bosses?"

"Neither," Ellen said. "I did."

There it was—the real reason my neighbor was so determined to prevent Gavin Howard from unearthing all of my great-aunt's secrets. *They're her secrets too.*

"And now you're worried that Ophelia will find out what really happened. That perhaps Gavin was sent here to confirm the truth and tell her, and the world. Some sort of agency clearing of the air, for whatever reason." I stood and marched over to Ellen's chair. "And you're terrified that Ophelia Sandburg will discover that she's mourned her first and perhaps only lover for no reason, and also realize just how horribly her dear friend Isabella used and betrayed her."

Ellen looked up at me, her calm expression belied by the pain in her blue eyes. "You see, you were wrong, Charlotte. You are definitely more than just my Watson."

Chapter Fourteen

Although I was so shaken by this confession that I had to shove my hands into my pockets to hide their trembling, I managed to promise Ellen that I would help her keep an eye on Gavin, particularly around Ophelia, before I fled her house.

After a night of restless sleep, I wandered into the kitchen bleary-eyed on Wednesday morning to help Alicia serve breakfast to our remaining guests. All three came down and actually sat at a table in the dining room, so Alicia whipped up some omelets to order, with me serving as her sous chef.

Thinking about the plan I'd made with Ellen, I reminded my guests about the tea party on Friday afternoon as well as the cocktail party Friday evening.

"I'm certainly willing to attend," Amanda said. "I have to stay in town anyway, so why not?"

Harper dabbed at her lips with her napkin before responding. "I'll be there. And Molly told me she'd come if you went ahead with those events."

"Good." I offered them my brightest hostess smile. "Sorry not to include you in the tea party, Tony, but this was just for Amanda and her fans. Of course you're invited to the farewell cocktail party on Friday night."

"No problem." Tony's fork clattered as he dropped it onto his plate. "I'll take the cocktails over the tea any day. Besides, I have business matters to deal with."

"Of course you do," Amanda said, under her breath.

I collected their plates and utensils before I left the dining room. After helping Alicia clean up, I told her that I planned to walk over to the police station. "There's some information I think I should share in person."

Alicia jerked her head to the right, directing my gaze to the side counter, where Tony loitered, coffee mug in hand.

"Just want to grab another cup," he said, as he fiddled with the spout on the percolator. "Hope that's okay. Didn't want to bother you with fetching it for me."

"It's fine," I said, shooting a questioning glance at Alicia, who'd made a zipper motion in front of her lips.

"He's still one of the suspects, isn't he?" she asked after Tony left the room. "I just thought maybe it was best if he didn't know all your plans for the day."

"Oh, right." I eyed her speculatively. "Smart thinking."

"I have my moments," Alicia said, as she grabbed a roll of paper towels and some disinfecting cleaner. "Anyway, we're all done here once I wipe down these counters, so if you want to run along . . ."

"Trying to get rid of me?" I asked, but flashed her a smile.

"Nope. I just remember you talking about needing to do some work in the garden and I expect you'd better do that early. Unless you want to pass out from a heat stroke or something."

"Ah, right. I should get out there before it gets too hot." I lingered for a moment, watching Alicia's vigorous cleaning of the counters. "Thanks for reminding me. And . . . thanks for all your hard work this week. I know it hasn't been the easiest time for anyone."

Alicia looked up from the countertop with a little twist of her lips that almost looked like a smile. "It's my job."

"But you go above and beyond," I said. "I don't think I've always been good about telling you how much I appreciate that."

Eyeing me speculatively, Alicia balled a damp paper towel in her fist. "I haven't always given you credit for handling things well, either. Let's say we're even and move on from there."

"Sounds like a great idea." I lifted my hand in a little salute before leaving the kitchen. I was happy that Alicia and I were slowly developing a less contentious relationship. *Perhaps in time we can even become friends,* I thought, as I headed to my office to complete some reservation and invoice paperwork, before doing a little weeding in the garden.

A few hours later, I walked to the police station, where I met with Detective Johnson to share the latest information on my guests. I mentioned the ghostwriting issue, although I did add the request that this not be made public knowledge unless it was absolutely necessary, and Lisette's treatment of Tony during their breakup.

"It does mean that both Amanda Nobel and Tony Lott could have reasons to want Lisette Bradford out of the way," I said, "but if it ends up having no bearing on the case, I don't want to expose the ghostwriting information to Amanda's fans. I mean, both Amanda and Tony, as well as the publisher, want to keep it a secret, which isn't illegal. Not to everyone's taste, maybe, but . . ."

"Not against the law," Detective Johnson replied. "And not uncommon, from what I've heard."

"Apparently not. Anyway, that's the latest information I have," I said, my thoughts circling around Ellen's concerns for Ophelia Sandburg. But that wasn't something I could share with the police.

Detective Johnson thanked me for stopping by. "By the way, I'm going to increase patrols in your area," she said, as she followed me to the door. "I don't think any of your guests, whether guilty of killing Lisette Bradford or not, would harm you or Ms. Simpson, but just in case . . ."

I paused on the concrete steps to shake her hand. "Thanks. It will be good to know that officers are nearby, if anything were to happen."

Popping on my sunglasses, I walked off at a brisk pace, following Pollock Street toward the waterfront for a block before turning right on Ann Street. Admiring the older homes that lined the street, I reached the corner of Ann and Craven before I heard footsteps close behind me. I spun around, almost bumping into Tony Lott.

"Charlotte, what luck," he said, as he pulled his straw fedora down low on his forehead. "I've been hoping for a chance to talk to you privately."

"Is that why you followed me today?" I asked, recalling his presence in the kitchen when I'd discussed my plans with Alicia.

Tony pulled a silk handkerchief from the breast pocket of his white cotton shirt and wiped his glistening brow. "Followed you? Really, I think you're imagining things, which isn't surprising, considering the heat." He flapped the handkerchief in the direction of the black iron-work fence that enclosed an area next to a church. "Why don't we step inside the cemetery. I bet it's a lot cooler under the trees. We can chat while we walk."

I pointed to the tall pole that held a historical marker. "It's called the Old Burying Ground. We can go inside, but just be aware that it's very old, so the paths are rough in places. Tree roots and rocks and that sort of thing. You have to pay attention to where you're walking, so too much chatting might not be the best idea."

"Don't worry; I won't allow you to stumble," Tony said, holding out his arm with his elbow bent, as if offering to escort me.

"I can manage," I strode ahead of him, passing through the open iron gate to step into the cemetery. "There are brochures there, in the holder, if you want more information on the graves."

"Nice, but not today," Tony said, as he moved close to my side. "I just want a quiet, and somewhat cool, place to talk.

I lengthened my stride, forcing him to increase his pace to keep up with me. It was cooler under the spreading limbs of the weathered trees, many of which were draped in thick wisteria vines. I paused in front of a pair of graves. "There's the headstone for poor little Vienna Dill, who was only two when she died of yellow fever, and near it is the memorial for Pierre Henry and his wife Annie Henry, African Americans who were the leaders of a school for emancipated slaves and their children."

"I'm not really interested in a history lesson." Tony's fingers clamped down on my bare forearm. "I just want to talk."

"About what, exactly?" I twisted my arm to break his grip and glanced around the area. Seeing no other visitors nearby, I slipped my hand into my pocket to clasp my cell phone.

"You playing amateur detective."

"What makes you think I'm doing that?" I slid out my phone, pressing it into the folds of my loose cotton tunic top to hide it from Tony's view.

Tony yanked off his hat and used it to fan his flushed face. "Come on, I know you've been talking to Amanda, and probably others, like that Harper chick."

The quiet of the cemetery was almost eerie. I gazed into the thick tangle of trees and shrubs that filled the spaces between the rough paths. "I was merely making conversation with my guests. It's what a good host is supposed to do."

"Right. And that's why Amanda once again accused me of having something to do with Lisette Bradford's death.

Just this morning, after talking to you yesterday. Which she admitted doing, by the way."

"And did you?" I asked, focusing my gaze back on him.

"Of course not." Tony's tone was full of bluster. "Why would I? She was nothing to me. I certainly had no reason to want her dead." His sparse eyebrows drew together. "I think it's much more likely that you're just looking to pin the murder on me to draw suspicion away from your friend, Roger Warren."

I tightened my grip on my phone as I forced myself to maintain a calm demeanor. "He isn't my friend. I just met the man the other day."

"Alright, the friend of your friend, Scott Kepler, then." Tony slapped his hat back on his head. "But whatever your motives, you whispering false ideas in Amanda's ear has to stop."

"I didn't have to do that. She already had those thoughts. In fact, she was the one who sought me out and told me she was afraid you were involved in Lisette's murder."

Tony's bark of laughter reverberated through the gloomy silence of the cemetery. "And did she say why? I bet she didn't, because I think you're making all this up."

Keeping the phone hidden, I pressed my free hand to my chest. "Amanda said you might want to harm Lisette because she humiliated you."

Tony took a step back, stumbling over one of the rocks that littered the ground. "What are you talking about?"

"You didn't have an affair with her, and then suggest to your company's editorial team that she write Amanda's latest novel?" I tipped my head and studied his face. His expression wasn't giving anything away, but he was perspiring freely. Although that could be attributed to the heat, it might also have indicated inner turmoil. "I heard that rumor from others, as well as Amanda, in case you're wondering."

Tony swore, before turning aside to stare at Vienna Dill's grave.

"Amanda said she felt incapable of writing another book in the *Tides* series by the publisher's deadline, but she didn't want to cause any trouble for her agent or publisher, so she agreed to a ghostwriting deal. Although she had no idea that Lisette had been selected to write the book and wasn't too thrilled with that choice, which she partially attributed to your influence. I mean, the publisher wouldn't have known about Lisette's fan fiction if it weren't for you putting forward her name and sharing her most popular work with them."

"Did she now?" Tony's tone was hollow. "How strange that she believes I could have any such influence. I handle publicity and marketing, after all. Nothing to do with editorial decisions. And as I said, I had no relationship, good or bad, with Lisette Bradford. On the other hand, Amanda's claims are a rather clever way to cast the blame on me. Lifts the cloak of suspicion off of her shoulders, doesn't it?"

"Why would she want to kill Lisette? Unless, as you shouted the other evening, it was jealousy. Although that seems like a weak motive to me. Why would Amanda fret over someone else writing a book for her when she approved the deal in the first place?"

Tony fixed me with a steely stare. "I don't know what you mean about shouting, and if you've been told that Amanda's thirteenth installment in her series was written by anyone other than her, you've been misinformed."

"It was Amanda who told me"—I held up my hand, palm out—"which seems like a pretty solid source."

"She's lying." Tony's cool façade cracked like ice under hot water. "I don't know why she'd say that, unless her mind is slipping, but I can assure you that all the *Tides* books have been, and will continue to be, written by Amanda Nobel."

I held his intense stare without faltering, but inwardly, my resolve crumbled. I knew, from what Julie had told me, as well as Amanda's own confession, that Tony was not telling the truth. Lisette Bradford had definitely ghostwritten Amanda's upcoming book.

But Tony Lott was never going to admit that to me. *Or anything about his failed relationship with Lisette,* I thought, considering how a desire to avenge the humiliation of being used and discarded could've fueled a murder. *And here you are, standing in a graveyard with a possible killer.* I backed away. "I think it's time I headed back to Chapters. You're free to stay and look around if you like. The Old Burying Ground is worth a proper visit."

"Thanks, but no thanks. I think I'd rather find a place for a proper drink," Tony said, before pointing his forefinger at me. "And just so you know, since you seem to want to dig into everyone's business, I know Amanda is hiding some secrets she might kill to protect. I heard that directly from . . ." Tony snapped his mouth shut and stared defiantly at me for a moment before speaking again. "Run along then, but just remember that I have a lot of power in certain circles. I know some travel journalists and bloggers who could trash the reputation of your bed-and-breakfast to the point where you'd be lucky to book one or two full weeks a year. So if you know what's good for you, you'd better stop spreading any salacious stories concerning me, or Amanda's books."

I held up my other hand, displaying my cell phone. "And if you know what's best, you won't threaten me, especially when I have the police on speed dial." I lowered my hand so he wouldn't notice it shaking. "Good day, Mr. Lott. I hope you will enjoy the rest of your day. But may I suggest that you don't try to talk to me privately again? I'm not sure I'll be able to keep my temper if you choose to spew any more of your misplaced anger at me." I turned on my heel and marched out of the cemetery, not stopping until I reached the iron entrance gate.

I paused then, to cling to the bars of the open gate until my wobbly legs felt strong enough to carry me home.

Chapter Fifteen

I hurried down Ann Street toward Chapters, skirting the clusters of tourists at the intersection of Turner Street. All I wanted was to reach the safety of my home, and perhaps grab a glass of wine. Sure, it was barely noon, but after the encounter with Tony I felt I'd earned a drink with lunch.

But as I approached Chapters, I noticed a man striding away from Ellen's house. The sun glinting off his curly hair told me this was Gavin, and when he made a sharp turn at the corner, I decided to follow him. He was headed in a direction that could easily take him to the Sandburg sisters' home, and I wanted to be able to alert Ellen if it looked like he was planning to visit them on his own.

I forced myself to walk slowly, not wanting to catch up with him or alert him to my presence. In fact, I lingered at the corner, peering down the street from that vantage point rather than moving closer.

Gavin halted in front of Bernadette and Ophelia's bungalow. Noticing that he seemed focused on their home,

I crept closer, making my way to the home next to theirs before sliding in behind a large azalea bush.

Bernadette answered the door, meeting Gavin on the front porch. From my vantage point, I could only faintly hear Gavin introduce himself and ask to speak with Ophelia.

But Bernadette's booming reply was loud enough for me to hear every word. "I'm sorry, Ophelia isn't here," she said. "There's a garden talk over in Swansboro today, and there's nothing she likes better, regardless of the heat and humidity." Bernadette's voice sharpened as she added, "I'd have thought Ellen would've told you that, since she's part of the garden club too."

Gavin said something that sounded like, "Thanks, I'll tell Ellen and we'll catch her later, then," before he turned and strode off the porch and out of the yard.

I stayed frozen in place until he marched by, only moving when he turned onto Ann Street. Then I scrambled after him, having decided that I could easily claim to have walked up from the waterfront if he questioned my sudden appearance behind him.

But when I turned the corner, he'd already crossed the street to reach a white compact car. I paused, realizing I'd seen that vehicle parked on the other side of the street and paid little attention to it, thinking it belonged to one of our neighbors' guests.

Obviously, it's a rental that Gavin's been using instead, I thought, as he jumped in the car and backed it up just enough to turn around in the quiet street. He drove off at some speed, toward the main part of town.

I suspected he was headed for Turner Street, which would lead him out of town and onto the road that connected with the bridge over to Morehead City. *And then on to Swansboro?* I questioned, picking up my pace. Reaching Ellen's house, I bounded up the porch steps and jabbed my finger against her doorbell.

"I think Gavin's stalking Ophelia," I blurted out as soon as Ellen opened the door.

She didn't even blink. "Let me grab Shandy and my purse, and we'll follow in my car," she said, before closing the door.

I only had to wait on the porch for a few minutes before she reappeared, clutching Shandy, who wore a neon-blue harness with a matching leash, against her chest. As I followed her down the steps and across the front yard, I filled her in on what I'd seen.

"Oh right, that garden club talk. I was thinking about going but changed my mind," Ellen said, as I slid into the passenger seat of her pale-blue sedan.

Ellen strapped Shandy into a contraption fixed to her back seat—rather like a child's booster seat, but sized for a small dog. "Keeps him from running around in the car, and it's much safer. Even a fender bender could toss a little fellow like him around," she said, as she climbed into the driver's seat.

"Good idea." I glanced over my shoulder at the Yorkie, whose black eyes, veiled by his long hair, were bright as polished buttons. He panted, his pink tongue hanging out of his mouth. "It is a bit warm, isn't it, boy?" I said, fanning my face with my hand.

"Despite parking in the shade, the car does get hot, but that'll soon be remedied," Ellen said, reaching across the dashboard to adjust the air conditioning.

Cool air blasted out of the vent in front of me. I leaned forward slightly to allow it to hit my face and neck. "Do you know where this garden club meeting is being held? I mean, I know it's in Swansboro, but is there a more exact location?"

Ellen backed out of her driveway and pointed the car toward the central part of town. "On the waterfront, near the town square." She cast me a quick glance. "Not that it would be hard to find an event happening in Swansboro. It's a pretty small town, and mostly residential, you know."

"I confess I haven't visited there yet, despite it only being a short drive away." I sat back and stared out the side window. "Don't you have to cross the bridge over Bogue Sound and take 58 all the way down to Emerald Isle?"

"That's the scenic route, and I prefer it if I'm just out for a drive, but there's a faster one we'll use today," Ellen said.

I studied her profile, noticing the tightness of her jaw. "Not driving alongside the beach, I take it," I said as we passed the entrance to the bridge that connected Morehead City to Atlantic Beach.

"No, but we'll turn off soon. Although not nearly as charming a drive, it's a more direct shot to Swansboro from here."

We traveled through a flat, rather sparsely populated landscape and then through the small towns of Cape Carteret and Cedar Point. As we drove, I shared the information from my encounter with Tony.

"It does seem that Mr. Lott has the requisite anger and control issues that might drive him to kill," Ellen said. "And he strikes me as a very proud, rather self-important man. I wouldn't be surprised if he didn't respond well to being used in a romantic relationship and then being humiliated."

Staring out over the water as we crossed the bridge that spanned the White Oak River, one of the major tributaries flowing into Bogue Sound, I tapped the glass. "He could've murdered her for revenge. But to play devil's advocate, wouldn't that also mean he was killing the goose before she laid any more golden eggs? If his employer hoped to continue the *Tides* series, and Amanda didn't choose to write more books, they'd need Lisette again, wouldn't they?"

"Maybe he didn't care about that. It wouldn't necessarily affect him personally. And besides, I'm sure the publisher could find someone else to fill that role. Let's face it—even if the quality of future books in the series fell off, they'd still sell. At least for a while. Maybe over time readers would drift away, but many will continue to follow a series they're so invested in, at least through another two or three volumes." Ellen sent me a side-eyed glance. "I'm more curious about Tony's comment alluding to Amanda hiding secrets. Did you get the impression that he learned this from Lisette Bradford when they were still dating?"

"Definitely, although he caught himself before he spoke her name. But I'm sure that's what he was about to say." I tapped the handle of my door with one finger. "Which means Lisette might have known something Amanda wanted to keep quiet."

"Would've killed to do so, perhaps?" Ellen asked.

"It's possible, I suppose," I replied, before falling silent for a few minutes.

"Oh, what a quaint town," I said at last, as I glanced across the car to look out the driver's side window. As we crossed the bridge, older wooden structures and docks set along the riverfront came into view, along with several streets filled with vintage-style businesses and homes.

"It was incorporated in 1783, and was a settlement that grew up around a plantation before that, so it's been around for a while." Ellen turned left, onto what was obviously one of the town's main streets.

"Front Street. Just like in Beaufort," I said, as we drove past several brick and wood-framed buildings set close to the sidewalks.

"Both are adjacent to the waterfront, so I suppose that makes sense," Ellen said. "I'm going to turn up a side street to park and then we can walk to the Town Square area. It's only a few blocks."

The streets were a little hillier than expected, until I remembered that this town faced the White River and part of the intercoastal waterway. River towns often featured bluffs, so these gentle hills weren't out of place. I followed Ellen and a frisky Shandy back to Front Street, where we trotted past a restaurant that featured a 1950s theme as well as several charming gift shops. Where the street ended, there was a stretch of grassy lawn rolling down to the water on one side, a strip of shops and a pub ahead of us, and a small park with an outdoor bandstand on the right, where the road intersected with another street.

"That's the town square," Ellen said, motioning toward the bandstand. "They hold concerts there every week during the summer months."

I pointed at a crowd gathered on the grassy area beside a two-story building that included shops on both floors and a deck that overlooked the river. "Is that the garden club group?"

Keeping a tight grip on Shandy's leash, Ellen shaded her eyes with one hand. "Looks like it. I remember our newsletter said that there would be a brief talk by a master gardener before a tour of some of the local properties."

"And there's Ophelia," I said, as a few people in the group moved aside, revealing the back of a tall, thin woman's head. "That fire-engine-red hair is pretty unmistakable."

"Definitely." Ellen let out Shandy's leash a little, allowing the small dog to sniff the surrounding grass. "I think I'll wait until the talk concludes before I try to pull her aside."

I glanced up the connecting road, which the signpost informed me was Church Street. "Is that Gavin's rental car, a block up from the stairs that lead to that pub?"

"Could be." As Ellen squinted in the bright sunlight. I realized she'd left the house in such a hurry that she'd forgotten her hat and sunglasses. "Although a lot of those rental cars look the same to me."

"You stay here and wait to catch up with Ophelia. I'm going to check out that car," I said, sprinting away before Ellen could protest.

When I reached the vehicle, the rental company sticker on the back window convinced me it was indeed Gavin's car, but it was locked and empty. I looked around, trying to catch a glimpse of him. Surely, if he'd trailed Ophelia to this town, he had some ulterior motive.

Leaning against the car, I peered inside. Not that I expected to see anything that would clarify the situation, but just because I was curious. What did a secret agent carry around in his rental car?

Nothing, apparently. As I straightened, a hand fell heavily on my shoulder.

"Thinking about stealing it?" Gavin asked, his voice calm and still as water in a tidal pool. "I wouldn't, if I were you. Rides rough, and the AC doesn't really cool well."

I turned, shaking off his hand. "I'm not in the market for a car, so, no. I was just . . . checking my hair in the reflection from the window."

Gavin's eyes were hidden behind his sunglasses, but I could read amusement in the twitch of his lips. "Really? You expect me to buy that?" He stepped back and crossed his arms over his chest.

"I don't care what you buy or don't buy," I said, with a swift glance to my left. *If I yelled, would any of the garden club members, hear me? Or maybe someone dining outside on the pub deck?* "Since you're the government agent, surely you can figure out my real motive."

"I refuse to have this conversation on a busy street. If you want to talk, follow me." He turned on his heel and strode down a tree-lined residential street.

"Hold up," I said, as I jogged to catch up to him.

"Did you tail me here from Beaufort?" He shot me a sharp glance. "And yes, I did notice you lurking in the bushes near the Sandburg sisters' house, in case you're interested."

"You didn't give any indication that you saw me."

"Of course I didn't. I wanted to see what you'd do next. I guess now I know—you alerted your friend Ellen and decided to follow me here."

"Only because we knew you were tracking Ophelia Sandburg, and we were worried about her."

"Perhaps *you* were; as for Ellen, I suspect the only person she's worried about is herself." Gavin stopped walking and whipped off his sunglasses as he turned to face me. "This playing detective has to stop, Charlotte. I don't know why Ellen would involve you in her problems, but I'm here to tell you it isn't safe."

I met his stern gaze with a lift of my chin. "I trust Ellen."

"You shouldn't. Not entirely." Gavin's light brown eyes glittered.

Not with charm, I thought. *With anger, or frustration.* "Speaking of trust, why should I listen to anything you say? I know you broke into Chapters and searched the attic."

"So I did hear something." Gavin narrowed his eyes. "I should've investigated, but I was too . . ."

"Involved in rummaging through my great-aunt's things?"

"Touché. But don't worry, I found nothing useful. It seems that one journal is the only piece of evidence Isabella Harrington forgot to bury, or burn."

Determined not to allow him to intimidate me, I stared boldly into his eyes. "According to my housekeeper, you visited Isabella once, not long before her death. It seems she thwarted you then as well."

"My, my, but you are a nosy one, aren't you?"

"I prefer the term curious, but if you insist." I placed my balled fists on my hips. "I plan to continue to be nosy where you are concerned, especially since you had the audacity to break into my house and search through my belongings, or at least my great-aunt's belongings. And, for your information, I know you're not Ellen's cousin. She was the one who told me that, by the way, while you've seemed quite happy to keep up your deception."

"Part of my job," he replied, slapping his sunglasses against his palm. "I'm on assignment. Did Ellen bother to tell you that?"

"Yes, and she even expressed her suspicions as to why."

Gavin slid the sunglasses into the pocket of his loose cotton shorts. "She may think she knows my mission, but she doesn't have the whole story."

"Why don't you tell me what that is, and then we'll all be in the loop."

"I can't do that," he said, taking off at a brisk walk.

"Can't or won't?" I huffed, struggling to keep up with his long strides.

"I don't have clearance to explain any more than what you already know. And, honestly, you shouldn't even know that." Gavin stopped at an intersection with another narrow street. "It was irresponsible of Ellen to share anything with you about her former operations."

I followed his gaze, noticing that the intersecting street ended at a marina, In the distance, the river and intercoastal waterway glittered under the July sun. the watery vista broken by clumps of islands and sandbars. "I think she wanted to warn me; to let me know that I needed to be on my guard around you."

"That's good advice." Gavin flashed me a cool smile. "But this particular mission isn't anything that should pose a danger to you. Not if you mind your own business."

"But what about Ophelia Sandburg? Do you, or your mission, pose a threat to her?"

Gavin took two steps back and looked me over, his expression unreadable. "Ellen told you about how she and your great-aunt used Ms. Sandburg in the past? How they embroiled her in espionage without her knowledge or permission?" He shook his head. "Yet you say you still trust Ellen. I'm sorry, but that makes no sense."

"Ellen admitted that she made mistakes," I replied, fighting to keep a defensive bite out of my tone. "Meanwhile, here you are, stalking poor Ophelia for some reason you won't disclose."

"Can't," he said, moving closer to me. "And I'm trying to protect Ms. Sandburg. I can tell you that much."

He was only an inch or two taller than me. I squared my shoulders and looked him in the eye. "But you can't say why she's suddenly in danger, after all these years?"

"Exactly. I've already said too much. I'd need approval from my bosses to say any more, and to be honest, I'm not sure I'll even bother to ask." Gavin tapped my lips with one finger. "Loose lips sink ships and all that."

"I don't spill secrets," I said, pushing my hand into his chest. "And I'd thank you not to touch me again in such an intrusive way without permission."

Gavin widened his eyes. "Yes, ma'am," he said, before giving me a little salute.

"It isn't funny. I don't know you from Adam, and you think you can grab me or whatever just because you have some sort of badge?" I shook my head emphatically. "I don't go for that sort of behavior and, trust me, I'm more than happy to share my concerns with the Beaufort police if you try anything again."

Gavin held up his hands in an apologetic gesture. "I'm sorry. I fell into operational mode, which obviously wasn't appropriate in this circumstance."

"Clearly not." I thrust my hands into the pockets of my lightweight slacks. "Now—I'm going to walk away and I suggest you don't follow." I looked him over for a moment. "I plan to rejoin Ellen, who's probably talking with Ophelia at this point. If you simply head back in the direction we came from, get in your car, and drive back to Beaufort, I'll promise not to tell Ellen everything that has transpired between us. Although"—I held up a finger, silencing the words Gavin appeared about to say—"I will mention I saw you, but say you merely waved and drove away."

“I can’t leave until I know Ophelia Sandburg is safe,” Gavin said, his jaw clenching.

“We’ll make sure she is, although since you won’t say from what, that may prove difficult.” I shoved a damp lock of hair away from my eyes. “But if you insist on keeping watch, stay out of sight. I can’t vouch for what Ellen might do otherwise.”

“I’m confused—you seem to think I’m the enemy here, so why would you want to protect me from Ellen Montgomery’s wrath?” Gavin’s tone, as well as his expression, lightened.

“I don’t know. I suppose because I know you’re only doing your job.” I walked a few paces before turning to add, “And because, if we’re being honest, I’m not exactly pleased with what Ellen, and my great-aunt, did all those years ago. They used a friend as an informant without her knowledge. That’s pretty . . . unacceptable in my book.”

“On that, at least, we can agree,” Gavin said, casting me a smile before slipping on his sunglasses.

“Just don’t think this makes us friends,” I said, spinning on my heel and marching away.

He called something after me that sounded like “not yet.” I didn’t bother to turn around and correct him.

Chapter Sixteen

When I caught up with Ellen, she told me that she'd promised Ophelia a ride back to Beaufort after the garden tour.

"She came with another club member, but agreed to ride back with us."

"Why'd she agree to that?" I asked,

"Because I told her I wanted to share some extra cut flowers with her and thought it would be easier if she traveled with us," Ellen said airily.

"Do you have them? The extra cut flowers, I mean?" I asked, as we wandered through one of the private gardens on the tour, trailing somewhat behind the others.

"Not yet, which is why I want you to offer her some lemonade on the porch while I go to"—Ellen cleared her throat—"collect the bucket."

"Wheels within wheels," I said, with a wry smile.

"It's one way to keep an eye on her today. While keeping Gavin at bay," Ellen yanked Shandy away from his investigation of a bee burrowing into a hollyhock blossom. "Even if he seemed about to drive off after he waved at you."

"That's what I saw, so I assume he left." I leaned over a rosebush and made a great show of sniffing one of its pale-yellow flowers. "Not much scent."

Ellen tightened her grip on Shandy's leash. "That's one of those hybrid varieties. They don't have the perfume of the older roses,"

This distraction was so successful, I continued to pepper Ellen with questions about the plants and shrubs we encountered as we trailed the larger group of garden enthusiasts through a few more gardens. *Anything to avoid questions about Gavin,* I thought, wondering as I did so why I felt any inclination to shield him.

Because what you told him was the truth—you don't feel comfortable about the way Great-Aunt Isabella and Ellen used Ophelia back in the day. I pulled a tissue from my pocket and dabbed at my eye, which was stinging from a drop of sweat that had rolled off my brow. *Because you believe he may have Ophelia's best interests at heart, while Ellen . . .* I shoved the wad of tissue back into my pocket as I stared at the determined set of Ellen's shoulders. *Who knows what Ellen Montgomery will do to protect her secrets?*

After the tour concluded and the garden club group had dispersed, Ophelia accompanied us on the short walk to Ellen's vehicle, chattering the entire way. When we reached the car, I insisted that she sit up front. "I don't mind sharing the backseat with Shandy," I said, giving the Yorkie's head a pat. I received a tongue lick across my hand in response. "See, he agrees with that plan."

On the drive back to Beaufort, Ellen kept the conversation focused on a critique of the gardens we'd toured earlier—a topic that Ophelia participated in with enthusiasm. Once I found I wasn't required to add anything to the discussion, I sat back and absently petted Shandy while staring out the window.

At Ellen's house, our prearranged ruse worked like a charm. Ellen had time to cut a few flowers from her garden while Ophelia and I relaxed, sipping lemonade on the front porch. When Ophelia finally left, toting the bucket of flowers around the corner to her house, I also made an excuse to leave, claiming some prior scheduled activity. It was a hasty lie, and not one I felt Ellen entirely believed. I didn't blame her, but the truth was, I didn't really have any specific plans. I just needed a little time alone to clear my head.

After checking in with Alicia, who said everything was under control at Chapters and, in fact, she was going to take a little time to just sit and read a book in the library for once while things were quiet, I retreated to my bedroom.

I took a shower and changed clothes before doing a little reading of my own—diving into a reread of John le Carré's *Tinker, Tailor, Soldier, Spy*. It seemed a good fit for my current entanglement with the espionage game, especially since I knew the book had been inspired by le Carré's own experiences with the Cambridge Five.

Absorbed in the intricate machinations of le Carré's wily intelligence officers, I almost didn't hear the buzzing of my cell phone. I grabbed it off my nightstand and answered just before it went to voice mail.

"Hey, I know this is last minute," Julie said, after we exchanged greetings, "but I wondered if you'd like to come over for dinner this evening? Scott is grilling some fresh-caught mahi-mahi and I'm making a salad. We'd love for you to join us."

"Sounds lovely," I said, as an unexpected sense of relief washed over me. I hadn't realized how desperately I'd wished for a conversation that didn't involve secrecy or borrowed guilt over the past indiscretions of a relative or friend.

"Great. Let's say six? We're going to eat out on the little patio behind Bookwaves, so casual attire is perfectly fine. And don't forget your bug spray."

I asked what I could bring, and Julie suggested a bottle of wine, which was never a problem since I had to keep Chapters well stocked for the guests.

When I left the house around a quarter to six, I paused on the front porch steps to survey the area. Seeing Gavin's white car parked across the street gave me a moment of relief, before I realized that he, like me, probably chose to walk to most places within the historic district. Which included the Sandburg sisters' bungalow.

Forget about that for one evening, I told myself, as I set off toward the waterfront. I made my way to Front Street, shifting from shoulder to shoulder the heavy canvas bag that contained three bottles of wine—two for the evening and one as a gift.

Reaching the building that housed Bookwaves as well as Julie's apartment, I slipped through the unobtrusive wooden gate that led to a narrow, brick-paved alley. Julie had decorated the alley with whimsical metal sculptures, colorful ceramic wall art, and shade-loving plants in hanging baskets. I smiled. This passageway always made me feel I was passing through a magical corridor into a fantasy world.

"Hi, and here, let me take that," Julie said, bustling forward to grab the canvas tote. "Ooo, party time!" she added, as she peered into the bag.

I rolled my shoulders to loosen my tensed muscles. "I thought we could crack open two this evening and you could keep one for future use."

"Thanks." Julie thrust the two bottles of white wine into a waiting bucket of ice before setting the red wine on her cedar serving table. "But I'll leave them all out here, just in case."

Scott, who was standing in front of an egg-shaped green grill, waved a metal spatula at me. "Good to see you, Charlotte."

I noticed his white chef's apron and smiled. "Grill Master General? Is that how you wish to be addressed now?"

"You can still call me Scott," he replied with an answering grin. "I don't require my friends to use the title."

"I call him a lot of things, not all repeatable," Julie said, wrapping her arms around his waist. She leaned her cheek against his back and flashed me a brilliant smile. "Not really. He's actually a pretty good guy."

I sat on one side of the small picnic table that filled the center portion of the tiny patio. "I'm aware. And I also know how you two like to spar with one another. So, trust me, I don't take everything you say seriously."

"That's good. Saves a lot of explaining." Scott carefully flipped pieces of fish. "This will be ready in just a sec."

"Here you go," Julie said, as she set a plastic wine glass in front of me. "Please, enjoy some of the chips and salsa too. I'm going to dash upstairs to grab the salad."

As Julie climbed the black iron stairs that led up to her apartment, I gulped in a deep breath of air, which carried the faint tang of the not-so-distant ocean. Above our heads, the globe lights Julie had strung from the Bookwaves building to the tall privacy fence enclosing the patio glimmered in shades of blue and green. Unlike my backyard, Julie had limited space, but she'd worked wonders, lining the solid wooden fence with enameled pots filled with flowers and herbs. Lime-green lounge chairs offered another bright pop of color, while the cedar serving and picnic tables provided earthy tones to ground the setting.

"I suppose your weekly guests are still at Chapters?" Scott asked, as he placed a foil-covered platter of fish in the center of the picnic table.

"All except Molly Zeleski, one of the fans. She lives in Morehead City so the police allowed her to go home."

"That must be fun." Scott poured a glass of wine before joining me at the picnic table. "I'm just glad I'm not under suspicion this time. Unlike Roger, who has been mysteriously incommunicado since Saturday."

"You still haven't spoken with him?"

Scott took a sip of wine, eyeing me speculatively over the rim of the glass. "Not since he called late Saturday night with that odd story about car trouble. I know he's in town, since I think the police told him not to leave. And I believe he's still doing some research at the Maritime Museum library. Another colleague mentioned seeing him there over the last few days, but even though he knows I'll be leaving for Asheville soon, he hasn't gotten back in touch with me."

"Do you really think he's capable of killing someone over threats of bad reviews?" I placed my elbows on the picnic table and leaned forward. "That seems pretty drastic."

"I'm sure if so, it wouldn't have been premeditated," Scott said. "I mean, I doubt he would've sought out Lisette Bradford with plans to harm her. But if he ran into her somewhere near the docks, and they argued . . ." Scott took another swallow of his wine. "I have seen him lose his temper. Once when I was with him, he struck out at someone, although that individual was hitting a dog, so I couldn't really blame him for lashing out."

"That's a very different thing," I agreed. "I might've been tempted to do the same in that circumstance."

"Me too, although Roger did kind of go overboard. His anger has been known to get the best of him." Scott slid his finger around the rim of his glass. "It has made me question whether he could've lashed out at Lisette and accidentally caused her to hit her head on something."

"And then panicked when he realized she was dead, and tossed her in the water?" I frowned. "He doesn't strike me as the type to lose his cool so completely, but of course I don't really know him."

"Don't tell me you guys are talking about the murder? I thought we agreed to avoid that topic tonight," Julie said, as she crossed the patio and plunked a wooden salad bowl filled with a mixture of greens and fresh vegetables on the table.

"Sorry, that's my fault." Scott slid over to allow Julie to sit beside him. "I mentioned Roger and, well . . ."

"Okay, but let's just drop it now." Julie shook her fork at him. "Oops, looks like I forgot my wine."

"I'll get it," I said, swinging my legs around so I could jump up from the attached bench. "What's your preference?"

"With the fish and the heat, some of the white." Julie fanned her face with her paper napkin. "Maybe this eating outside wasn't such a great idea."

"But it's lovely out here," I said, as I set a full wine glass in front of Julie. "And once twilight falls, it will cool off."

"But that won't happen for another hour, at least." Julie thrust a set of wooden tongs into the salad. "It's just fish and salad. I hope that's okay. I did buy some fresh peach ice cream for dessert."

"Looks delicious," I said, as I filled my plate. The salad was dressed with Julie's homemade vinaigrette, which she knew was my favorite.

Scott unwrapped the foil from the fish and handed me the metal spatula. "Here, help yourself. There's plenty, and it's better fresh, so don't stint."

"Perfectly grilled." I slipped a large portion of the fish onto my plate.

"One of Scott's many talents," Julie said, saluting him with her wine glass.

Scott leaned over to give her a quick kiss on the cheek and Julie beamed in response.

We focused on our food after that, chatting about everything except the death of Lisette Bradford, which was a relief. But as we polished off the ice cream, obviously homemade and topped with fresh peaches, Julie raised a question I wasn't really prepared to answer.

"That Gavin guy," she said, waving her spoon at me, "what's up with him? I've seen his spiffy boat at the docks, so I know he doesn't need to shack up with Ellen, and she doesn't seem that fond of him. What's the story there? Is he really a cousin?"

I thought about the le Carré book I'd just been reading. The British intelligence officers had called their American counterparts *the cousins*. I smiled. "In a way."

Scott lifted his russet eyebrows. "What do you mean? You're either someone's cousin or you aren't, or so I've always believed."

"Well, I don't think they're related by blood," I said, before licking the last little bit of ice cream from my spoon.

Julie spun around on the bench so she could stand up. "He certainly doesn't have Ellen's flair. Rather a dull sort, I thought." She swept up the paper goods and plastic utensils and piled everything on one plate. "Keep talking—I'm just going to dump this, and then fill up everyone's glasses." Balancing the leaning tower of trash between her hands, she slowly walked over to the garbage can placed to one side of the alley entrance.

"I figured Gavin for an accountant," Scott said. "But apparently he's some sort of freelance researcher. Which is an equally low-key personality type of job, I guess."

"Unlike an author?" I asked, with a wry smile.

"Not all authors are quiet types. Take me, for example," Scott said, before his next words were cut off by the slam of the garbage can lid.

"Who are you and what are you doing here?" Julie's words were staccato as drum beats.

Scott spun around and leapt to his feet while I stared over to where Julie had faced off with a man standing in the alley.

Sliding off the bench, I also jumped up. The man, wearing a navy-blue hoodie despite the warm weather, looked vaguely familiar.

Billy Bradford, I thought, curling my fingers into fists as he marched forward, ignoring Julie.

He strode up to Scott, who'd rushed to intercept him. I unclenched my fingers and thrust my hand into the pocket of my jade-green linen pants, my fingers scrambling to clutch my cell phone.

"What do you think you're doing?" Scott asked, in a tone I'd never heard him use before.

"Looking for your pal, Roger Warren," Billy used one hand to yank back the hood shading his face. "I've tried to track him down but haven't had any luck. Saw you come in and out of here several times over the last few days, though, and when I heard voices, I thought I'd see if you could clue me in."

Guess you didn't think to check the library at the Maritime Museum. Of course I didn't voice those words aloud. "The police are looking for you," I said instead.

"Right, 'cause they think I killed Lizzie. Which I didn't. Never would, whatever she might've told those weird followers of hers."

"This is private property," Scott motioned for Julie, who was still standing by the back wall of the building, to move behind him., but she shook her head. "You're trespassing, which is a crime, in case you didn't know."

Billy hitched up his drooping jeans and glared up at Scott. "Tell me where I can find Roger Warren and I'll be happy to leave."

"So you can do what? Attack a man old enough to be your father?" Scott squared his shoulders. "No way. I'm not telling you anything."

"Protecting that murderer, are you?" Billy spat at the ground near Scott's feet. "Guess I shouldn't be surprised, all you high-and-mighty types always stick together."

"What makes you think Roger murdered Lisette?" I asked, as I slipped my phone out of my pocket and held it behind my back.

"Heard people talking while I've been hiding out. Lizzie supposedly threatened to do something bad to his books. Something to do with reviews or whatever. Figured that might tick him off. And more than that"—Billy wiped the back of his hand under his nose—"I saw them, arguing, down by the waterfront that night. Lizzie had just come out of a restaurant with some other people, including that ridiculous Amanda woman, but they didn't stick together. All went their separate ways, leaving Lizzie by herself."

"Were you stalking her again?" I asked.

"Not stalking. Just keeping an eye out, so I could find the right time to talk to her."

Scott harrumphed. "From what I hear, Lisette didn't want to speak to you. Ever."

"That's what those other broads might've told you, but you shouldn't pay them no mind. They love to exaggerate," Billy said, shuffling his feet.

"Wait." I waved my free hand. "You saw Roger Warren talking to Lisette after she left the restaurant?"

"Yeah, the group split up. Went their separate ways, like I said. Anyway, Lizzie wandered down to the end of the boardwalk, where those excursion boats are docked. There weren't many people around there at that point, so when that older fellow strode up and began talking to Lizzie, I hung back behind the ticket booth and kept watch. Heard her call him Dr. Warren, so I was able to figure out later who he was."

"If you saw him harm your ex-wife, you should tell the police," Scott said.

"Like they'd believe me." Billy snorted. "They've already convicted me. The angry abusive ex, or so they probably think."

I glanced over at Julie, who held up her cell phone before mouthing something that looked like, "keep him talking." Realizing that she'd probably already contacted the police, I nodded.

"But you have pertinent evidence," I said, catching Billy's eye. "That could change everything."

"But I didn't see the old man kill Lizzie. Just overheard them arguing. I had to sneak away before they split up, 'cause there was some cop on patrol headed my way." Billy met my inquiring gaze with a twist of his lips. "Hid out for a bit, and when I got back to that spot, the Warren guy was nowhere to be seen. I didn't see Lizzie either, but there was this excursion boat blocking my line of vision. I was about to get closer, to see if she was still around anywhere, but the cop walked past again, on his way toward the main part of town, it looked like. I didn't want to be seen by the police, so I split while I could."

Flashing lights from the street caught my eye. A police cruiser, not blaring its siren, had pulled up and parked.

The thud of booted footfalls alerted Billy, who spun around, coming face-to-face with several uniformed officers.

He shouted, unleashing a colorful string of swear words. But there was no way for him to escape through the alley, which was blocked by cops. In desperation, Billy scrambled toward the stairs to the apartment, where Julie barred the way, holding the lid of the garbage can in front of her like a shield. Scott, obviously fueled by adrenaline, leapt forward and tackled Billy to the ground.

"Thank you, Mr. Kepler, but we'll take it from here," said Detective Johnson, looking regal and stylish in a pale-yellow sheath dress and heels. I wondered if she'd been pulled away from a night out, and considered how law enforcement officers, like teachers, were often called on to do much more than a nine-to-five job.

Scott sat back, scooting out of the way while two police officers handcuffed Billy before helping him to his feet. Detective Johnson read Billy his Miranda rights as he was marched out to the street and the waiting patrol cars.

"So much for our calm and relaxing evening," Julie said, tossing the lid back on the can with a bang. She looked over at me with a wink. "Good thing you brought that extra bottle of wine."

Chapter Seventeen

When I finished helping Alicia clean up after breakfast on Thursday I decided to walk to the Maritime Museum. Despite Scott's comment about Roger Warren using the museum library frequently, I knew finding him there was a hit or miss proposition. But a walk wouldn't hurt, whatever the outcome.

I strolled the few blocks to Front Street. The Maritime Museum, located right across the street from the waterfront, didn't charge admission. But I always paused at its plexiglass donation box to drop in a dollar or two, happy to support the museum's preservation of history and its educational programs. Glancing up, I admired the main hall's tall, open-timbered ceiling, which reminded me of the interior of an old sailing ship.

As I crossed to the other side of the building, I cast a quick glance toward one of the most popular displays, which chronicled the history of the *Queen Anne's Revenge*. The flagship of Edward Teach, better known as Blackbeard, the ship was believed to have been purposefully run aground in

1718 in the waters of Beaufort Inlet. The pirate and his crew escaped, but the ship sank. It was not rediscovered until 1996, when the wreck site was claimed by the state of North Carolina as it fell within the three-mile state waters limit. Many of archeological finds from the *Queen Anne's Revenge* were kept on display in this building, making the museum a popular tourist attraction.

I crossed the lobby to reach the area that housed the museum's research library. Its balcony-style second level, positioned along one side of the room, was accessible via a wooden staircase that looked like it belonged on an old sailing ship. However, only staff could access the upper level, even though the ground floor, with its wooden bookshelves, large study table, and an inviting fireplace, was available for use by visitors.

Seated in a leather upholstered desk chair, Roger Warren was bent forward, poring over the books scattered across the wooden table before him.

"Hello, Dr. Warren," I called out in a hushed tone. Even though there wasn't anyone else in the room, somehow being a library made me keep my voice down.

He lifted his head, pushing his glasses up his nose with his forefinger. "Yes, may I help you?" He turned his head with a puzzled expression that cleared after he looked me over. "Ah, Ms. Reed, isn't it? We met at the Amanda Nobel event, if I recall correctly."

"We did." I crossed to the other side of the table and sat down across from him. "Scott Kepler introduced us. He's a friend of mine."

"And mine," Roger said, absently stroking his short white beard as he examined me. "What brings you here today, Ms. Reed? Doing a little research related to your B and B's events? I hear you like to focus on books and authors, but I imagine historical reenactment events would also go over well."

"Please, call me Charlotte. And no, I'm not here to conduct any research. I just wanted to talk. Scott told me you'd been using the library a lot this week, so I stopped by on the chance that I might find you here."

Roger crossed his arms and rested his chin on one hand. "I suspect you want to question me about Lisette Bradford's murder. Why you're so interested in this case, I can't imagine, but I can assure you that I had nothing to do with her death."

"She was my guest. That's reason enough for me to want to discover the truth, don't you think?"

"Perhaps. Although I'd leave such business to the police if I were you."

I opened my mouth to say something about helping the authorities, with their blessing, but thought better of it. If Roger Warren had any hand in Lisette's death, I'd be a fool to tip him off to my, or Ellen's, amateur sleuthing. "I just feel a certain responsibility for those who stay at Chapters and, of course, I want to ensure the safety of my guests."

Roger quirked one bushy white eyebrow. "To protect them from the deadly machinations of a batty old professor?"

"That's not what I meant. It's just that I find it a little strange that Scott's leaving town soon and has been trying to get in touch with you, to no avail." I grabbed a well-worn bookmark off the table and fanned the back of my neck. "He told me you missed your dinner date Saturday night, by the way."

"I had car trouble. I hope he told you that as well." Roger leaned back in the chair, lifting the front legs slightly off the floor.

"He did. But he also said that you haven't been in touch since, which he, and I, found a little strange."

Roger's expression hardened into a stone mask. "I've been busy, and despite our friendship, I'm not in the habit of checking in with Scott every day, or even every week."

"I'm sure that's true, but the thing is"—I tapped the corner of the bookmark against the table—"someone else said they saw you down at the waterfront Saturday night . . ." I held up the bookmark in an instinctive protective gesture when Roger rattled the table by dropping down the front legs of his chair. "To be fair, I suspect the person who told me this isn't the most truthful individual, so I wanted to ask you about it directly. Before I say anything more to the police."

"Who said that?" Roger leaned forward, stretching his arms across the table.

"I don't think I should tell you that." As I scooted back my chair, its legs scraped against the wooden floor.

"But you're more than happy to share this story with the police, is that right?" Roger's eyes narrowed behind the thick lenses of his glasses.

"I have to at least admit I heard it, if I'm asked. Other people were present, for one thing. Besides, I imagine the speaker will be sharing the information with the authorities, if only to help his own cause."

"I see." Roger stared down for a moment before banging one fist against the tabletop.

I jumped to my feet. "I'm sorry. I didn't mean to upset you. I thought if you had a good explanation for being at the waterfront and talking to Lisette . . . Well, I know for a fact that someone claims they saw you there, so if you can just explain it to me, maybe I could help you. If I know the truth, I could speak to the police on your behalf."

Roger sat back, his glare hot as the July sun. "Being innocent, I'm not too worried about what you do or do not tell the authorities. Share your rumors if you wish. It won't make a scintilla of difference." He stood to face me across the table. "The upshot is, I do not need your help, Ms. Reed. Nor do I desire your company. If you would simply walk away and leave me to my research, that would be much appreciated."

I studied his stony expression, trying to determine whether his disdain was based in justified anger, or guilt. The truth was, I couldn't tell.

A failed mission, I thought, as I mumbled a goodbye and scurried out of the library. *You've learned precisely nothing.*

Except that Roger Warren appeared to have a temper, as Scott, and Ellen's friends, had said. *And perhaps the self-assurance that allows someone to murder and proclaim their innocence without displaying a crack in their façade.*

I stepped outside the museum, blinking in the bright sunlight. Jamming my sunglasses over my eyes, I strode across the street, where a gray barn-like building housed the Harvey W. Smith Watercraft Center. Leaning against the wood siding, I stared into the cavernous structure, where masters of the craft restored boats and demonstrated shipbuilding techniques to visitors.

As soon as I returned to Chapters I planned to share the details of my encounter with Roger Warren with Ellen. I hoped she could give me some insight as to whether Roger's actions should move him to the top of our suspect list.

But before I dove back into the troubled waters of our sleuthing partnership, I decided to walk to the end of the boardwalk to clear my head. *Because after what Ellen herself told you, and what Gavin said, you aren't quite as trusting of Ellen as you once were, are you?* I sighed and tucked a few tangled strands of my wind-blown hair behind my ears.

When I reached the docks, I paused for a moment to stare out over the flotilla of boats, musing about how lovely it would be to jump on one and sail away. *Leave it all behind, even Chapters,* I thought, as I leaned against the weathered top of the wooden railing.

A waving arm and familiar voice caught my attention. I stared at the figure casting off the line from the cleat mooring his vintage cabin cruiser to the dock.

"Charlotte, so glad to see you here. Saves me coming to look for you." Gavin motioned for me to join him. "I have information I can now actually share."

I hesitated for a moment before walking over to the opening in the rail and making my way to his boat slip. Thankfully, I was wearing sneakers with grips on their soles, so I wasn't too worried about my feet sliding out from under me on the water-slicked wood planks.

"Heading out?" I asked, when I reached him.

"I was, and still am, if you'll join me." Gavin held out his hand. "Just a short trip out into the sound, I promise."

I examined his face for any sign of deception, but once again, sunglasses hid his eyes and I couldn't read his expression. It seemed a little dangerous, getting on a boat with a comparative stranger, but . . . *If he were to harm you, he'd have to answer to Ellen.* Assuming that consequence alone was an effective deterrent to any rash action, I took hold of his hand and allowed him to help me onto the boat. My curiosity over what he had to say overwhelmed any sense of caution.

As I stepped in, I noted the name painted across the stern of the vessel—*Anna-Lisa Marie*—and idly wondered if this was a reference to someone, or even multiple someones, in Gavin's life.

Gavin cast off the rest of the line and directed me to follow him into the covered area that held the wheel, which he informed me was called the helm, as well as other controls. Not having grown up near the water, I was fairly ignorant about boats, although I did know that port meant the left side, starboard the right side, and the front of the boat was called the bow while the back was the stern. But that was about the extent of my knowledge.

Fortunately, Gavin seemed to know what he was doing.

I took a seat on one of the padded benches that ran along both sides of the covered portion of the deck. "Is this yours, or a loaner from your agency?"

"She's all mine," Gavin said, as he steered us away from the docks and out into Taylor's Creek.

"I didn't realize intelligence officers were so well paid," I said, admiring the beauty of the polished wood and chrome interior.

Gavin cast me an amused glance. "They aren't, but I live on her when I'm not working, so that makes it feasible."

"No other home?" I turned sideways and stared out the window before adding, "I thought maybe with that name on the stern . . . I mean, I wondered if it referenced someone significant in your life."

Focused on something on his control panel, Gavin didn't look at me. "The name came along with the boat. I figured it meant something to the original owner, so why not keep it?".

"Ah, so I guessed wrong. *Anna-Lisa Marie* isn't your wife or significant other."

Gavin fiddled with something that looked like a compass. "No, I don't have one of those. Just a boat."

"Less trouble, I suppose," I said.

Gavin side-eyed me, his lips curving into what looked suspiciously like a smile. "Not always. She takes a lot of upkeep and doesn't give much in return."

"Except this." I swept my hand through the air, indicating the vista we could see as the boat rounded the far end of Carrot Island. Ahead, the channel opened up into more open waters, although I could still see strips of land in the distance. "What do they call this—the Back Sound?"

"That's correct. It lies between Harker's Island and the Shackleford Banks, and connects to what is called the Core

Sound, which separates the Outer Banks from the mainland." Gavin cast me a glance. "It's all the same body of water, really. It's just been given different names in various locations."

"And you can sail out to sea from here, right? I did that once, on one of the sightseeing cruises."

"Through the Beaufort Inlet, which separates the Banks and the end of Atlantic Beach. You do need to know what you're doing though. Currents can be treacherous there at times." One hand still on the helm, Gavin turned to face me. "Most boaters use the intercoastal waterway to travel up the coast instead, unless they really want to put out to sea."

I drew in a deep breath of air, relishing the slight hint of salt. Overhead, the harsh call of seagulls broke the stillness. "The Beaufort Inlet is where they discovered Blackbeard's ship."

"Right. Rumor has it he intentionally grounded it, so it wasn't a typical wreck, although there are plenty of those scattered all over the area."

"That's one good reason to maintain the Cape Lookout lighthouse, I guess." I stared back out the window. "Are you stopping?"

"Just slowing down so we can talk. I don't like to use too much speed when I'm not totally focused on navigation."

I pressed my back against the wood paneling covering the space between the window and my seat. "You said you could give me information. I assume this is about the situation involving my great-aunt and Ellen?"

"It has more to do with Ophelia Sandburg, but yes." Gavin's gaze was fixed on the expanse of water visible through the windshield of the boat. "I asked my superiors if I could share a few facts with you and, surprisingly, they agreed." He shot me a questioning look. "There was something said about you discovering that journal last year and sharing it with them? I think that turned the tide in your favor."

"I actually gave it to Ellen, so I think she's the one who deserves the credit. But I did find one of Isabella's old coded journals in my attic. I couldn't read it, of course."

"It seems one of our codebreakers could, or so I'm told." Gavin's hand, resting lightly on the helm, twitched. "I haven't seen it, but apparently it contained something that clued the agency into the identity of someone they were looking for—the woman connected to a man called Leo Evans back in the late sixties."

"Ophelia Sandburg." I plucked at the scoop neckline of my navy short-sleeved top. Although the moving boat provided a pleasant breeze, my neck and collarbone were damp with perspiration.

"Right." Gavin turned to look at me again. "I take it Ellen took it upon herself to fill you in on Ophelia's relationship with Leo, and how she and Isabella leveraged that to their advantage?"

"She did. She also said that she's sorry for that now." I frowned, trying to remember if Ellen had ever explicitly stated this. "At least, she seems to harbor genuine regrets."

"That's all very well, but not the real problem." Gavin slipped off his sunglasses and hung the frames from the pocket of his light-weight white cotton shirt. "If this was just some unfortunate past operation, I wouldn't have been sent to Beaufort."

"Exactly why were you sent here? To dig up dirt on Ellen after all these years?" I tapped my sunglasses against my palm. "Honestly, that doesn't make sense to me."

Gavin's fingers tightened on the helm, blanching his knuckles. "That isn't my mission. Water under the bridge, no matter how murky. No, I was deployed here to keep tabs on Ophelia Sandburg."

"To spy on her?" I fought, and failed, to keep disapproval from frosting my tone.

Looking me over, Gavin sighed. "No, to make sure no one *else* was stalking her. And, if necessary, to protect her."

I slid to the edge of the bench seat. "Protect her? What do you need to protect her from?"

"Someone who wants to make sure she can't blow his cover." A shadow clouded Gavin's light brown eyes. "A man who wants her dead."

Chapter Eighteen

I leapt to my feet, allowing my sunglasses to fall from my lap and clatter to the deck. "Who in the world would want to kill Ophelia?"

"Leo Evans, now known as Leonard Ellis-White. Who abandoned his communist sympathies, but not all his business ties to the Soviets, after the Iron Curtain fell." Gavin grimaced. "Not to mention, once he found a way to make more money off of capitalism than espionage."

"He still lives in England?" I asked, as I scooped up my fallen sunglasses.

"And has accumulated a tidy fortune in a few not-so-tidy ways." Gavin fiddled with something near the helm. "Hold on, I'm going to stop and drop anchor while I explain this."

He sprinted out to the stern, where he worked something obviously connected to the anchor. Once he completed that task, he returned, telling me that we could now talk without worrying about the boat. "Of course, I'll keep an eye out so we don't drift too far, but it looks pretty calm out there right now," he added, as he crossed to the captain's chair.

"There are a few other boats, but not near us," I said, after a swift glance out across the water.

"I think I can manage not to run up on any of them," Gavin said dryly, before clearing his throat. "Now, let me try to explain the situation. But I must warn you—it's convoluted and might be a little hard to follow."

"I think I can manage," I said, earning a swift smile.

"All right, where to begin . . ." Gavin gripped the back of the captain's chair. "I imagine Ellen told you about Leo's connection to Paul Peters?"

"She said he was Paul's protégé."

"Very true, at least at that time. But once he was recalled to England, he cut ties with Peters. I suspect Leo was angry with his former mentor for forcing him to leave."

"Do you think Leo truly cared for Ophelia?"

"At the time, yes. However, he soon moved on." Gavin met my inquiring gaze with a roll of his eyes. "He somehow managed to marry an heiress, which kick-started his financial rise. He believed in expediency and personal gain more deeply than love, it seems."

"If he stopped spying for Russia, why is he on your agency's radar now?"

"Because once you're on it, you're on it for life. And because he's still engaged in business transactions with several major Russian companies. Also"—Gavin released his grip and flexed his fingers—"because his name came up amid some disturbing chatter."

"Something involving Ophelia, I take it."

"We didn't know who the woman was at first." Gavin circled around the chair and sat down, swiveling it to face me. "You see, Leo, or I should say Leonard, has become a person of influence in Britain. Not fame—he never sought that, for what I think are obvious reasons. But he's mingled with the movers and shakers for many years. Long enough to make the kind of connections that might lead to something more than wealth. Something like a knighthood."

I tapped my chin with one finger. "The possibility of which would evaporate if anyone learned of his earlier indiscretions?"

"Exactly. MI6, along with the U.S. intelligence communities, also wanted to make sure his current connection to Russian interests was strictly based on business, and not something more."

"But why didn't they expose him earlier? They knew who he was, and what he was up to when he worked with Paul Peters."

"True, but he never really did anything important enough to risk burning British, or even American, double agents, which could've happened if we'd outed him." Gavin leaned forward and clasped his knees with both hands. "Leo Evans was a low-level spy-in-training. He never actually achieved the rank where he was entrusted to do anything more than help Peters. Also, as I'm sure Ellen has told you, we didn't want to expose Peters. He was more useful to us as someone to whom the U.S. could feed disinformation, courtesy of your great-aunt."

"I see. Not to mention, Leo's now wealthy and well-connected, which means he has powerful friends."

"Right. He's firmly established as Leonard Ellis-White, respectable businessman." Gavin flashed me a sardonic smile. "Well, not entirely respectable, but powerful enough to maintain the façade. MI6 wouldn't even bother, but they've noticed a disturbing trend in his business practices lately. A few too many contracts given to Russian companies. Throwing parties that bring together people British and U.S. intelligence would rather not see fraternizing."

"They're afraid he might be up to some old tricks?"

"Yes. Which is why they want to put a stop to his ability to wield influence." Gavin's smile was grim. "They could do that easily, if they could connect him to the former junior spy, Leo Evans, but that has turned out to be a difficult task."

"Unless someone can positively identify him," I said thoughtfully. Meeting Gavin's gaze, I widened my eyes. "Someone like Ophelia Sandburg."

"She's the only person alive who can do so. Peters is dead, as is Isabella Harrington. Ellen Montgomery, despite working with Isabella, never actually met the guy." Gavin swiveled his chair and checked the boat's position before turning back to me. "It seems Ellis-White somehow learned of our interest in the former girlfriend of one Leo Evans and decided to eliminate this threat to his glorious future."

"You're saying he planned to kill her?"

"To have her killed. He wouldn't do the deed himself, not now. But apparently he knows how to find and hire people willing to do it for him."

"Is that what you heard in the 'chatter,' as you call it?"

Gavin nodded. "We learned of a murder-for-hire plot. We couldn't go public with it, for obvious reasons, but no one at the agency wanted to see an innocent woman killed for the benefit of Mr. Leonard Ellis-White, Esquire."

"So you were sent here to bring her in and have her confirm that Evans and Ellis-White were the same person?"

"No." Gavin stood and paced the deck. "Honestly, I believe it's best to keep her in the dark, for her own sake, as well as national security." He stopped in front of me. "I was sent to Beaufort to watch over Ophelia and, if necessary, protect her from whatever harm might materialize. While some in my agency may want to tell her the truth, that was never my plan, and thankfully my superiors agreed. We have been trying to neutralize Ellis-White's rise to power for some time, primarily because of his close ties to Russia. He seems far too interested in promoting that country's business and political interests, and there's some concern that he may be helping them in attempts to destabilize other nations. He's been upping the ante lately, and consequently received a back-channel warning." Gavin exhaled a gusty sigh. "Unfortunately, that tactic seems to have backfired."

"Because it drove him to hire someone to kill Ophelia, the only living witness who could link him to Leo Evans?"

"Yes. We underestimated the lengths he would go to. Which is why I was sent here."

"As well as to snoop through my great-aunt's things, it seems," I said, keeping my tone neutral.

Gavin cast me a rueful smile. "That was my idea. I thought since you'd found one coded journal, perhaps there were more. Something that would help us tie Ellis-White back to Leo Evans more definitively, without ever having to consider involving Ophelia, now or in the future. But unfortunately, I didn't find anything."

"So while you're here, watching over Ophelia, I assume others in your agency are working to find and arrest the assassin?" I asked, looking up at him.

"Maybe not arrest. That isn't really our thing," Gavin said, with a humorless smile. "But you're correct—I was waiting to hear that the danger had been eliminated."

I studied his calm face for a moment. "Or to take action if said danger appeared to be imminent?"

"That was the plan." Gavin ran his fingers through his curly hair. "Fortunately, I've been informed that the would-be killer is safely contained, and there's no other on the horizon. Which is one reason I can now tell you this."

"Ophelia is safe?"

"At the moment. We're still endeavoring to directly tie Ellis-White to the murder-for-hire plot, which will not only effectively destroy his hopes for a knighthood, but will also ensure he doesn't try anything like this again."

"You won't arrest him?"

"Like I said, that isn't our thing, and we don't want to bring in the British authorities if we can help it. No, it's more of a secret pact, I suppose. If we let Leonard Ellis-White know we have damning evidence on him, he'll be forced to toe the line." Gavin frowned. "Honestly, the real hope is that he will quietly retire to his country estate and no longer participate in the affairs of big business or politics. My superiors believe they can force him to halt his interference if they hold the fact that he can be outed at any time as a former spy over his head. And, trust me, they'll make sure he doesn't try to harm Ophelia Sandburg again. Even a whisper of him planning to do something like that and they will lock him up forever."

"I don't know if I like that fact that he doesn't have to pay for trying to have Ophelia killed," I said.

"Oh, he'll pay. A word in the right ear and his hopes of advancing in British politics or society are dashed. He may not face prison, but he'll be thoroughly ostracized."

"That still doesn't seem fair." I shifted on the cushioned bench seat. "Don't you think he should pay more dearly for attempting an assassination?"

"Do I think so? Yes. But my superiors have other plans for him. Information can be powerful leverage."

"They want to use him somehow." I didn't frame this as a question.

"Undoubtedly. How and why, I'm not sure." Gavin's smile was grim. "Above my pay grade."

"I see. Well, I suppose as long as Ophelia is safe, I won't worry about Leo Evans or whatever is name is now," I said, sinking back against the wall.

Gavin sat down on the bench beside me. "I'm leaving his sorry carcass for others to deal with. Personally, I was more concerned over the danger to Ophelia. It's one reason I requested this assignment."

I side-eyed him. "You asked to be sent here?"

"I did. As you've learned, my ties to the Leo Evans case go back a few years. And, although you may find it hard to believe, the idea of innocent civilians being harmed due to intelligence operations does concern many agents."

"Some, anyway," I conceded, reading honesty in his eyes. "But if the would-be killer has been apprehended, won't you be leaving town soon?"

"Not yet. I'm waiting for word that Ellis-White has been informed of his new marching orders."

"Wait—does that mean you may still have to tell Ophelia the whole story in case you eventually have to ask her to identify him?" I shifted in my seat to face him more directly. "Because I think that could be quite devastating for her."

Gavin stood and strode back to the helm. "That's not my plan. I don't want to involve Ophelia Sandburg if I can help it. Ellis-White might think she's a threat, but I don't want to use her that way." He cast me a reassuring smile. "I asked that my colleagues try getting the hired killer to identify him first, and only use Ophelia as an absolute last resort."

"I find it curious that you have the power to request that," I said, eyeing him with interest.

"I have a little clout." Gavin grinned. "Just a little, but it's enough in this case."

I rose to my feet and crossed to stand beside him. "I appreciate your kindness, and if she knew, I'm sure Ophelia would too."

Gavin frowned. "Don't be fooled—I'm not always so nice. Now, if you'll excuse me, I must weigh anchor so we can return to Beaufort."

After he returned to the helm and fired up the engines, I fixed Gavin with an inquisitive stare. "I have to admit I'm still surprised that you don't want Ophelia to identify Leo Evans, or I suppose I should say Ellis-White. That would seem to give you more leverage over him in the long run."

Gavin maneuvered the boat into a turn, pointing it back the way we'd come. "Again, let's just say that I dislike involving civilians in these matters."

"You're involving me," I said, my gaze wandering back to the glittering expanse of water before us.

"True. I suppose I should examine my reasons for doing that more closely." Gavin tapped the wheel with his fingers, drawing my attention back to his face. "Perhaps it's because I feel you're something of an ad hoc colleague. You did turn over Isabella Harrington's coded journal and have kept your mouth shut about it. Among other things."

"I was protecting my great-aunt and Ellen," I said, shifting my weight from foot to foot. "I don't know if that proves my ability to keep a secret or my loyalty."

"Both, I think." Gavin cast me an appraising look. "Which isn't a bad combination, in my line of work."

I met his gaze with a lift of my chin. "Are you trying to recruit me?"

"I thought Ellen had already done that."

"No, she's pretty tight-lipped about anything involving intelligence work. She only told me about my great-aunt because I'd stumbled upon that coded journal and a few other things. I guess she decided it was better that I know the truth so I didn't spill any secrets inadvertently."

I brushed back my hair with one hand. "She's involved me in sleuthing local murder cases, both last year and now, but that's a different matter."

"I see. And no, I won't try to recruit you into any serious intelligence operations, even though I think you might make an excellent spy." Gavin flashed me a bright smile.

I shook my head, refusing to be charmed. "You should tell Ellen what you've just told me. About Ophelia being in danger and you protecting her, I mean. I think she suspects you have more nefarious intentions."

"I'm sure she does, which is fair," Gavin said dryly. "To be honest, I didn't tell her upfront because I was suspicious of *her* motives. I knew what she and Isabella had done, using an innocent young woman as an unknowing informant all those years ago. I wasn't sure she truly cared for Ms. Sandburg, and I didn't want to risk her tipping off the wrong people."

"Ellen would never do anything that would harm Ophelia," I said, bristling.

"Maybe not now. But she had no compunction about putting her in harm's way in the past. So I had to be sure."

I opened my mouth and shut it again as I considered his words. Gavin obviously hadn't known Ellen personally before this mission. All he knew was what he'd read in agency records. "Which is why you decided to stay with her instead of on the boat," I said at last.

"Correct. I needed to take her measure; to see if I could trust her."

"What have you decided?"

Gavin turned his head to look me in the eye. "That while her behavior in the past might've been rash and reckless, she is no longer that ambitious young officer. From what I've observed, I would say that she'd now do everything in her power to protect Ophelia Sandburg."

"I believe she would. You should talk to her. Perhaps she can help with your mission."

"Which is nearly over. But yes, I will speak with her as soon as we get back. Thanks," Gavin added, with another swift smile. "That was the other reason I asked you on this little boat trip—to determine if your opinion of Ellen Montgomery matched my own observations."

"Not a friendly overture, then?"

"I didn't say that." Gavin lifted one hand off the wheel and reached out, but before he clasped my forearm, he asked, "May I?"

I nodded, and he gave my arm a gentle squeeze.

"You'd be surprised how rare it is for me to spend any time with an attractive and intelligent woman who isn't a colleague or part of my . . . research," he said, lifting his fingers.

"The lonely life of a spy," I said lightly, pulling my arm closer to my side.

Gavin arched his eyebrows. "Not what I call myself. Sounds too much like something out of a James Bond film. And trust me, my life is nothing like that."

"But you are alone." I stepped away, moving closer to the side bench and windows.

"As are you, from what I hear."

I shot him a sharp glance over my shoulder. "I suppose that means you've dug into my past?"

"Of course. I had to know who I was dealing with." Gavin motioned toward the bow. "We're going to be rounding the island soon, and since there are sandbars and shoals. I'd better stay on my toes."

"In other words, you don't want to discuss what you know about my life?"

Gavin side-eyed me. "I know about your late husband, if that's what you're wondering. But this isn't the time and place to talk about that tragedy."

"There's no time and place for that, ever," I said, slumping down on the bench seat. "At least not with a virtual stranger."

Gavin lifted his hands. "Forgive me, I didn't realize your feelings were still so raw."

"It's only been four years." I pressed my back into the paneling behind me. "You may think that's long enough to grieve. A lot of people do. But"—I swore silently as my voice cracked—"it really isn't any time at all. Not when you loved someone so much . . ." I choked back a sob, determined not to cry in front of this man.

Gavin didn't say anything in response. He kept his eyes focused on the view in front of us, guiding the boat through Taylor's Creek and back into the Beaufort harbor.

I followed him out to the stern deck after he docked at his slip and securely moored us to the cleats on the wharf. I had to admit that his skill handling the lines and everything else impressed me.

As Gavin helped me onto the deck, my foot slipped, and he placed his hands on my waist to steady me. Which was the proper thing to do, of course. But then his fingers lingered for a moment and he looked me up and down with an expression that sent a little jolt of electricity down the back of my neck.

No, you can't let this happen, I thought, as I pulled away and stepped back.

"Thank you for the information," I said. "And the boat ride. I just want to be clear that I'm not looking for . . ."

"A relationship?" Gavin offered me a wan smile. "Don't worry. Not something I really do. And as I said, I know a little bit about you, including your love for your admittedly heroic late husband. Besides, once I get the all clear, I'll be leaving Beaufort."

"Oh, right. Your mission is almost complete." I fixed him with an intent gaze. "Don't forget to talk to Ellen, though, before you go anywhere. I think you owe her that, even if you don't approve of her past actions."

"I will. I'll even shake on it." Gavin held out his hand, but when I gripped his fingers, he clasped mine for a moment instead of giving them a shake. "Be careful, Charlotte. I know you're working with Ellen to investigate the Lisette Bradford case. I worry you both might be in over your heads."

"We are sharing anything we discover with the police," I said, freeing my hand from his grasp. "Besides, Ellen is quite skillful in negotiating a crisis."

"She's still an older woman, and all her smarts won't stop a bullet," Gavin said, holding up his hands in surrender.

"All right, I won't say anything else about it. But if you do run into trouble, and I'm still in town . . ."

"Don't worry. You won't be called on to play knight errant and ride to our rescue," I said.

"Pity. I rather like horses." Gavin slipped on his sunglasses.

Once again, I couldn't see his eyes. But there was something in his expression that told me he was amused.

Which was, I had to confess, irritating and intriguing in equal measure.

Chapter Nineteen

By the time I returned to Chapters that afternoon, I had to rush to finish several tasks I'd planned to complete sooner, like confirming the menus for Friday's events with Alicia and Damian.

I got Damian on the office speaker phone while Alicia sat in my chair and propped her feet on the desk. "What?" she said, when I raised my eyebrows. "I think I'm owed a little rest, especially since I had to pull double duty today when you disappeared for hours on end."

"Fair enough," I said, before greeting Damian. With Alicia tossing in some choice comments, I quizzed him on his plans for snacks and hors d'oeuvres for both the tea and the cocktail party scheduled for the following day.

"I can manage the sweets," Alicia said, when Damian expressed concern over the idea of petit fours. "You just whip up all the little sandwiches and other finger foods and handle the drinks and we'll be good to go."

"I'll help too," I said, earning a snort from Alicia. "Seriously, don't base anything on today. I just ran into an unplanned distraction. I promise I won't even leave the house tomorrow, unless we need something from the market."

"Whatever. As long as you play hostess, I won't complain," Alicia said. "I don't mind the other work, but don't expect me to entertain anyone."

"You really think Charlotte would ever expect that?" Damian's voice was filled with good humor.

"Just make sure you get here on time," Alicia replied in a frosty tone.

But her lips twitched into a smile when Damian said, "Good things are worth the wait."

With the menus set for both of Friday's events, and arrangements for how Alicia and I planned to tackle the necessary cleaning confirmed, I decided to retreat to my room. Friday was going to be a marathon. Before that tsunami of activity, I wanted a little time to process the information I'd gathered earlier in the day.

Just as I sat on my bed with my laptop, my cell phone rang. I sighed and set the computer aside to answer the call.

"Hello, Ms. Reed, just thought I'd give you an update," Detective Johnson said.

"Good news, I hope."

"Not bad, anyway. We do have Billy Bradford in custody, of course. The trespassing and threatening behavior actually were a help, since we don't have enough evidence yet to hold him on murder charges."

"But this way you can keep him off the street while you question him further. That's definitely a positive," I said.

"What about Roger Warren? Billy claimed he saw him arguing with Lisette down by the harbor on Saturday night."

"Oh yes, Billy's been telling us all about that, and we have the statements concerning his comments from you, Ms. Rivera, and Mr. Kepler as well. We did bring Dr. Warren in for questioning today, but again, we can only detain him so long without more evidence."

"Does that mean this is another warning call?" I asked, focusing on Brent's smile in the photo on the opposite wall.

"It is, but I wouldn't be too concerned. We'll keep tabs on Dr. Warren when we release him. I just wanted to give you a heads-up in case he slips past our surveillance and decides to stop by Chapters for a chat."

"Chat, huh? You've met the man, right?"

"He does have a short fuse, but"—the detective softened her tone—"I'm not convinced he had anything to do with the murder. We've checked out his alibi for the rest of the evening, after he said he left Ms. Bradford quite alive at the docks, and he apparently did have car trouble. The service company confirmed it."

"Unless he didn't leave her alive . . ."

"Exactly. There's that short span of time that's unaccounted for, so we need to follow up with anyone, in addition to Mr. Bradford, who might have seen him near the waterfront on Saturday evening."

"Or who saw Billy Bradford, I suppose."

"We're checking into all of that with people who were in the general area, and examining any CCTV camera footage from businesses in the area as well."

"Do you still want Ellen Montgomery and me to collect any information we can gather at the two parties I'm hosting tomorrow? All of the current or recent guests will be in attendance at one or the other."

"Definitely. Anything that sounds interesting, let me know right away."

"I will." I stared at my phone for a moment as another thought occurred to me. "Have you cleared anyone to leave town? I'd like to know, just in case one of the guests decides to make a sudden exit."

"They can actually all leave, if they want. With Bradford in custody, and our eyes on Dr. Warren, I think we have the most likely suspects in our sights. Of course, the others have been warned that they must remain available for future questioning, if needed, but if your lodgers want to leave town, we have no legal reason to force them to stay."

"Not even Tony Lott?" I asked. "I told you about that incident in the Old Burying Ground and his possible motive for harming Lisette."

"We're following a lead that may give Lott a solid alibi, so I think we have to give him the benefit of the doubt at the moment. Not to say we won't keep him on our suspect list, but right now he's not our top candidate." Detective Johnson coughed, then apologized before continuing. "Darn allergies."

"They can be tough," I said sympathetically. "All right, we'll proceed as if the culprit is in custody, but Ellen and I will still do a little sleuthing during tomorrow's parties."

"Thanks, that will be helpful. I don't have the resources to have anyone infiltrate events at Chapters and anyway,

I'm afraid my officers would stand out like the beacon of a lighthouse, whereas Ellen Montgomery . . ."

"Can be your unobtrusive super spy?" I chuckled. "Good use of what you have at hand, I'd say, Detective."

"I am practical to a fault. Or so I'm told," Detective Johnson said, before wishing me a good evening and hanging up.

I rearranged my pillows behind my back and pulled my computer onto my lap. While I had a few minutes to myself, I thought I'd do a little more internet searching into the more esoteric aspects of the case.

After falling down the rabbit hole that opened when I dug deeper into the information on Lisette Bradford's Amanda Nobel fan club, I paused for a moment to clear my head. Glancing over at the still-to-be-read books stacked on my nightstand, the ARC of Amanda's upcoming book caught my eye. *Written by Lisette,* I thought. *Sad that she got a chance at publication only to be killed before that book came out, and without ever getting her name on a cover.*

Turning my focus back onto the online information, I noticed a link in one comment that I'd overlooked before. Clicking through, I was intrigued when it actually led to an in-depth examination of the similarities between one of Amethyst Angel's stories and a popular piece of fan fiction written by Lisette.

The writer of the blog post compared the two stories in detail, offering a side-by-side analysis. Reading through both texts surprised me—it turned out to be a damning indictment of Lisette Bradford. The similarities were far too close to be mere coincidence. Lisette's story even included passages identical to those written by Amethyst Angel, give or take a word or two. The author of the article also offered time-stamped evidence that Amethyst Angel's piece had been published at least six months before Lisette's similar story.

"Definitely plagiarism," I told Brent, who smiled back from his portrait with his well-remembered charm.

I knit my brows and once again considered the possibility that Molly Zeleski had written fan fiction under the Amethyst Angel pen name. That would certainly explain her vigorous defense of that author's work, as well as her disdain for Lisette Bradford. But I was still unsure that such behavior on Lisette's part, no matter how unethical, was enough to drive someone to murder. Especially since it had been some time since the plagiarism charges had flared up.

But what if there was a more recent wound . . . I glanced again at the pile of books on my nightstand. Stealing someone's work was always despicable. Still, in the fan fiction world, that didn't typically translate into a loss of income. But Lisette Bradford *had* received a payment of some kind for ghostwriting book thirteen in the *Tides* series. Whether a lot or a little, it was still money. She'd also garnered a professional writing credit, probably with promises of more to come.

"Think about it—if what Amanda told you is right, Lisette used Tony to get her name in front of Amanda's publisher. Then she was probably hired primarily on the basis of that one fan fiction story," I told Brent's picture. "It was apparently extremely popular, and may have convinced the editorial board that Lisette had the skill to write the next *Tides* book. Unfortunately, what they didn't know was that it wasn't Lisette's original creation. She'd stolen the concept, and much of the language, from someone else."

I frowned. Lisette hadn't just taken away another author's source of pride and accomplishment. Although those were important things, they paled in comparison to the betrayal and anger Amethyst Angel would undoubtedly have felt if they'd learned that Lisette had also financially profited from her appropriated creation.

It wasn't hard to imagine anyone feeling this was the ultimate blow—the final betrayal. Lisette's contract with the publisher, and the possibility that it would open up future professional writing opportunities, would, I was sure, have felt like being stabbed through the heart.

The death of a dream, I thought as I stared at the paperback ARC. *And if that isn't enough to drive someone to murder, nothing is.*

Chapter Twenty

After cleaning and baking Friday morning, Alicia and I set up the front parlor for the afternoon tea. Once we'd arranged all the chairs and side tables, we pulled in one of the round tables from the dining room and draped it in a lace table covering.

"Isabella said this tablecloth was a gift from some Englishman," Alicia told me as she placed a tiered silver-plated platter in the center of the table.

I rubbed the intricately worked lace between my fingers, wondering if the Englishman had been Paul Peters. *Or even Leo Evans,* I thought, releasing the fabric. "It's quite lovely."

"You don't find handiwork like that these days." Alicia stepped back and studied the table. "I think we can fit all the tea pastries and sandwiches here, along with the lemonade pitcher and glasses. But we'll need something else for the tea set."

"How about the side table?" I pointed to a tall, narrow mahogany sideboard set against one of the parlor's wainscoted walls.

"That will work. We'll need something to cover it as well." Alicia shoved one of her springy curls back up under her hairnet. "I think there's a lace-edged table runner in the linen closet."

"Thanks. If you'll take care of that final detail, I'll run out and cut a few more flowers for a centerpiece on the sideboard. We can put the tea set on one side and the cups and spoons on the other." I looked around to make sure we'd arranged enough chairs to accommodate our guests before I thanked Alicia again and left the room.

I glanced at my watch as I walked down the hall. Fortunately, I had more than enough time to gather some flowers and create an arrangement before I needed to shower and change my clothes. Grabbing my woven straw basket and clippers from the back porch, I headed outside.

As I laid a stalk of white daisies on top of a pile of lavender, cherry-red hollyhocks, coral zinnias, and greenery, I heard a voice call out my name.

"Good afternoon, Charlotte," Gavin said, as he jogged over to the rose-draped fence that separated Ellen's garden from mine.

"Hello." I shifted my basket to my other arm. "Have you talked to Ellen yet?"

"Jumping right to the point, I see," Gavin said, with a smile. "Yes, I've filled her in on the real reason I'm here. Needless to say, she wasn't pleased, but to be fair, her anger was directed more at herself than me."

"I know she regrets her past actions in relation to Ophelia. So—now what?"

Gavin pulled off his sunglasses. "Now I wait to hear if I'm free to leave Beaufort."

I stared into his light brown eyes. They gave nothing away, which I supposed was one reason he was good at his job. "I thought everything was under control."

"It is, but there's still the matter of leveraging our information to keep Ellis-White in line. Until my superiors feel they've accomplished that mission, they want me to stick around." His lips twitched. "I hope you don't mind."

"Of course not," I said, staring down at my cut flowers. "I just think Ellen will be happy when all this is resolved."

"I imagine so, although she seems to be focused on your murder mystery at the moment. Perhaps to distract her mind from other thoughts? Anyway, I understand she's attending a couple of parties at your B and B today."

"A tea party this afternoon and then a cocktail party in the evening," I said, looking back up at him. Studying his calm face, I considered the fact that he'd requested this mission to protect one of my friends. "The tea is for a select group of guests, but if you want to attend the cocktail party later, I don't mind."

"Thanks, I just might do that." Gavin's lips curved into a smile. "Especially since I know that both the Sandburg sisters plan to attend. A good way to continue my surveillance, even if it isn't such a high priority now."

"All work and no play, I see." I wrinkled my nose. "I suppose you ferreted that information out of Ellen?"

Gavin quirked one eyebrow. "Maybe. Or maybe I have other sources."

"No doubt. Now, if you'll excuse me, I need to carry these flowers inside and create an arrangement before the tea party." I slipped my clippers under the stack of flowers. "The cocktail party starts at six PM. Very casual, so don't worry about dressing up."

"Good, because I don't do that often. Unless work demands it, which is rare." Gavin's smile morphed into a broad grin. "It's not like in the movies."

"No James Bond bespoke suits or tuxes?" I asked with a lift of my eyebrows.

"Almost never. At least for my missions. I'm usually playing the understated, average guy. Slipping past observers because of my very ordinariness."

I looked him over. "I can see that. I imagine a lot of people underestimate you."

"To their regret, sometimes. But you said you have work to do, so I'll say goodbye for now." Gavin slipped his sunglasses back on. "I do think I'll pop over for a drink later, though. If I have more news on the Ophelia Sandburg situation, I'll share it with you then. Discretely, of course."

"Of course," I said, before wishing him a good afternoon and leaving the garden.

After creating an arrangement in a jade-green ceramic bowl, I grabbed a shower and dressed in an understated outfit consisting of a silky, amber-colored blouse and beige linen slacks. Fluffing my hair in the mirror, I mentally prepared myself for the upcoming parties. I felt tired but knew I had to remain alert if I wanted to pick up on any information that could assist Detective Johnson with the Lisette Bradford case.

"Wish me luck," I told Brent's photo, pressing two fingers against the frame for a second as if metaphorically drawing on his courage before leaving my room.

In the parlor, Alicia had already filled the tiered tray with small, crustless sandwiches, delicate pastries, and other tea party fare. Damian, wearing his white chef's jacket over a black T-shirt and trousers, greeted me with a smile.

"I hope you like the sandwiches. I tried to create a good variety." He pointed at the serving tray. "Cucumber and cream cheese, egg salad, tuna salad, chicken salad, and even a little homemade pimento cheese. Not strictly a tea party staple, but since we're in the South . . ."

"It looks lovely, thank you," I said.

"Made the bread myself." Damian adjusted the white chef's hat that covered his dreadlocks. "Tried out a new recipe at home yesterday and it came out well, so I thought, why not use it for the party?"

"I should reimburse you for the ingredients," I said absently, my focus pulled to the hall as the front door opened. "I think some of the guests are arriving."

"No need, I was the one who wanted to experiment with a new recipe," Damian said with a bob of his head. "Anyway, before too many people get here, let me run back to the kitchen to grab the lemonade. That will be everything, except for the tea, and I think Alicia plans to wait to bring that out once everyone arrives."

Molly brushed past him as he exited the room. "Hello again, Charlotte," she said, pausing just inside the doorway to survey the room. "How lovely. Perfect setting for a tea party, especially with the antique furniture and that awesome baby grand." Her eyes sparkled with enthusiasm. "Do you play?"

"Not really. I can pick out a melody, but that's about it. I do sing, usually in choruses and choirs, although I haven't done much of that recently."

"That's a shame. But I guess running the B and B takes a lot of time." Molly sat down but bounced up again as Amanda and Harper entered the room.

I greeted them and told everyone to help themselves to the food. "Tea will be out momentarily," I said. "We're just waiting on my neighbor Ms. Montgomery, and Julie Rivera. I hope you don't mind that I invited them to join us."

"Of course not." Amanda, who was looking very chic in a periwinkle blue dress with a short-sleeved white jacket, motioned toward the serving table. "Everything looks so perfect; I almost hate to touch it."

"You'd deeply disappoint Alicia and Damian if you don't eat their creations," I said, with a smile.

"In that case . . ." Amanda picked up a rose-patterned china luncheon plate and plucked some of the tea-time delicacies from the tiered tray.

As Harper and Molly, who'd waited for Amanda to fill her plate, followed suit, Alicia bustled in with a steaming pot of tea. She set the silver-plated teapot on a matching platter on the sideboard. "Here you go," she said, as Ellen and Julie appeared in the parlor doorway.

"Thought we'd better hang back and give Alicia plenty of leeway with that hot pot," Julie said, flipping her long braid behind her shoulders.

Alicia muttered something about *people making a fuss over nothing* and left the room.

"Can I pour anyone tea, or would you rather do that yourselves?" I asked, when all the guests had filled their plates and set them on the small tables placed beside each chair.

Ellen waved her hand through the air. "We can handle that, can't we, ladies?" She sauntered over to the sideboard and surveyed the tea set-up. "Lemon, cream, sugar, and even some mint leaves—something for everyone, it seems." She cast me a sidelong glance. "Just the thing to accompany an enlightening conversation."

Once everyone was settled with their tea cups as well as finger food, I kicked off the conversation with an innocuous discussion of favorite authors and books.

"Well, Amanda is my favorite, of course," Molly said, between bites of cucumber sandwich. "Nobody even comes close for me."

Amanda lifted her china cup. "Thank you, but I know there are much finer authors than me. I certainly don't compare myself to the true greats."

"I don't agree with that assessment." Molly clinked her teaspoon around in her cup. "You just have this magical way of writing that captivates me. I don't think anyone else can match it."

"Lisette thought she could," Harper, sitting next to me, said under her breath. But when Amanda asked her what she'd said, Harper took a sip of tea before replying. "Changing the subject a little, I'm interested in this new book you mentioned the other day, Amanda. I know you don't want to say too much, but could you give us a tiny clue as to what it's about?"

Amanda set down her tea cup and leaned back in her armchair. "I can tell you it isn't a romance in any way, shape, or form."

"Really?" Julie, about to take a bite from a pink petit four, halted her hand inches from her mouth. "Not whatsoever? That's a big change from your other work."

Amanda shrugged. "Change can be good, don't you think?"

"Most definitely," Ellen said. "And in my opinion, romance isn't the be all and end all of life, despite what the media would have us believe."

"I so agree." Amanda turned to Ellen, her blue eyes bright as sapphires. "Our society makes it out to be the only thing that matters in life, but I think there's so much more."

I studied the author for a moment, intrigued by her enthusiasm over this topic. "I take it you want to explore other things in your writing now?"

"I've always wanted to," Amanda said, shifting her gaze to me. "It's just . . . Well, I wrote *Tides of Time* when I was young, still rather foolishly hoping to prove something to myself as well as others. I didn't expect it to take off like it did, and never envisioned such a long series."

"But you're known as the queen of romantic adventure," Molly said, widening her eyes. "Why would you want to mess with a perfect formula for success?"

Julie used her linen napkin to dab a few cake crumbs from her lips as she gazed at Amanda with a thoughtful expression. "I think I can understand it. Perhaps Amanda almost feels like a hostage to that success?"

"I confess I sometimes do." Amanda's smile was lovely but sad. "I know it sounds terribly ungrateful, especially when there are so many people struggling to break into the publishing world with little or no success."

"That may be true, but you're still allowed to feel how you feel," Ellen said firmly. She stood, tea cup in hand. "I understand the publishing business can be tough, isn't that right, Julie?"

"Definitely," Julie said. "Like everything else, it's driven by the market. While there are many well-written bestsellers, there are some that aren't, and yet are still inexplicably popular. And you know, trends come and go. What's popular one day can change the next."

Ellen poured another cup of tea before turning back to face the group. "Not to mention, from what I've read online, there's a lot of scams and people looking to take advantage of authors." She stirred her tea as she allowed her gaze to sweep over the room. "I've even heard of people outright stealing other authors' books and simply changing a few names and words before republishing them under their own name." She strolled over to her chair, teacup in hand. "Does that really go on?" she asked Amanda, widening her eyes in feigned innocence.

She's good, I thought. *If I didn't know better, I'd buy her act.*

Before Amanda could reply, Molly jumped in. "Definitely true. And in the fan fiction community it can be even worse." She shot a glance at Harper. "Right?"

"I've heard something about that but don't know for sure." Harper stirred her tea so vigorously that a little sloshed over the rim of her cup.

Amanda pursed her lips. "As I've said before, I don't read fan fiction based on my own works, or on anything else, really, so I wouldn't know about that. But I wouldn't be surprised. Where there's money to be made, or fame to be acquired"—she shrugged—"I suppose anything's possible."

Keeping my head down, I surreptitiously glanced at all my guests to gauge their reactions to this discussion. Molly, her eyebrows drawn in over her eyes, fidgeted in her chair while Harper sat still as a statue. Amanda stared down into the cup she balanced between her hands, her lowered lashes veiling her eyes.

"There are some unscrupulous people, like in any business," Julie said. "But I believe any reputable publisher would cancel a book's publication or drop it from their catalog if they thought it included any stolen material." She plucked a delicate shortbread cookie from her plate. "Books have been canceled because of things authors have said or done too. You know, like making hateful statements about individuals or groups of people. That really isn't tolerated anymore and, honestly, it shouldn't be."

As Amanda bent forward, her body wracked by a paroxysm of coughing, Harper leapt to her feet and rushed to the author's side.

"I'm fine, I'm fine. Sorry," she said, waving Harper back. She pressed her napkin to her lips for a second. "Forgive me. Tea just went down the wrong way."

I stared down into my own empty cup. Amanda's obvious consternation over Julie's remark was a clue I couldn't dismiss, no matter how much I liked the author. *Tony said she had secrets. What if those included the kind of statements that might cause a backlash if revealed? Amanda did confess to confiding in Lisette at one point in her career. If Lisette knew something, had some kind of proof of Amanda making ugly remarks . . . Anger over such a situation could've led to an argument and, perhaps, murder.*

And it might damage the publisher's reputation too, I thought, realizing this also gave Tony Lott another motive, although I wasn't sure he was *that* loyal to his job. I glanced over at Ellen, whose gaze was fastened on Amanda.

"Then there's ghostwriting," Ellen said, her tone light as a meringue. "But I suppose that's a very different thing. I'm told it's perfectly legitimate, even if some readers, like me, don't care for it."

Harper shot Ellen a sharp look before striding back to her chair. "Sometimes it's just a necessity. There's such a demand for writers to churn out new works. I think authors can get burnt out and need a break after writing a string of books."

Ellen set her tea cup in its saucer and wiped her fingers on her napkin. "I hadn't thought of it that way. What do the rest of you think?"

Molly finished off a tea cake before answering. "I suppose it's understandable, although I can't imagine you'd do anything like that, would you, Amanda?"

I adjusted my expression, hoping to appear only vaguely interested, as both Molly and Harper fixed intent gazes on

Amanda. I couldn't tell, from either of their faces, whether they were unaware that Lisette had written Amanda's upcoming book, or whether one or both were faking. *Maybe they're just testing Amanda,* I thought, *in order to gauge her own knowledge of the situation. That's what I'd do, if I suspected the truth, especially if I were Lisette's killer.*

Amanda fiddled with the handle of her tea cup. "If I did, it's not something I'd talk about, is it?" She lifted the cup to salute her two fans. "Wouldn't want to disappoint my readers."

I shifted my gaze back to Molly and Harper. Molly's glower made me wonder, once again, if she was actually Amethyst Angel. Perhaps she already knew all about Lisette writing Amanda's upcoming book. If she'd also somehow heard the rumors about how Lisette caught the attention of Amanda's publisher, and especially how their interest was captured by her most popular piece of fan fiction, she could easily feel *she* should've been the one offered that job.

A compelling motive to murder Lisette, who stole Amethyst Angel's work and profited from that theft, I thought, before focusing on Harper. Her expression was essentially unreadable, but I noticed that she'd gripped her hands together so tightly that her knuckles had blanched.

Of course, I reminded myself, *both women could just be disturbed by their idol being so cavalier about the idea of someone else writing her books.* I cast Ellen a questioning glance before looking back at Amanda. While she hadn't vehemently denied the ghostwriting in front of her fans, she also seemed unwilling to admit it. Perhaps because she didn't want to disappoint them. *Although there is also another possibility,* I thought, with a frown. *If she killed to keep Lisette from spilling her secrets and creating a scandal, Amanda might've decided not to broadcast Lisette's connection to her, as well as her latest book. Sure, she told me earlier, but that doesn't mean she hasn't since reconsidered and decided on a different strategy.*

Ellen casually crossed one leg over the other and examined her painted toenails. "But do you think an author is ever pressured to acknowledge the ghostwriter in some way, like with a coauthor credit?"

Ellen lifted her head in time to connect with Amanda's astonished gaze, while Molly gasped and Harper spat a swallow of tea back into her cup.

"What a peculiar question, Ellen," Julie said. "Don't feel compelled to answer, Amanda."

Amanda swept back her golden fall of hair with both hands. "I'm fine. And as for that query, Ms. Montgomery, I'm not sure what I'd do in such a situation. I'm just glad that I'll never have to deal with that sort of dilemma."

She turned to Julie, asking about current sales in various genres and anticipated trends in the book market, while I shared a glance with Ellen.

I felt I could almost hear what my sleuthing partner was thinking. If it was along the lines of my own thoughts, it would be something like: *If Lisette had something on Amanda, could she have been using that to force Amanda to acknowledge her contribution to the new* Tides *book? What if Amanda had grown tired of this blackmail and snapped?*

Ellen met my gaze with a tilt of her head toward Amanda.

The author, chatting cheerfully with the others, seemed oblivious to our sudden lack of participation in the conversation, but after answering one of Molly's questions, she shot Ellen and me a look that betrayed her awareness of our intent.

She's on to us, I thought.

Ellen rose to her feet. "More tea, anyone?"

Chapter Twenty-One

The tea party continued for another thirty minutes without incident, but as soon as the guests dispersed—Julie to her bookstore, Amanda to her room, and Molly and Harper out to do a little shopping in local boutiques—I huddled with Ellen to discuss our thoughts.

"Amanda reacted strongly to your mention of a ghost-writer forcing an author's hand," I said. "I think we both came to the conclusion that perhaps that was what Lisette was trying to do to her. Maybe she wanted Amanda to ask her publisher to offer a coauthor credit?"

"That thought did cross my mind, although of course we don't have any proof. But my comment did affect her, which is a clue." Ellen poured a glass of lemonade.

"Could've led to an argument," I said, as I gathered up used teaspoons and placed them on a serving tray.

"Which could have led to an unplanned murder." Ellen swirled the lemonade in her goblet. "What about the two younger women? They both appeared edgy to me as well."

I stacked a few plates next to the spoons. "I agree. But maybe we'd better talk about this in more detail later," I said, nodding my head toward the door, where Alicia had appeared, gripping a large metal tray lined with a kitchen towel.

"Leave all that. I'll get it," she said, as she hurried into the parlor.

I backed away from the sideboard. "No problem, I just thought I'd help."

Alicia audibly sniffed. "I know how to best stack things so the china doesn't get broken." She glanced at me, her stern expression softening. "I appreciate the offer, but I'm sure you'd like to get a little rest before you have to play hostess at tonight's cocktail party. Damian and I can take care of this."

I murmured my thanks before glancing around the parlor to make sure none of the guests had left any valuables behind.

"Well, I have to be running along," Ellen said, as she grabbed her large straw purse from the floor beside her chair. "I probably should write a few notes before I freshen up for the next event." She gave me a wink. "It's a never-ending party around here, it seems."

As Alicia told her goodbye, I realized she probably thought Ellen meant she'd be writing thank you notes or some other type of genteel correspondence. *Not notes on a criminal case,* I thought, with a smile. I told Ellen I looked forward to seeing her later as I followed her out into the hall.

"Don't worry, I'm sure we can find a better time, and a quieter spot, to compare our theories at the cocktail party," she said, before heading out the front door.

I walked back to my bedroom, so distracted that I almost bumped into Damian, who was coming out of the kitchen with a trash bag in his hand.

"Clean up number one today," he said, waving the empty bag. "Glad you're making this worth my while, Charlotte."

"Oh right, I did promise you a bonus." I looked him over. "I think you deserve it, dealing with two parties on the same day."

"I think so too, but not all my employers are as generous." Damian grinned. "Which is why I prefer to work for you whenever possible."

"Good for you, but also good for me," I replied with an answering smile.

I spent the remainder of the afternoon resting in my room and trying to focus on my le Carré book. But I couldn't concentrate—the bits of information I'd accumulated concerning the Lisette Bradford murder swirled around in my mind like the colorful shards in a kaleidoscope. I finally gave up and just rested for a half hour before freshening up for the next party.

On a whim, I changed into a full-skirted sundress I hadn't worn since Brent had died. Glancing in the mirror, I noticed how its tropical floral pattern gleamed against my pale shoulders. *I look a little too much like I'm going out on a date rather than playing hostess,* I thought, with a frown. *Perhaps I should wear a wrap.* But I ultimately decided against it. It was hot, and the sundress was cool and comfortable. Besides, wraps could become a bother, always slipping down and needing readjustment. Not to mention that this was the farewell party capping off a decidedly atypical week at Chapters. Who cared what I looked like?

But Alicia did shoot me a raised eyebrow glance when I stepped into the kitchen to check on the final preparations for the cocktail party.

"La-di-dah," she said as she tweaked the cotton lace edging the top of her full-length white apron. "Aren't we daring tonight."

I made a face as I studied the tray of hors d'oeuvres she'd placed on the kitchen island. "I was just tired of being too hot at these things."

"Well, you look very hot to me," Damian said, as he placed a bottle of rum into a wire mesh basket.

I shook a piece of fresh broccoli at him. "Behave, young man. You know I'm almost old enough to be your mother."

"Not unless you were a teen when I was born. And anyway, I tell my mom she's hot too, because she is." Damian counted the bottles filling the basket before looking up at me. "But I apologize if I offended you."

"Don't be silly. I appreciate the compliment," I said, before nibbling on the broccoli.

"All that charm, and no girlfriend in sight," Alicia said, after a swift glance at Damian. "What's up with you young men these days?"

"Some of us may have other preferences," Damian said, meeting my interested gaze with a wink.

Alicia muttered something about *kids these days* but appeared unphased by this revelation. If it was one, which I actually doubted. Alicia might be older, but she wasn't oblivious. "Haven't noticed you escorting *anyone,* if it comes to that," she said.

"Just haven't found the right person yet." Damian hoisted the heavy basket of liquor. "I'm going to cart this outside. If you could grab that tray of glassware, Charlotte, that would be awesome."

"Sure thing." Gripping the tray with both hands, I had to kick open the back porch's screen door with one foot as I followed Damian outside.

A miasma of heat and humidity permeated the flagstone-paved patio, making me glad I'd decided on the sundress. As I carried the tray of glassware over to our outdoor bar, I noticed that Molly had already arrived and was making a beeline for Damian.

He looked up from arranging bottles on the shelves under the solid surface bar top. "Hello, Molly. How are you? I know we've just missed crossing paths this week."

"I'm good." Molly, who'd twisted her curly blonde hair up into a messy chignon, was wearing a different outfit than she'd worn for the tea party. Unlike the simple white top and red skirt from earlier, she was now sporting a daringly low-cut pink sundress. I wondered if it was something she'd purchased on her shopping trip with Harper.

"Good to hear. I guess we haven't really seen each other in what? More than fourteen years, I think."

Molly fanned her face with her hand. "Goodness, you make me feel ancient."

"You don't look it," Damian said, earning a smile from her.

"Anyway, I wasn't even sure if it was you when I was here earlier in the week," Molly said. "I mean, you were just a kid when we were in school together. You've gotten so tall," she added, looking him up and down.

"Had a growth spurt at seventeen." Damian took some tumblers from the tray I'd set on the counter. "Can I get you anything?"

"Screwdriver?" Molly cast me a glance as she fidgeted with one of the curls that had fallen out of her updo. "I think that's one of the more refreshing drinks, don't you?"

"Good for a hot day," I replied, stepping around the bar to assist with putting away the other glassware as Damian fixed Molly's drink.

"I also wanted"—Molly bit her lower lip, her peaches-and-cream complexion coloring as she eyed the tall, dark-skinned chef—"to apologize."

"For what?" Damian asked, as he handed her the drink.

"Treating you pretty poorly back in school," Molly said, before taking a long swallow of her cocktail.

"Oh, don't worry about that." Damian, who'd removed his white chef's coat and hat, looked very slim and sophisticated in his black T-shirt and trousers, accented with a pale-yellow vest. "We all do some stupid stuff when we're kids, right?"

"Some of us more than others." Molly focused on me. "I don't know if Damian told you, but I was kind of a pain as a child. Got angry a lot and said and did things I really regret now."

"I'm sure it wasn't as bad as all that," I said, resisting the urge to confirm her suspicion. I didn't see any need to let Molly know that Damian had talked to me about her past behavior.

"Oh, it was." Molly plucked the slice of orange off the edge of her tall glass and squeezed it into her drink. "Which is why I thought I should apologize to Damian. I wasn't very nice to him when we were in school," she said, dropping the orange wedge into her glass.

"Apology accepted, and no hard feelings," Damian replied, his tone mild as milk.

I shot him a side-eyed glance. Damian had his own issues with his temper, so I was surprised he was so quick to forgive Molly.

But then again, maybe that's why, I thought, as I bent down to rearrange some of the glassware on the shelves. *He might understand her better than most.* I straightened in time to catch Amanda walking onto the patio, with Tony trailing her. She was wearing the same outfit from the tea party, and looked just as cool and elegant as she had earlier.

Tony, on the other hand, appeared decidedly uncomfortable, in gray trousers and a blue and white striped button-down shirt with its sleeves rolled up above his elbows. He clutched a white handkerchief that he pressed to his forehead every few seconds. I wondered if it was the heat or guilt that had him perspiring so profusely.

"So I should soon be free of all the annoying questions," Molly said.

I realized that my observation of the other guests had made me lose track of the conversation. "I'm sorry, what?"

"Molly was just saying that she's hooked up the authorities with someone who can vouch for her whereabouts when Lisette was killed," Damian said. "She should soon be cleared."

"Really?" I examined Molly's round face for any trace of deception. "There's a witness?"

"Yeah. They were out of town for a few days, so when I told the police where I was, they couldn't confirm it. But once they talk to Diane, everything should be cleared up." Molly finished off her drink and plunked the glass down on the top of the bar.

"Another?" Damian asked.

Molly nodded but fixed her gaze on me as she picked up a cheese-topped cracker from the hors d'oeuvre tray. "I know people suspected me, because I wasn't fond of Lisette, and I do have a temper. Which I'm working on controlling these days, by the way. Anger management classes."

"Funny, I'm trying that too," Damian said, as he fixed her another screwdriver.

I cast him a swift glance. I hadn't heard this before, but it did explain why his behavior had been less problematic lately. "Good for you."

"It is a good thing." Molly smiled at both of us before finishing off her cracker and picking up the refilled tumbler. "I'm finding it very helpful, anyway. But what I really wanted to let everyone know is that once my neighbor, Diane, tells the police about seeing me back at my house in Morehead City after that dinner on Saturday night, I shouldn't be any sort of suspect anymore."

I drummed my fingers against the countertop, only stopping when Damian shot me a questioning look. "That sounds like a positive development. Being under suspicion can be very distressing, as I unfortunately know."

"Me too," Damian said. "So good on you for getting out from under that."

Molly smiled brightly. She certainly looked innocent, but I still wasn't convinced. I'd wait for Detective Johnson to confirm her alibi before I struck her off my own list of suspects.

"Is the bar open, then?" Tony asked, as he sauntered up, almost elbowing Molly when he reached the counter.

Damian's smile faded to professional politeness, but he dutifully fixed the drink Tony ordered while Molly slipped away to join Harper, who'd just walked outside.

Harper was wearing an indigo-blue gauzy cotton tunic dress that was trimmed with braiding and tiny mirrors. With her long, straight hair parted in the middle and hanging loosely about her shoulders, she looked waifish and charming.

I stepped out from behind the bar and crossed the patio to greet Julie and Scott, who'd parked near the carriage house.

"Everything old is new again," Scott said, as they joined me at the edge of the patio. "That dark-haired gal could have posed for a fashion ad back in the sixties."

"That's what it reminds me of too. I was trying to pinpoint why it looks so retro but also familiar," I said, as Scott leaned in to kiss my cheek.

"Come on, you weren't alive in the sixties, Charlotte," Julie said, before giving me a hug.

"No, but I've seen plenty of family pictures." I replied with a smile. "You know Great-Aunt Isabella was a bit of a flower-child back in the day."

Julie made a tutting noise. "Really? She must've been close to forty then."

"Never stopped her from wearing the most current fashions." I glanced over my shoulder at the sound of approaching footsteps. "Isn't that right, Ellen?"

Looking very fashion-forward herself in a vivid geometric print top and white palazzo pants, Ellen nodded. "Isabella never let age deter her from doing as she wished."

"Sounds like my kind of woman." Scott slipped his arm around Julie's waist. "Too bad I didn't get to meet her until she was in her nineties." He tapped his temple with the fingers of his other hand. "Although, come to think of it, when I rented the carriage house for my initial research on the book, she was still pretty flamboyant. I remember a pair of cheetah-print leggings . . ."

Julie giggled. "Maybe I should invest in some more dramatic outfits? It made a lasting impression, it seems."

"Hard not to," Scott said, his smile widening into a grin. "But forgive me, Ellen, I haven't said hello yet. Distracted," he added, tilting his head toward Julie.

"And why wouldn't you be? You look quite stunning in that red dress, Julie." Ellen turned to me. "I understand you invited Gavin to join us tonight?"

"I hope you don't mind," I said, without thinking. Noticing Julie and Scott's confusion, I added, "Ellen and Gavin don't always see eye-to-eye, even if they are family."

"Probably *because* they're family," Scott said, before offering to get Julie and Ellen drinks. "I'll let you fend for yourself, Charlotte. Hope you don't mind, but I only have two hands." He held up said appendages and waved them like a dancer in a Hollywood musical extravaganza.

"It's fine. I think I'll wander over and see how my other guests are doing, anyway." I motioned toward Harper and Molly, who were huddled together, animatedly discussing some topic.

Something I should probably check out, I thought, sharing a glance with Ellen.

As I walked toward the two young women, who were standing near the large lilac bush that flanked the entrance to the garden, I was stopped by Ophelia and Bernadette.

Ophelia, despite her red hair, looked like an old-fashioned schoolmarm in a floral-print dress with a white lace collar. She pressed her palms together as if in prayer. "Thanks so much for inviting us. I'm glad to have a chance to speak with Ms. Nobel again before she leaves town."

"And of course, your parties always have top-notch food and drinks." Bernadette, wearing her customary white polo and khaki Bermuda shorts, raised her plate filled with snacks.

"Thanks, I hope you enjoy yourselves. I wanted to invite everyone who attended the book discussion. Unfortunately, Sandy and Pete couldn't make it, but I think everyone else is here." Glancing over at the bar, I noticed Gavin strolling over from Ellen's yard.

"Even Ellen's cousin, or whatever he is," Bernadette said, fixing me with a stare that told me she questioned Gavin's supposed familial connection to Ellen. I sighed. It was hard to put anything over on Bernadette. "He's certainly eyeing you, Charlotte, but then again, you are looking sexier than usual. That's quite a dress," she added with a wicked smile.

"Don't be silly." I forced myself to avoid glancing at Gavin. "I'm glad you're here, but let's talk more a little later. Right now I need to check in on a few other guests," I said, walking around the two sisters to continue my trajectory toward the garden.

As I approached Molly and Harper, I noticed that Molly was still sipping on her second drink while Harper nursed a glass of white wine. I opened my mouth to call out a greeting but halted my words, and my steps, when I overheard what they were discussing.

"And you're really convinced that Amanda knows?" Harper asked.

"How could she not?" Molly brushed a damp curl of hair away from her forehead. "Even if all she did was peruse a few of the discussions on her fan clubs back in the day . . ."

Harper's long hair swung to veil her face as she vigorously shook her head. "But she said she ignores the fan fiction side of things. Don't you think it's possible she never heard about that controversy?"

"What controversy?" asked a voice behind me.

I turned my head to catch Amanda striding forward to confront both Harper and Molly.

Harper lifted her chin and met Amanda's gaze squarely. "The plagiarism. Years ago, Lisette ripped off another fan fiction author's story and passed it off as her own. So if the rumors are true and you chose her to ghostwrite your latest *Tides* book, well, I hate to tell you, but that book is going to benefit a thief."

Amanda stopped short, a few feet away from the younger women. Although she worked her lips violently, she said nothing, instead opening her hand, allowing her glass, which was filled with some clear liquid, to crash to the flagstones.

Chapter Twenty-Two

Apparently the crash activated Gavin's protective detail gene. He flew across the patio to Ophelia's side, but with her having no knowledge of the danger that had recently stalked her, she simply stared at him with frightened deer eyes. He apologized and backed away, almost bumping into Ellen, who had come up behind him. She laid a hand on his shoulder and drew him away from the Sandburg sisters, loudly proclaiming that he should join her for another drink.

At the same time, Tony ran over and grabbed Amanda and yanked her away from the broken glass now lying at her feet, Damian rushed forward with a dustpan and whisk broom to clean up the mess, and Molly and Harper retreated so far back into the lilac bush I was afraid their bare arms would be scratched by its limbs. I managed to sputter out a question, asking Amanda if she was okay, while taking in the chaotic scene unfolding around me.

"I'm perfectly fine," Amanda said, as she freed her arm from Tony's grasp.

Julie appeared at my elbow. "What's all this about?"

"Not sure," I said. It was only a partial lie. I was certain Harper's revelation was what had triggered Amanda, but it wasn't clear to me whether the information about Lisette's plagiarism of another fan fiction author was news to her, or whether she was simply upset that others knew about the ghostwriting deal.

Scott, joining us, pointed toward Amanda and Tony with his glass of wine. "Something I need to do here? Looks like Ms. Nobel would like her watchdog to take a hike."

"Don't worry, he wasn't actually manhandling her. I think he's just making sure she doesn't cut herself on the glass shards, especially since she's wearing those strappy sandals." I placed my hand on Scott's tensed forearm, knowing he was the kind of guy who'd rush to Amanda's aid if he thought she was in any sort of danger.

A moment later, I left Damian sweeping up the rest of the glass under the supervision of Ophelia, who was chatting incessantly while Bernadette rolled her eyes and held the dustpan.

I crossed to the lilac bush to check on Molly and Harper. Both young women appeared stunned by Amanda's reaction.

Harper rallied first. "I didn't mean to shock her. I thought for sure she knew all about that old controversy over Lisette's fan fiction, no matter what she says about not paying attention to that stuff."

"But what does that have to do with Amanda?" Molly looked genuinely confused.

I examined her with interest. Coupled with her comments about having an alibi for the time Lisette was killed, Molly's obvious shock over this revelation convinced me that she really *was* innocent. *Amanda's violent reaction, on the other hand . . .*

Harper stared down at her feet. "I know it may seem hard to believe, but I have it on good authority that Lisette actually penned the upcoming book in Amanda's series. As a ghostwriter, of course."

"It's true," I said, when Molly looked to me with wide eyes. "Amanda confirmed it in a recent conversation with me."

"I had no idea. But it does explain a few things." Molly rubbed her forehead as if trying to banish a headache. "That weird argument between Tony, Lisette, and Amanda at dinner Saturday night—remember, Harper?"

"Yes." Harper lifted her head. "I thought it was odd at the time too, but just dismissed it as another disagreement between those two."

Molly turned to me. "Harper and I had left the table to go to the restroom. When we returned, I heard Amanda say something about feeling pressured. Then Tony mentioned legal repercussions after Lisette said nothing bad would happen if everyone did the right thing. I found it all perplexing. But now it makes sense. Amanda and Tony were afraid Lisette was going to talk." Molly yanked the pins from her messy bun, allowing her hair to tumble down to her shoulders. "Wow, that means both Tony and Amanda had a solid motive to kill Lisette, right?"

I glanced over at these two possible suspects, now separated. Amanda was talking with Julie and Ellen, while Scott had cornered Tony. I didn't know what they were discussing, but from Tony's expression, I assumed he wasn't thrilled about whatever it was.

"But how could Lisette threaten to say anything about the ghostwriting deal? I mean, she had to have signed a contract," Molly said, as she shoved the hairpins into the pocket of her sundress. "Wouldn't she be the one to be slapped with a lawsuit if she talked?"

I almost spoke up to offer my theory that Lisette was threatening to disclose something else, some secrets that could damage Amanda's career, but decided it was wiser to stay silent on that topic.

"Probably why Tony was warning her," Harper said, in a distant tone.

"It seems you already knew all this information about the new *Tides* book, Harper." Molly's eyes narrowed. "You didn't share a peep about it to me."

"I'd heard the rumors about Lisette ghostwriting Amanda's book." Harper's face was a study in concentration, as if she were still trying to puzzle out a few details. "And I figured, if it was true, that Amanda had to know that part. But I wasn't sure she knew about the plagiarism scandal in Lisette's past." She shrugged. "I sort of posed that question in my comment, just to see how she'd react."

"She seemed genuinely shocked," Molly said.

Harper took a long swallow of her wine instead of replying.

"Regardless, Amanda wouldn't be to blame if someone else used stolen material in the sample she chose to pitch her writing," I said, hoping to gauge the two young women's feelings on the matter. "It's not like Lisette was going to use that material in the actual *Tides* book."

"No, but it seemed like Amanda was pretty unhappy with whatever Lisette was saying at the restaurant. I wonder if Lisette knew something else. You know, from working with Amanda on the book or something." Molly tapped her chin with one finger. "She was talking in this sneaky, wheedling tone, like she was trying to manipulate someone."

Before Harper or I could respond to this speculation, Molly loudly cleared her throat and made a surreptitious cutting motion with her other hand.

"Please, forgive me," Amanda said, as she joined us. "I was just taken aback by your comment, Harper."

Before Harper could respond, Molly stepped forward and poked her forefinger into Amanda's shoulder blade. "Was your upcoming thirteenth book really ghostwritten by Lisette Bradford?"

Amanda pursed her lips as she looked Molly up and down. "Yes, it was. I'm sorry if that disappoints you, but I truly needed a break from the series, and my publisher really wanted one more book, sooner rather than later."

Molly crossed her arms over her chest. "But I take it you didn't know anything about Lisette stealing stories from other fan fiction authors in the past?"

Amanda's pleasant expression iced over. "I don't think I need to answer that, Ms. Zeleski. You may be a fan, but that doesn't mean I'm required to share everything from my personal life."

"Perhaps we should drop this for now," I said, determined to avoid fanning the flames of this conflict. "Why don't we all head over to the bar and grab another drink and then take a little walk around the garden or something? It's our next-to-last evening together, and I'd like to end the week on a more pleasant note."

"Last night for me," said a voice off to my right. I turned to see Tony sauntering toward our group. "The police have told me I can leave, and I plan to do so early tomorrow morning. Sorry to leave you in the lurch, Mandy," he added, raising his glass. "But I've had enough of this situation."

"I'm sure I can manage without you." Amanda stepped away from Molly, Harper, and me to face off with him. "I assume everything is set up for the next stop on the tour?"

"You may need to check with someone else at the publishing house about that. So long, Mandy," Tony said, before turning on his heel and striding off toward Chapters's back door.

Amanda stared after him, a puzzled expression wrinkling her brow.

"What did he mean by that?" Molly asked.

Amanda shook her head. "I have no idea."

"It almost sounds like he doesn't plan to continue with the tour." Harper twisted a lock of her long dark hair around her finger.

"It does, but why . . ." Molly widened her eyes and motioned to the other side of the patio. "Who's that? The guy who flew into action when Amanda dropped her glass. I don't think I've seen him before tonight."

Following her gaze. I noticed that Gavin was casually leaning back against the bar while Damian fixed him some sort of mixed drink.

"He was at the book club discussion, the one you missed." Amanda said. "Some cousin of your neighbor Ellen, right, Charlotte?"

"Yes, Gavin Howard. It's okay, he's supposed to be here. Just let me go and say hello," I said, before crossing the patio.

"Interesting party," Gavin said, when I reached him.

I tugged up the drooping strap of my sundress. "Especially your contribution. Flying into action like a ninja. I think that took several people by surprise."

"I'm sure." Gavin thanked Damian, who'd just handed him a drink.

I walked a few paces away from the bar, heading for the maple tree near the garden fence. Gavin followed but remained standing when I plopped down on the bench placed under the tree.

"You thought it could've been a gunshot, didn't you?" I asked, keeping my voice low as I looked up at him.

Gavin swirled the liquid in his tumbler. "If I'd analyzed the sound, I'd have known better, but I just reacted. Instinct."

"Or training," I said. "You thought Ophelia might be in harm's way, even though you told me the danger was past."

"It is, as far as I know." The ice cubes in Gavin's drink clinked against the glass. "But I wasn't going to hesitate, on the off chance . . ."

"Your colleagues were wrong? I guess I have to appreciate your concern, no matter how strange your actions might've appeared to others."

He turned slightly, his gaze shifting to the clusters of people on the patio. "I simply like to do my best, especially when the situation involves innocents."

"The funny thing is, not everyone here is necessarily innocent. At least not when it comes to the Lisette Bradford murder."

"Oh?" Gavin raised his eyebrows as he glanced back at me. "Perhaps you should fill me in on that. Ellen isn't very forthcoming. I suppose she doesn't quite trust me," he added, as he sat beside me.

"Can you blame her? She thought you were sent here primarily to discredit her or some such thing."

"As did you, when we first met." Gavin took a sip of his drink before returning his focus to me.

"I suppose." I met his intent gaze with a smile. "But strangely, I've come to see you as one of the good guys."

"A grave error on your part," Gavin replied with an answering smile. "I'm not anyone's knight in shining armor. Despite my commitment to protecting innocents like Ophelia Sandburg, I'm not Mister Clean. I wouldn't want you to get the wrong impression."

"Oh, don't worry. I suspect your armor is a bit dingy. More gray than white, perhaps?"

“That’s a good guess.” He stood, holding out his free hand to help me to my feet. “I do what needs to be done,” he said, as he continued to clasp my hand. “Sometimes that doesn’t cast me in the role of hero.”

“That’s okay,” I said. “I don’t consider myself heroine material either.”

Gavin released my hand. “Well, perhaps we should hang out together then. I hear that spending time with someone whose company you enjoy makes life more interesting.”

“I’ve been told that before.” I turned away and allowed my gaze to sweep over the patio full of guests. “But lately, I haven’t felt like testing out that theory.”

“Perhaps it’s time to consider it,” Gavin said, as he stepped up beside me.

“Perhaps,” I said, not glancing at him before I walked away.

Chapter Twenty-Three

Strolling past Bernadette and Scott, who were chatting with Damian at the bar, I caught up with Ellen, who'd joined the other guests clustered around Amanda. *Doing some discreet investigating, no doubt,* I thought, as I sidled up beside her.

"I think I'm going to have to beg off," Amanda said, pressing her fingers against one temple. "I'm afraid I've developed the most dreadful headache."

Molly and Harper made sympathetic noises, while Ophelia trailed Amanda across the patio, asking if she wanted any of the headache powders she just happened to have in her purse.

Amanda gracefully declined this offer before heading inside, leaving Ophelia standing rather forlornly near the back door. She looked around for a moment before joining her sister and Scott at the bar.

"I think I'll call it a day too." Molly rattled the ice cubes in her empty glass. "I have to drive back to Morehead, so I shouldn't overdo it."

"Good idea," I said. "Looks like the party is winding down anyway."

"Yeah, everyone's disappearing." Molly gave Harper a quick hug. "Don't know if I'll see you again anytime soon, since I don't plan to drive back over before you leave Sunday morning."

Harper remained still, not responding to this show of affection, but she did tell Molly good luck as well as goodbye. "I hope all your plans work out," she added, as Molly walked away.

I side-eyed Ellen, wondering if she'd learned what those plans might be. But she simply wished Harper a good evening and strolled toward the bar.

"I don't have to drive anywhere," she said, when I caught up with her. She asked Damian for a vodka and tonic, which he fixed before running into the house to grab some more ice.

As we sipped our drinks, Ellen and I chatted briefly with Scott, Bernadette, and Ophelia before they wandered off toward the entrance to the garden, where Julie was animatedly discussing something with Gavin.

I narrowed my eyes, wondering what my friend was up to. Julie tended to want to match me with any available and, at least in her eyes, suitable, bachelor. Which I found equal parts sweet and annoying.

"Uh-oh, maybe Scott had better watch out," I said lightly, when Ellen appeared to follow my gaze.

Ellen shot me a look over the rim of her tumbler. "Really, Charlotte? Don't think I haven't noticed that Gavin's interest is otherwise engaged."

"Nonsense," I said, refusing to rise to this bait. "So, now that we're finally alone, tell what you found out tonight, if anything."

"Not much, or at least not anything more than what we already know." Ellen set her half-full glass down on the bar. "Except it does appear that we can strike Molly Zeleski off our suspect list."

"If her story about having a solid alibi holds up," I said, finishing off my drink.

"I think it will. Just a feeling I have. Now, as for the rest—the jury's still out."

"Do you think Lisette was really using Amanda's prior confidences to blackmail her in some way? Because if so, I think that definitely could provide a motive for a serious argument that got out of hand, if not a premeditated murder."

Ellen's expression grew thoughtful. "From what you told me about your graveyard conversation with Tony, I suspect there's something to that theory."

"As for Tony, I still haven't struck him off the list. He doesn't seem like the sort of man who would handle humiliation well. He could have easily met up with Lisette after the dinner party and gotten into an argument with her." I set down my own empty glass. "We know Roger did."

"If Billy Bradford is to be believed. He may be trying to cover his own tracks." Ellen looked like she was going to add something more to this discussion, but tightened her lips when Ophelia and Bernadette approached the bar.

"We're going to head home now, if that's alright with you, Charlotte," Bernadette said. "Fee has a garden club event at the crack of dawn tomorrow."

"And Bernie's actually going to join me," Ophelia said, offering us a bright smile.

"Only because it's a volunteer opportunity. Upkeep on one of the local historic sites," Bernadette said. "I'm not much for gardening, as you know, but I like to help out with those sorts of things."

"I'm sure the town appreciates it," I replied, before wishing them a good evening. Once they were out of earshot, I turned to Ellen. "I'm just glad, if what Gavin tells me is correct, that Ophelia's no longer in any danger."

Ellen lifted her glass and took a long swig. "As am I," she said, thumping the empty tumbler down on the bar. She glanced over at me, her blue eyes cloudy. "I know you probably think less of me after you learned how Isabella and I used Ophelia, and honestly, I don't blame you. But at the time . . ."

"You thought it was necessary. Yes, I know." I absently tugged on my dress strap. "I have to admit I was taken aback when I heard about the situation with Ophelia, but"—I shrugged—"I decided I shouldn't allow that to destroy our friendship. Especially since I can tell you're truly remorseful."

"Remorseful about what?" Scott called out as he and Julie walked up to the bar, arm-in-arm. "Don't tell me you've had one too many, Ellen."

"Wouldn't really matter," Julie said, flashing a smile. "You can easily stagger home, and even have an escort." She flung out her free hand to indicate Gavin, who had strolled up beside her.

"I'm sure I won't need any such assistance," Ellen said, her expression stiff as starched linen.

Damian, crossing the patio with a bucket of ice swinging from one hand, stopped to look over our little group. "Seems like everyone could use another drink," he said, with a lift of his eyebrows.

"Not for us. We need to leave, I'm afraid," Scott said. "Julie's arranged for us to meet some people for dinner."

Julie's face brightened. "A possible investor in the bookshop. Someone who wants to put in some money but remain hands-off. My kind of sugar daddy," she added, with a grin.

"Hey now, I didn't think that was part of the deal." Scott's answering grin told me that he wasn't concerned about the situation.

"One never knows," Julie said airily. She rose on her toes and gave him a swift kiss on the cheek. "Of course you know we're only kidding around," she told the rest of us.

"I should hope so," Ellen said, her expression still a little troubled.

I thought I knew why, but of course had no intention of mentioning my late great-aunt's liaison with Paul Peters. Although she had actually been under orders to play a role and keep tabs on him for U.S. intelligence, a lot of her peers might have assumed he was Isabella's "sugar daddy." Something her handler, Ellen, knew and had encouraged, on orders from her agency masters.

After Julie and Scott left, Damian fixed another round of drinks for Gavin, Ellen, and me. "Wouldn't do that if you weren't walking home," he said. "Now, if you don't mind, I think I'll cart some of these bottles and glasses back inside. Alicia said she wants to start up the dishwasher sooner rather than later." He filled a couple of wire baskets and carried them in through the back-porch door.

"So it's just us," Gavin glanced from me to Ellen and back again. He lifted his drink. "What should we toast to? Keeping secrets?"

I clinked the rim of my glass against Ellen's tumbler. "And uncovering them."

"I'll drink to that one," she said, shooting Gavin a haughty look. "I'm out of the secret keeping game now, you know."

Gavin examined her for a moment before tapping his own glass against hers. "My instincts tell me otherwise, but we can pretend if you want."

I sipped my drink and said nothing. In this chess game, I knew I was outclassed.

* * *

Tony checked out the next morning, thanking me for my hospitality without looking me in the eye. He scuttled out the front door, clutching his suitcase like a lifeline.

That left me with two guests. Alicia, who'd made waffles from scratch, grumbled over the fact that while both Amanda and Harper had come down for breakfast, they'd only toyed with their food.

"Fresh berry compote barely touched," she said, holding out the offending bowl while I checked the percolator.

"I'm sure they appreciate it, but there's only two of them and neither eats that much, from what I've seen," I replied, keeping my tone mild. "I'm going to take in some more coffee and see if they're really done," I added, pouring some into a serving carafe.

I placed the carafe, along with extra sugar and cream, on a tray and carried it into the dining room. As I set the tray on an adjacent table, I observed Amanda and Harper examining a brightly colored tourist map of the area.

"What do you think, Charlotte?" Harper asked, looking up at me with her icy eyes. "Amanda thinks we should spend our last evening in Beaufort participating in a ghost tour of that historical cemetery."

"The Old Burying Ground? It is a fascinating local attraction. If you haven't seen it yet, I'd say it was worth a visit." I motioned toward the coffee tray. "Can I get either of you a refill?"

Both women agreed. As I poured out the coffee I glanced over their shoulders at the map. "Does it say what time the tours happen? I don't remember seeing that."

Amanda stirred cream into her coffee and took a sip before replying. "I checked on it yesterday with the Historical Association," she said, her gaze still focused on the map. "The tour starts at seven PM, so I suggested Harper and I go out to dinner first. I thought that might be a nice touch for our final evening."

"I think you probably need tickets," I said, as I gathered up the tray.

"Too bad Tony decided to run off," Harper said. "I thought it was part of his job to take care of such things."

"Never mind about Tony. He was really just along to make sure the tour succeeded, not to manage my social life." Amanda swept one hand through the air. "I can make my own arrangements for personal activities." She lifted her head and offered me a brilliant smile. "I'm not helpless, whatever some people might think."

"I'm sure Mr. Lott didn't see you as helpless," I said, shifting my weight from foot to foot as I balanced the tray between my hands.

"Just annoying, then." Amanda cast Harper an apologetic glance. "Sorry to talk trash about a colleague. I don't usually do that. But that man got on my last nerve."

"Don't worry, I wasn't fond of him, either," Harper turned her attention to me. "Thanks for the coffee, Charlotte. And please thank Alicia for breakfast. It was delicious."

"Yes, it certainly was," Amanda said.

What little you ate of it, I thought, but simply nodded and left the room.

"They wanted me to make sure to thank you for breakfast," I told Alicia as I set the tray on the counter. "Said it was delicious. So your efforts weren't in vain."

Alicia snorted and turned to face the sink. "Pecked at it like birds, but I suppose that's their prerogative. They're both checking out tomorrow, I take it?"

"Yes, quite early. I think we just need to put out some cinnamon rolls or other baked goods and have to-go cups for the coffee. Nothing too fancy."

"Suits me," Alicia said. "Just leave those remaining breakfast things on the counter. I'll rinse them and stack the dishwasher." She cast me a half-smile over her shoulder. "You can take a break. Imagine you need it after yesterday."

"You also did a lot of the work for those parties," I said.

"But I didn't have to entertain anyone. I expect that's a lot more exhausting. Is for me, anyway."

"Okay, thanks. Just don't worry about fixing anything for lunch or dinner tonight. Our remaining guests will be out, and I can forage for myself."

"It's a deal," Alicia said. "In fact, if you don't mind, I'd like to take the rest of the day off. Once I finish cleaning up from breakfast, I mean. My family mentioned something about a cookout later, and I wouldn't mind joining them for a change."

"No problem." I poured myself a mug of coffee. "Leave whenever you want."

"Thanks, appreciate it." Alicia gave me a little wave as I left the kitchen.

I headed for my bedroom, planning to call some of my own family members, but as soon as I set my mug on my nightstand, my cell phone rang.

It was Detective Johnson. "Hello, sorry to bother you on a weekend," she said.

"Oh, it's just another workday when you run a B and B." I settled on my bed, anxious to hear whatever news the detective had to share. "By the way, Tony Lott checked out early this morning. He told me you had cleared him to leave town."

"Yes, that's partly why I called. We've cleared him, along with Molly Zeleski. Neither had any involvement in Lisette Bradford's death."

"Really? I know Molly said that one of her neighbors could provide an alibi, but I wasn't sure if that had been confirmed."

"It has. And it's not just that one neighbor, but also someone else who lives across the street. Both vouched for her whereabouts around the time Ms. Bradford was killed. She was definitely in Morehead City. Nowhere near Beaufort harbor."

"I see." I picked up my mug and took a sip of coffee. "What about Tony Lott?"

"We've also confirmed his alibi. It seems he was involved in a long phone conversation during the time the murder was committed. We've talked to the person he claimed to be speaking to and also double-checked the phone records, so we know it's the truth."

"But why wouldn't he mention that? I mean, he was under suspicion, at least from Amanda and the other guests. Why not clear that up right away?"

Detective Johnson cleared her throat. "I suspect he wanted to keep that conversation a secret, especially from Ms. Nobel. You see, he was chatting with a representative from another publishing house. Something about a new job, if I understand correctly."

"Ah, so he was looking for a new position on the sly. That explains a lot." I thought back to Tony's behavior and his comments over the past week. While he'd appeared eager to fulfill his obligations to Amanda's publisher, he'd shown little personal regard for the author. *He just wanted to do what was required; what would look good to a new employer,* I thought, downing another slug of coffee.

"Apparently he got the job, from what I hear," Detective Johnson said. "I guess that's why he felt free to bail on Ms. Nobel a day early."

"And wasn't concerned over arrangements for the future stops on her tour." I felt a pang of sympathy for Amanda, but it was washed away by a more pressing thought. "That narrows the field of suspects. Of course you still have to consider Billy Bradford and Roger Warren, but I wonder"—I set down my mug and sat back against the iron spindles of my headboard—"if perhaps we've missed an obvious suspect."

"You mean Amanda Nobel?" Detective Johnson asked, proving once again that she was no slouch in the sleuthing department.

"She had the opportunity. All of the dinner guests apparently split up after they left the restaurant, and no one's said anything about where Amanda was between dinner and her return to Chapters."

"Very true. She told us she was just walking through the town, but we haven't found anyone who can establish an alibi for her whereabouts at that time. And according to what you shared with me, she also had a motive."

"To prevent Lisette Bradford from betraying her secrets, whatever they are." I tapped the side of my phone with one finger. "Which apparently, if disclosed, might've had a negative effect on Amanda's career."

"I'm guessing they were something that could've gotten her blacklisted in the publishing community." Detective Johnson paused, as if considering this angle more thoroughly. "When we talked to Mr. Lott in his final interview, he alluded to Lisette Bradford having the ability to hold something over Ms. Nobel, but he didn't know the specifics."

"I have to wonder if perhaps Lisette was pressing Amanda to give her a coauthor credit. Some authors do that when they have help writing a book. Maybe Lisette was threatening to expose Amanda's secrets if she didn't go to bat for her with the publisher."

"I see where you're going with that, at least as far as it might've played out in Ms. Nobel's mind. Eliminating Lisette Bradford would remove that danger, since it seems no one else knows what these potentially scandalous confidences were."

"The murder didn't even have to be premeditated," I said. "Amanda may have just confronted Lisette over the situation and things got out of hand."

"We have been considering an unplanned attack scenario," Detective Johnson said. "The crime didn't look particularly well thought-out, and we've discovered that Ms. Bradford actually died from hitting her head as she fell against the dock, after a previous blow probably knocked her off balance."

"So, I guess that puts Amanda up there on the list." I sighed. I liked the author but knew that didn't mean she couldn't be a killer. *After all, you're close with people who have allowed their friends to fall into unpleasant situations in the past . . .*

"Along with Mr. Bradford and Dr. Warren. We still haven't ruled them out," Detective Johnson said.

"Do you still want to allow Amanda Nobel to leave town tomorrow? That's her plan."

"Let me think about that. We may want to question her again, but if so, I'll have someone in the department set up the arrangements. You don't need to do anything. In fact," the detective's voice sharpened, "please don't give Ms. Nobel any indication that we've spoken, and definitely don't let her know that you suspect her of anything. I'd rather not spook her."

"Okay, I'll try to keep everything light and friendly," I said before thanking the detective and wishing her good luck with the investigation.

I stared at the phone for a moment after we completed our call. I'd have to put on an act around Amanda, but it was only for one day, and with her evening plans, she'd be out most of the time.

Still, acting had never been my strong suit. I punched in Ellen's number.

"Hey," I said, when she answered. "Want to give me some tips on how to dissemble?"

"Come over and I'll see what I can do," she replied, before adding. "If you're looking for some techniques on handling suspects you don't want to tip off, we could also ask Gavin for pointers."

"Sure, why not?" I said. "When it comes to subterfuge, I suppose two spies are better than one."

Chapter Twenty-Four

I checked my answering machine before I left Chapters, jotting down a few future reservation requests I'd have to respond to on Monday. As I walked out the back door, I noticed Harper and Amanda strolling down the driveway, heading toward the street.

"Hello again," I told Ellen, who was standing just inside her fence. Shandy leapt up against the gate, barking a welcome. "Were you just chatting with Amanda and Harper?"

Ellen bent down to pick up the Yorkie. "Saw them heading out and asked about their evening plans. Apparently, they're going out to dinner and then taking an evening tour of the Old Burying Ground. I guess that's safe enough, even if we are looking at Amanda as a more viable suspect."

"It would seem so. They'll be surrounded by people at any restaurant as well as on the tour."

Ellen nodded as she snuggled Shandy closer. "I thought we'd sit on the front porch. Just let me take the pup inside and ask Gavin to join us."

I smiled as the small dog licked Ellen's chin. "Okay, I'll walk around and grab a seat."

On the porch, I settled onto the swing, leaving the Adirondack chairs for the others. But when Gavin walked out behind Ellen, he strolled over to the swing.

"I hope you don't mind," he said, as he sat beside me. "But I love these things. Reminds me of my grandma's house. She had a porch with a swing too, although not quite so elegant."

"And where was that?" I asked, as I scooted over.

Gavin just quirked an eyebrow and shook his head. "Sorry, privileged information. I still have family there."

"What, you think I might send a hit man after them?"

Ellen tutted. "Now, children, no arguments," she said genially, ignoring the glower Gavin cast her way. "We're here to figure out how Charlotte should handle Ms. Nobel this evening, just in case she is our murderer."

"I don't quite understand how she's become your top suspect," Gavin said, crossing his arms behind his head as he leaned back. "It seems more likely to me that the ex-husband is the culprit, or even that professor. Men are far more likely to resort to violence than women, you know."

I dug my heels into the porch floorboards to stop the motion Gavin's action had caused. "Really? I'm not sure that's true, and while both Billy Bradford and Roger Warren did have reasons to attack Lisette, Amanda's possible motive feels more pressing to me."

Ellen tapped the arm of her chair with her violet-painted fingernails. "I agree with Charlotte. A scandal over something Amanda said or did in the past—something both Amanda and Lisette thought damning—could damage Amanda's career more than a few poor reviews would hurt Roger Warren."

"It would hurt her publisher too, at least financially. If her career was destroyed, I mean," Gavin said thoughtfully.

"Yes, and that's why we kept Tony Lott on the list so long. But he's been cleared, along with Molly Zeleski, according to Detective Johnson."

Gavin slid forward, setting the swing in motion again. "What about the other guest? The young dark-haired woman with the Cher hairstyle—Harley something."

"Harper," I said, crossing one ankle over the other. "I suppose she did have the same opportunity as any of the others, but I can't imagine a motive for her to kill anyone."

"You did tell me that she seemed to dislike Lisette Bradford," Ellen said.

"True, but if dislike was a popular reason for killing"—I lifted my feet, allowing the swing to rock—"we'd have a lot more murders."

"There are plenty based on nothing more substantial." Gavin stared up at the ceiling fan spinning lazily above us. "I wouldn't rule anything out when it comes to killing. Most of it doesn't make much sense."

I scraped my sandal soles across the porch floor, slowing the swing. "But getting back to Amanda—any suggestions for how to talk to her without betraying my suspicions?"

"One trick is to keep any conversation on safe ground," Ellen said. "Don't mention anything connected to her books or even writing in general. Just ask about her evening out with Harper. That should be enough material for a friendly discussion, especially since she's leaving tomorrow morning."

"But if I could find out something that would help the investigation . . ."

Gavin shook his head. "You've done enough already. Let the authorities handle it from here. If Ms. Nobel is guilty, you certainly don't want to clue her in to your suspicions. That could turn you into a target." He laid a hand on my forearm. "The sad truth is, once someone has resorted to murder, it can become easier for them to kill again."

"Gavin's right. We don't want you to become another victim," Ellen said, worry lines creasing her brow.

"I hardly think anyone would try to kill me in my own house, especially with other people present. Remember, Harper and Alicia will be at Chapters tonight too." I turned my gaze on Ellen. "You were chatting with Amanda and Harper right before they left for dinner. Did you pick up on anything interesting?"

"Not really. Harper was wearing an interesting necklace that I admired, and we chatted briefly about it." Ellen absently pleated the silky material of her tunic top between her fingers. "That was really all that was said, other than Amanda expressing excitement over the ghost tour. She said it could be research, since she might try to work something about an old graveyard into her next book."

"Another *Tides* book?" I asked, widening my eyes. "I thought she was over writing those."

Ellen lifted her shoulders. "I don't know if it was another book in that series, or part of her new venture. She didn't really say."

Hearing someone calling my and Ellen's names, I glanced toward the street. Pete and Sandy Nelson waved at us from the sidewalk.

Ellen pressed a finger to her lips before turning and calling out, "Out for a walk?"

"Yep, the evening constitutional." Pete stepped onto one of the pavers that led from the sidewalk to Ellen's house. "We try to walk every day, regardless of the weather, but this summer's been so darn hot, it's been a challenge." He dabbed at his forehead with a crumpled tissue.

"Come and sit for a minute to cool off." Ellen pointed up to the porch ceiling. "The fans produce a nice breeze."

"Thanks, I think we will," Pete said, sprinting up to the porch with Sandy following more slowly. "Ahhh . . ." He took a position under one of the fans and tipped his head back.

"It does feel good, although I'm still burning up," Sandy said, when she reached the porch. She yanked off her floppy fabric hat and used it to fan her flushed face.

Ellen stood and waved her hand toward the Adirondack chairs. "Please, have a seat."

"No, no, we don't want to disturb you," Sandy said, casting an inquisitive glance at Gavin and me.

"You aren't. We were just chatting." Ellen's bright smile gave nothing away. "Can I get you something to drink? Water or lemonade or something stronger?"

"Water would be wonderful," Pete said, as he flopped down into the chair Ellen had vacated. "Uh-oh, this is a mistake. Now I won't want to get up again."

"I'm afraid you must. We'll have to walk back home, if nothing else." Sandy tugged down the hem of her Dancing Dolphin T-shirt as she leaned back against the porch railing. "It seems you're having a nice long holiday, Mr. Howard."

If I didn't know better, I'd have said Gavin's smile was perfectly sincere. "It's been lovely. Ellen's such a gracious host."

I caught a glimpse of Ellen's face before she headed inside and fought an urge to laugh. "They're cousins, you know," I said.

Gavin nudged my foot with the toe of his sneaker. "Visiting family is always the best, isn't it?"

Pete rolled his eyes. "If you say so, although that hasn't always been my experience, Mr. Howard."

Lifting his foot, Gavin sat back, causing the swing to rock again. "It's Gavin, and I suppose there are a few families who aren't as hospitable as mine."

"Yeah, like Sandy's bunch." Pete shot his wife a grin. "They're a trip. They put the fun in dysfunctional, I always say."

"Really, Pete," Sandy said, tossing her hat at him. "As if your mom wasn't always looking at me like I had three eyes."

"Here we go," Ellen said, bustling out the front door with a water bottle in each hand. "I don't usually go in for these plastic bottles, but I thought it was something you could carry with you on your walk."

Pete leapt to his feet. "Is that a subtle hint for us to go?"

"No, just a practical suggestion," Ellen said, as she handed the bottles to him and his wife. "I don't want to hear about either of you passing out on the sidewalk from heat stroke."

Sandy took a long swallow of water before focusing her piercing stare back on me and Gavin. "Do you finally have a night off, Charlotte? I noticed Chapters appears unusually quiet this evening. Are all your guests gone?"

"Not yet," I said, sliding closer to the arm of the swing, and farther from Gavin. No point giving Sandy any ideas. "A couple have left, but I still have two lodgers tonight. They'll be checking out tomorrow morning."

Pete motioned for Ellen to sit back in her chair before crossing to the railing to stand beside Sandy. "Can you take a few days off then, or do you have more guests arriving soon?"

"No one this week. I wasn't happy about that when I originally looked at my schedule." I shrugged. "No customers equal no money, as you know. But now I'm glad to have a little breather before my next group."

"And what about you, Gavin? Are you leaving soon as well?" Sandy arched her feathery brows. "Or are you planning to stay and enjoy the area and its attractions a little longer?"

Oh dear, she already has ideas, I thought, my lips tightening into a grimace.

"I'll probably be heading out tomorrow as well." Gavin's tone was as laconic as his posture. "I don't want to impose on Ellen too much longer."

"Well, before you go, you should stop in at our café." Sandy pointed to the logo on her T-shirt. "I don't think you've been in yet, or at least I haven't seen you."

"I haven't had that pleasure," Gavin said.

"Then you should come for lunch tomorrow. Our treat." Sandy cast a warning glance at her husband, who'd opened his mouth as if to offer a protest over this invitation. "Bring Ellen, and . . . well, Charlotte should be free by early afternoon, so let's say one o'clock?" she added, fluttering her lashes in a show of innocence I didn't buy for a minute.

Neither did Gavin, if his amused expression was any clue. But he offered Sandy a gallant smile. "Sounds like a wonderful idea. Thank you."

I lifted my hands. "I'll have to see if I can make that. There's a lot of cleaning and so on that I need to help Alicia with right after the guests depart."

Sandy shook her water bottle at me. "Nonsense, you said you have all next week off. That's plenty of time to catch up."

"Okay," I said in a resigned tone. "If that suits Gavin and Ellen."

Ellen waved aside any concerns with a sweep of one hand through the air. "Of course, it's all right with me, and I doubt Gavin will object to a free meal. Or the company," she added, casting me a wicked grin.

It seemed she'd forgiven him for his meddling in her affairs. Probably because, like me, she'd come to appreciate his active concern for Ophelia Sandburg's safety. "I'll have to make sure my guests actually check out by noon, of course."

"Just tell them you'll charge them extra if they don't," Sandy said.

"So where are your remaining two tonight anyway?" Pete handed Sandy her hat. "I'd have thought they'd want to lie low, what with being questioned about that murder and all. But then again"—he cast his wife a quick glance—"I didn't expect to see Roger Warren any time soon, but there he was, large as life, at the Dolphin today."

"He does live here," Ellen said.

Sandy took a quick swig from her water bottle. "Yeah, but I think this is the first time he's visited our café. And he was glancing around the whole time he was there, as if searching for someone. He even asked me if I'd seen that famous author or any of her fans in the last day or so."

I shared a look with Ellen. If Roger Warren was the killer, perhaps he was trying to track down anyone who might've had vital information from that Saturday night. Information they could share with the police as the investigation progressed. *Like Amanda and Harper,* I thought, a pang of concern tightening my chest. Maybe he was keeping tabs on both women, which wasn't good, especially since they'd headed out on their own this evening.

"They went out to dinner. Not sure where. Then they were going on a tour," I said, fighting to keep anxiety from coloring my tone.

"Tour?" Sandy pulled her hat back over her light-brown hair. "Was it something in Morehead City or Atlantic Beach or what?"

"No," I said, sharing another quick glance with Ellen. "It was here in Beaufort. One of the historical group's events."

"That can't be right. I volunteer with the Historical Association, taking care of their online calendar and other things." Sandy frowned as she met my questioning gaze. "I don't remember anything scheduled for this evening."

"It's a ghost tour of the Old Burying Ground," Ellen said. "Or at least, that's what the women told me when they left to go to dinner."

Sandy wrinkled her pert nose. "Impossible. We don't have any of those planned until the fall."

"But Amanda said she'd spoken to someone at the Historical Association . . ." I jumped up, sending the swing, and Gavin, crashing back into the porch rail.

"She had to be mistaken, unless something was scheduled without my knowledge. I suppose that's remotely possible, but it does seem odd." Sandy patted Pete's shoulder. "Anyway, I think it's time for us to run along, dear. Despite the lovely company, we aren't getting any exercise just standing here."

Pete grunted and took another swig from his water bottle before agreeing with her.

"But we expect to see all three of you tomorrow at one." Sandy waved gaily as she and her husband said their goodbyes and left.

I strode to the edge of the porch and gripped the railing so I could lean out and make sure Pete and Sandy had disappeared before I turned back to Ellen and Gavin.

"You heard her—Sandy claims there is no ghost tour tonight," I said, my voice shaking. "Which means that Amanda . . ."

Ellen's grim expression conveyed her own concern. "Lied," she said.

Chapter Twenty-Five

"Let's not panic." Ellen stood and crossed to me, briefly laying a hand on my shoulder. "There may be perfectly reasonable explanation. Perhaps Amanda was simply confused over the dates for the tour."

I shook my head. "She explicitly said that she'd called the Historical Association about tonight. But . . ." I pressed my hands to my temples, as if to contain my swirling thoughts. "Maybe she just wanted to muddy the waters in case the police were trying to track her down. It could have nothing to do with Harper, except for using her company as a cover story."

"Right." Ellen glanced at Gavin. "As far as we know, there's no connection between Harper and Amanda, other than Harper being a devoted fan."

"So there's no reason to suspect Harper is in danger. Unless Roger Warren really is stalking them." I shook my head. "Which is another problem."

"I'm more concerned about why Amanda Nobel would lie so blatantly about a nonexistent tour." Gavin's eyes narrowed. "It doesn't seem logical, and when things don't make sense, I get worried." His gaze shifted from Ellen to me. "I think I should jump in the rental and cruise around Beaufort for a bit. See if I can find them."

"We should alert the police," I said.

"Sure, but it wouldn't hurt to have another person out looking." Gavin held up his hands. "If I see them anywhere in town, I'll call the police before I call you, Charlotte. Just let me grab my keys and phone and I'll be off."

As he dashed into the house, Ellen took a deep breath. "I could take my car and search as well. Don't worry, I'll call the police if I spot them, or Roger, rather than try to confront any of them myself."

"I can search as well." I met Gavin's determined gaze as he walked back out onto the porch. "Perhaps we should coordinate our routes?"

"Ellen and I can do this," Gavin said. "You should stay at Chapters."

Ellen cast him an approving glance. "With 911 on speed-dial, in case Amanda and Harper return to the house, or Roger decides to show up here."

I opened my mouth to protest, but closed it again when I realized they had a point. We didn't know where Amanda and Harper had dined, or where they'd gone after that. We didn't even know if they were still together. If they'd walked anywhere near the Old Burying Ground, Harper would've quickly seen there was no tour, since the cemetery gate would be locked by this time of day. She might've realized something was up and left Amanda at that point.

"All right. You two go. I'll wait at Chapters. But I'll also call Detective Johnson and give her the heads-up."

After we all shared phone numbers, Gavin conferred with Ellen for a moment more about covering different sections of Beaufort before sprinting to his car.

"I need to grab my purse and lock up, but then I'll hit the road too," Ellen said, as he drove off. "Like Gavin suggested, I'll call the police first if I spot Harper, Amanda, or Roger, then give you a ring."

"At least they were walking, so they couldn't get too far." I crossed to the porch steps. "They really didn't mention anything about where they were dining when they talked to you at the garden gate earlier?"

"No, like I said, we mostly chatted about Harper's necklace." Ellen paused with her hand on the front door latch and looked back at me. "That may seem kind of frivolous, when I was supposed to be digging for clues. But you know I love unusual jewelry and that piece was certainly unique. Apparently, Harper inherited it from her great-grandmother. It was lovely—a rather large amethyst in a white gold filigree setting."

I stopped dead on the bottom step and spun around to face her. "A what?"

"Amethyst necklace," Ellen said with a lift of her eyebrows. "Why? Does that mean something?"

"Don't you remember what I told you about the pen name of the fan fiction author Lisette plagiarized?"

Ellen shook her head. "I'm afraid not. I recall you saying something about it, but I can't remember the name."

"Amethyst Angel," I said, as realization illuminated Ellen's face.

"It's Harper. The wronged author is Harper," she said.

"Which means Harper also had a motive to kill Lisette." I tapped my chin with my finger. "But it gives Amanda a reason to harm Harper too, if only to tie up all the loose ends related to a possible scandal. Maybe Amanda was afraid Harper was holding more information than she let on. Harper was able to hide the fact that she knew about Lisette's ghostwriting, and the plagiarism accusations, from Amanda for quite some time. Amanda could be afraid Harper knows even more. Either way, we have two people wandering around, one of whom might be a killer. Not to mention that even if they're both innocent, it's possible they're being stalked by someone else." I threw up my hand in a swift goodbye. "Go. I'll phone Detective Johnson as soon as I get home to alert her to these new possibilities."

"And tell her either Gavin or I will call if we see anything," Ellen called after me as I ran across her lawn to reach my own front yard.

As soon as I locked the front door behind me, I rang the detective and filled her in on our recent revelations. She thanked me and promised to send out some officers to join in the search for Amanda, Harper, and Roger.

"Stay home and call me when or if either woman returns to Chapters, or if you see any sign of Roger Warren," she said before hanging up.

I walked through my silent house, staring blankly at random pictures and other objects as I attempted to process the information about Harper and her connection to Amanda and Lisette.

I was certain Harper had written the fan fiction story that Lisette had appropriated, and later used to land a ghostwriting deal. The amethyst necklace, an heirloom Harper apparently treasured, was the defining clue.

"And she knew about Lisette ghostwriting Amanda's upcoming book," I told Brent's photo when I finally wandered into my bedroom. "Molly didn't know about that, but Harper somehow discovered that information before this week. Which means"—keeping my gaze locked on Brent's portrait, I flopped down on my bed—"Harper was well aware of Lisette's misdeeds before she showed up this week at Chapters."

Absently pulling on one tufted knot in my chenille spread, I mulled over this information. It certainly explained Harper's less-than-cordial attitude toward Lisette. "She was actually pretty chill about it, considering," I told Brent. "I mean, Lisette had not only stolen her story, she'd benefited from that theft financially. Not to mention the fame Lisette accrued in fan fiction circles based mainly on that one story. She also had the advantage of using the ghostwriting to launch her own writing career. Harper had every right to be furious."

But that fury, while righteous, could also have been a motive for murder.

Harper and Amanda were off somewhere together, and there was no doubt in my mind that at least one, if not both of them, was in danger.

And more importantly, one of them could be a killer.

* * *

I called Detective Johnson again, but only reached her voice mail. After leaving a message, I tried to reach Ellen, but also got no answer. Of course, she was in her car. I knew from riding with her in the past that she, like me, refused to answer her phone while driving.

I considered calling Gavin and decided against it. He was already engaged in a search and had promised to contact the police and me if he spotted the two women, or Roger Warren. I could fill him in on these new details if he called.

"The truth is," I told Brent, as I jumped up off the bed and padded over to his portrait, "I guess I just don't want to talk to him right now." *No, the truth is,* I told myself, when I touched the picture frame before leaving the room, *you do, which is a revelation you don't like all that much, do you, Charlotte?*

Not wanting to pursue this line of thought, I allowed my agitation to drive me into the kitchen, where I yanked open the refrigerator to reveal a plate of food Alicia had apparently prepared and left for me. A canary-yellow sticky note affixed to the plastic wrap read: *Thought this might be appreciated.*

Which it was, of course. But more than that, it was a reminder to express my gratitude to Alicia more often—not just for the dinner, but also for all the other things she did to help me keep Chapters up and running. We hadn't started out on the best footing—I'd always assumed she thought she should've inherited Chapters instead of me, and suspected she saw me as a dilettante—but over time it seemed we were becoming friendly colleagues, if not actual friends.

I leaned into the open fridge for a moment, allowing the chilled interior to cool my face. My anxiety over the fate of two of my guests gnawed at me, making me restless as well as heated. Closing the refrigerator door, I decided to take a turn around the garden. While I knew I shouldn't leave Chapters, a walk in the garden certainly wouldn't do any harm. Since the front door was locked, Harper and Amanda, or, for that matter, Roger, would either have to wait on the front porch or come around back to find me. Either way, they wouldn't be wandering around inside Chapters on their own. Besides, the front porch was visible to anyone passing by. Surely neither would attempt an attack where they could easily be seen.

I didn't plan to be outside for long; just enough time to clear my head. I checked the pocket of my cotton shorts to make sure I had my phone as well as my house keys.

As a precaution, I locked the back door behind me. I didn't typically bother with locking that door when I was in the garden, but this evening I wanted to make sure no one could slip inside Chapters unnoticed.

The wind, carrying a faint tang of salt air, offered a cooling breeze as I paced the garden's pea gravel paths. Despite this, a trickle of perspiration rolled from my hairline to a spot between my shoulder blades, forcing me pluck my scoop neck top away from my back. From the trees, their leaves silvered with dust, bird caws and whistles wafted over my head. I kept one hand thrust in my pocket, my fingers clutched around my cell phone, as I gazed over the tapestry woven by the colorful summer flowers.

There was a peace I found in the garden that was only matched by being near or on the water. I drew in a deep breath of the perfumed air and allowed my gaze to roam from clusters of bee balm and other butterfly attracting blossoms, to a bed of culinary herbs, and then a clump of spear-like foliage from the spent irises.

This reverie was broken by the ringing sound of raised voices. Identifying them as belonging to Amanda and Harper, I instinctively decided to hide. I slipped behind a weigela bush, a well-established shrub taller than me. With its thick lattice of limbs laden with leaves it created a barrier between me and the two women entering the garden.

As I peeped out from behind my natural screen, my gaze was drawn to a flash of light. I squinted at the sunlight glinting off the surface of something Harper held in her right hand. Confused for a second, I clapped my hand over my mouth when my brain finally recognized the shiny object.

Harper was holding a gun.

Chapter Twenty-Six

I fumbled with my cell phone, pressing the button that brought it out of a snooze, glad I'd switched to silent mode. Certain that the weigela was thick enough to hide me, I was shocked to hear Harper call out my name. "Get out here, Charlotte," she said. "Unless you want me to shoot Amanda right now."

I stepped out from behind the bush, hands up.

"Move closer," Harper commanded. "And toss that phone on the ground."

Keeping my gaze fixed on Amanda, I silently complied, crawling out from behind the bush and walking close to the two women before dropping my cell phone to the ground at my feet.

"You don't have to do this." Amanda's voice was astonishingly calm. I had to give her credit for remaining so cool under pressure. Meanwhile, my heart ricocheted against my ribs and my vision blurred. Afraid I was about to pass out, I flexed my knees

Amanda shared a swift look of concern with me before addressing Harper again. "As I said before, I didn't know anything about Lisette Bradford stealing your story. If I had . . ."

"You'd have done the same thing." Harper's voice was taut as a violin string. "Because she had some sort of hold over you, didn't she? And instead of standing up to her and dealing with whatever the fallout happened to be, you just caved and allowed her to manipulate you. Which meant the truth about how she got the ghostwriting gig based off a story she stole from me would never be revealed."

"I keep telling you I'm sorry. I never meant for any of this to happen. If I'd known from the beginning . . ."

"But you did. I think you knew about Lisette stealing my story, and still let the project go forward." Harper pressed the gun against Amanda's temple. "I didn't think you knew that part, not until this week. You always claimed you didn't engage with fan fiction stuff, so I believed you were innocent on that point. Even though I knew about the ghostwriting and Lisette getting that deal based on a story she ripped off from me." Harper lowered the gun but still kept it trained on Amanda's head. "Molly told me when we were out shopping that she'd heard rumors about Lisette having some dirt on you, and she wondered if you or Tony could've killed her because of that. But she didn't have all the pieces. She didn't know about Lisette ghostwriting your latest book. Not until the cocktail party."

"But you knew, didn't you, Harper?" I asked, hoping to draw her attention away from Amanda. "And you also somehow learned that Lisette used the story she basically stole from you to land the project. After she seduced Tony to get him to put her name forward to the publisher, of course. You knew, and you argued over that with Lisette Saturday night." I didn't frame this as a question.

"I just wanted to talk to her. To let her know I was aware of her bad behavior. That she hadn't simply put one over on me, like she had poor Tony." Harper's fierce stare didn't falter. "What did she have on you, anyway? Must've been something pretty serious."

"It was," Amanda said. "She and I corresponded via email early in my career, and she'd saved them all. It was during a time when I was . . . lost." Amanda clasped her trembling hands in front of her. "I'd gotten too famous too fast, and it didn't feel real. Or right, I guess. Anyway, I was experiencing a serious case of impostor syndrome. I foolishly tried to manage it by sharing far too many negative comments with Lisette, who I thought was a friend."

"That doesn't sound like much of a secret," Harper said with a sniff.

"Doesn't it?" Amanda's smile was brittle as a dead leaf. "I said things about my fellow authors, my editors, my publisher, even my readers—horrible things that would destroy my career if they got out today. I thought I was being oh-so-clever and witty, but it was all just ugly attacks meant to bolster my own fragile self-esteem."

"And Lisette threatened to expose all of that?" Harper's face softened for a moment before she raised the gun higher again. "I don't care, you should've owned up to it. That would've destroyed her hold over you."

"And destroyed my career in the process," Amanda said.

"Not necessarily. But it would've meant you could've demanded that she be dropped from the project. At least then she wouldn't have been allowed to profit from her theft of my work." Harper's voice cracked like badly fired pottery. "Anyway, stupid me, I wanted to protect you at first. I believed you were just as blindsided as me, so I tried to keep you out of it. You were my idol, after all." Harper's lips curled into a sneer. "But Lisette confessed some of what she knew about you, at the end. And she told me about using that fan fiction story, *my* story, to get the contract to ghostwrite your book."

"I didn't realize she'd stolen anything from you, Harper. I swear." Amanda turned her head until she was staring directly into Harper's eyes. "I didn't hear about any accusations of plagiarism against Lisette until this week. Of course, then I did a little digging, but all I discovered was that Lisette had been accused of stealing from another fan fiction author, who used the handle Amethyst Angel. I tried to find out who that was, but I failed. Then, this morning at breakfast I saw your pendant and put two and two together. I realized you were the author Lisette had wronged."

The gun dipped slightly. "So you invited me on a nonexistent tour tonight to do what? Silence me somehow?"

"No, no." Amanda took a deep breath. "I wanted to find a way to make amends."

"Likely story." Harper once again pressed the pistol to Amanda's temple.

It was time to draw her attention elsewhere. "Is that why you brought the gun? Because you were afraid of what Amanda might do?" I forced myself to keep any trace of accusation out of my tone.

Harper's gaze slid to me. "I wasn't going to be caught unaware again. When I tried to talk to Lisette, she attacked me. I just wanted to have a civil conversation, letting her know I wasn't fooled, but she flew at me, all nails and teeth, like some harpy."

"And you fought back to protect yourself." My cell phone, lying at my feet, vibrated against my sandal. Fortunately, Harper didn't notice.

"Yes, I struck her. What else was I supposed to do?" Harper's hand remained steady. She obviously knew how to handle a gun, which was not a particularly reassuring thought.

"After she attacked you, which makes it self-defense, not murder," Amanda said, hope brightening her voice. "Just tell the police the truth and it can all be cleared up."

"Be quiet," Harper snapped. "It was an accident, but I covered it up. I know what that means."

"You just panicked," I said, in the voice usually reserved for de-escalating student altercations. "Anyone would understand that."

A sharp bark of laughter escaped Harper's lips. "Sure, because no one is ever falsely accused or convicted."

"We can vouch for you." While her tone retained a soothing sweetness, Amanda's rigid jawline and glassy eyes betrayed her fear.

Harper lowered her dark lashes, veiling her pale eyes. "You say that now. But just like before, I'm sure you won't risk your own interests to support or defend me when it comes down to it."

"I would have, if I'd known the truth and known what Lisette had done to you," Amanda said.

"Don't give me that crap. You were perfectly happy to keep things quiet, even after learning that Lisette was a plagiarist. You didn't care anything about someone as unimportant as Amethyst Angel." Harper pulled back the gun and stared at the author with disdain. "You didn't lift a finger when you thought it was just some poor, random writer who'd been wronged. You only cared when you knew it was me, and only then because you were afraid I'd share your secrets with the world. Of course, the irony is that I didn't really know anything about what Lisette was holding over you, while you knew plenty that could've derailed all of Lisette's plans."

I considered tackling Harper, but decided that was foolish. She was shorter than me, but obviously strong and fit. Not to mention, she had a gun. Even if I could knock off her aim, she might still be able to fire off a shot that would harm Amanda, or me.

Amanda wiped a bubble of spittle from the corner of her mouth. "I swear I had no knowledge about any of this until this week. And I certainly didn't know that the story Lisette used to secure the ghostwriting contract was stolen from someone else. As soon as I realized the truth, I was determined to somehow right that wrong. Which is why I lied about this evening. I wanted a chance to talk to you somewhere away from crowds." Her gaze flickered over to me, "And away from the B and B, because I'd noticed Charlotte being far too observant about too many things. I just thought the cemetery would be the perfect spot."

"You didn't realize it would be closed by the time you got there, I guess," I said, as my phone vibrated against my foot again.

Amanda gave a little shake of her head. "I had no idea. Honestly, I wasn't trying to deceive Harper. I just noticed a mention of a ghost tour and didn't check into the details."

"You wanted to get me alone so you could threaten me," Harper said, nudging Amanda's shoulder with the pistol. "Admit it."

"Not at all. I only asked you to come with me this evening so I could talk to you in private; to allow us to work something out between us with no outside interference." A few more cracks in Amanda's stoic demeanor had appeared—her left eye twitched and a sheen of perspiration glistened on her forehead and upper lip. But her voice remained calm.

Harper, on the other hand, was sweating profusely, and her free hand shook so violently she shoved it into the pocket of her denim shorts. "But now we have a bigger problem. You both know I killed Lisette. Accidentally, but still . . ."

I bit my lip to avoid blurting out the truth—the police knew as well, or at least they were aware of my suspicions and would follow up on them. There was no way out for Harper, but I couldn't let her know that. It might cause her to take immediate and drastic action. We had to keep her talking, at least until the authorities arrived.

Amanda appeared to have reached the same conclusion. "It was self-defense. And if Charlotte and I don't press charges over this little misunderstanding, you won't be in that much trouble. Why not put the gun away and end all this? We can have that serious conversation about more positive things, like future book collaborations. I still need a ghostwriter, you know."

Another burst of manic laughter escaped Harper's chapped lips. "Sure, as if that's going to happen now. What publisher would want to hire me after this? No, it's all over." She lowered the arm holding the pistol. "It's all over now."

Watching the anger that suffused her face dissolve into despair, a new danger flared in my mind. Harper might not shoot Amanda or me. But that didn't mean she wouldn't do something else equally drastic, like take her own life.

The barrel of the gun was pointing toward the ground. This was my chance. I lunged forward, prepared to knock the weapon from Harper's hand, but she was too quick for me. She swung up her arm, shoving the pistol into my chest.

A vision of Brent's smiling face filled my mind. *Might see you soon,* I thought, as Harper shouted for me to back off.

Out of the corner of my eye, I spied a monarch butterfly. It flitted past my ear and landed on my shoulder, orange and black wings outstretched.

Not an angel, I thought, as a sense of detachment swept over me. *But maybe the next best thing.*

The butterfly appeared to have distracted Harper. She instinctively lowered the gun as she stared at its fluttering wings. It was only a moment's reprieve, but it was enough.

Just long enough for Gavin to leap the fence between Ellen's garden and mine.

I grimaced, thinking of the thorns that must've pierced his skin when he vaulted over the rose-draped barrier. But this thought was swept away as he shoved me to one side, sending me tumbling to the ground while he rushed forward to deal with Harper.

Ellen, who'd come from the same direction, but obviously used the gate, also ran into the garden, her speed belying her age.

While Ellen pulled Amanda out of range, Gavin grappled with Harper, grasping and twisting her wrist to force her to drop the gun. He then pulled her hands behind her back with an efficiency that told me he'd done something similar many times before.

The wail of police sirens filled the air. "I called them," Ellen said, as she strolled over to help me to my feet. "You weren't answering your phone, for me or Gavin. We found that a trifle disturbing and decided we'd better head on back to Chapters to check on you."

"Thank goodness," I said, brushing some pea gravel from my bare knees. I was going to suffer from a few scratches and bruises, but that was a small price to pay. Glancing up, I followed the flight of the monarch as it lazily sailed away.

"Thank you," I said softly, repeating this sentiment in a louder voice when I turned my gaze on Gavin and Ellen.

"We'll take over from here," Detective Johnson said, as she strode into the garden followed by several uniformed officers.

Gavin kept his hold on Harper until she was secured by the police. She remained silent as she was escorted to a waiting cruiser, but in the tears cascading down her cheeks I could read the truth—she'd finally realized the tragic denouement of her own story.

"We'll need statements," Detective Johnson said. "So please stay put until we can deal with that, but then you can all get some much-deserved rest." She stared at Gavin, who'd wiped his hand on his shorts, leaving a trail of blood. "Any of you need medical attention?"

"Just a few scratches from thorns," Gavin said, holding up his hands. "Minor stuff."

"I'm fine," Amanda managed to say before she burst into tears.

Ellen put her arm around Amanda's shaking shoulders and hugged her close. "There's absolutely nothing wrong with me," Ellen told the detective.

"No, there isn't." Gavin cast her an approving look before strolling over to me. "You okay too, Charlotte?"

"I'm fine," I said, not resisting when he pulled me into gentle embrace. "Perfectly fine," I murmured into the folds of his cotton shirt.

"You're better than fine," he whispered in my ear before lifting his head and telling Detective Johnson that he'd be glad to give a statement, but she'd have to call his bosses first.

"Not another one," the detective said, in an exasperated tone. But when I pulled away from Gavin and turned to look at her, she was smiling.

Chapter Twenty-Seven

The next day, Amanda checked out early, as she'd planned.

"Thanks for everything," she said, clasping my hand as she told me goodbye.

I felt a pang of sympathy. Amanda had seemed like someone who had it all, but right now she looked wan and defeated. Late Saturday night, after the police had left, she'd told me she'd advised her publisher to halt the release of book thirteen in her series, pending the conclusion of the murder investigation, as well as a consideration of Lisette Bradford's alleged plagiarism of Harper's work. "I know the book doesn't really contain anything that was stolen from Harper, but it just feels tainted to me. Anyway, it seems wrong to allow it to go forward, given the circumstances. I may have to regroup and write the thing myself," she'd said, her eyes bloodshot from weeping.

I wished her well and said I hoped she'd get a chance to write the book of her heart, sooner rather than later. She simply smiled sadly and left, walking with her slumped shoulders to meet the waiting taxi.

With my final guest on her way to the airport and the next leg of her tour, I wandered into the kitchen to find Alicia. "Would you mind terribly if I invited a few people over for a get-together around three this afternoon?" I asked her.

"Not if I don't have to cook," she replied, casting me a questioning glance.

"You won't. It's going to be very casual. I'll just use some of our leftovers from the cocktail party and whatever else I can put together." I opened the refrigerator and examined its full shelves. "There's plenty here to work with, and we have wine and beer, along with water and soft drinks. That should be enough."

"Sounds good. I'm happy to help clean up after." Alicia slipped her apron over her head. "Just thought I might go to church this morning. After all that's happened, I figure a few prayers wouldn't do any harm."

"Say some for me too," I said.

"Will do." Alicia looked me over. "I was just thinking—since we don't have any guests this week, maybe you should take the opportunity to visit your folks or something. Get out of town for a few days. You look like you could use a change, and I don't mind hanging around Chapters on my own."

I considered this for a second before offering her a warm smile. "That actually sounds like an excellent idea. Thanks."

Alicia turned away, busying herself pulling a few serving platters from the drying rack. "No problem."

I left her finishing the kitchen chores and headed into my office. It was time to catch up on some paperwork. After checking over future reservations, I scribbled a list of the people I wanted to invite for my afternoon get-together. It was primarily the book club group, although I intended to include Scott as Julie's guest, as well as Gavin.

Since it was still early, I knew I'd have to wait to call or text most of the group, but decided to go ahead and contact Pete and Sandy. I figured I could reach them since they had to get up at dawn to prepare for the Sunday breakfast rush at the café.

"Afraid we'll have to skip that free lunch," I told Sandy when she answered the phone. "After everything that happened yesterday evening, I think I'd rather just hang out at Chapters today. But I'm throwing a little impromptu event around three PM and want you and Pete to come."

"We'd love to," Sandy replied. "Especially if you'll provide all the juicy details about whatever happened yesterday."

I promised I'd give a full report, or at least as much as I knew, during their visit.

Completing some budget work took up another hour, after which I called the others on my invite list, including the Sandburg sisters, Julie and Scott, and Ellen.

"I suppose I should bring Gavin along as well?" Ellen asked, in a perfectly innocent tone.

"Of course. I mean, he was just as involved in this case as we were, in the end. And I guess I owe him some food and a drink or two, since I canceled our lunch at the Dancing Dolphin."

"True. It will also give you a chance to say goodbye. He plans to leave Beaufort tomorrow," Ellen said.

"I assumed as much." I squashed a tiny pang of disappointment at this thought. "Okay, see you both around three."

As soon as I hung up, I got a call from Detective Johnson, who filled me in on the latest developments in the Lisette Bradford case.

"This will be all over the news later today," she said. "But I thought you deserved to hear it straight from me, after the help you and Ms. Montgomery and Mr. Howard gave us."

I laid down my pen and stared at the paper I'd used to write down names for today's get-together. It was covered in random doodles including, I was dismayed to see, a few hearts. "I appreciate that."

"Basically, it's now a pretty open-and-shut case. Ms. Gregg confessed to striking and shoving Ms. Bradford during a heated argument. Apparently, Ms. Bradford then fell and hit her head against a dock cleat. When Ms. Gregg realized Ms. Bradford was dead, she panicked."

"She tossed Lisette's body in the water and then cleaned up the area?"

"So she says. There was plenty of water available, of course, and apparently someone had left a bucket and deck mop beside one of the slips. It's good we have her confession, since it seems no one was around to catch Ms. Gregg in the act, and there are no CCTV cameras in that area. Not to mention that the two women were arguing out on one of the docks, and a large excursion boat hid them from view."

"Did you ever confirm the story about Roger Warren arguing with Lisette a little earlier?"

"Yes, and although he was gone by the time Harper Gregg approached Ms. Bradford, apparently that earlier argument had agitated her. When Ms. Gregg confronted her, it seems Lisette Bradford was already angry and basically looking for a fight."

"Which just escalated things, I guess." I sighed deeply. "It doesn't sound like Harper was planning to hurt Lisette."

"No, she swears she only wanted to talk—to confront Ms. Bradford over the theft of that story you told me about." Detective Johnson softened her clipped professional tone. "It's a sad case. I hope the prosecutor will go for manslaughter, but we'll see. Covering up the situation after the fact, and then threatening you and Ms. Nobel doesn't help Ms. Gregg's case."

"I guess not." I crumpled the scribble-filled paper and tossed it in the wastebasket. "Is it okay if I share this information with others, like Ellen Montgomery and my book club group? You said it would soon be on the news."

"Sure, no problem. And thanks again for all your help," Detective Johnson said, before wishing me a good day.

I swiveled my rolling chair and stared at one of the photos of Great-Aunt Isabella that adorned the far wall of the office. In it, she was standing arm-in-arm with a few unidentified people who looked vaguely familiar. *Probably some celebrities or tycoons,* I thought, studying their elegant attire and general air of wealth and power.

"How'd you do it?" I asked my great-aunt as I rose to my feet and crossed the room to examine the photo. Isabella was wearing a vivid turquoise cocktail dress and a sapphire pendant that was probably worth more than my former annual teacher's salary. She stared back at me, her lips curved in an enigmatic smile. "How'd you play that role for years, knowing you were under imminent threat if you were discovered? How did you live a life filled with constant danger?"

Just like Ellen's life was once. Just like Gavin's probably is now, I thought, pressing my forefinger against the glass covering the photo. "I have to give you credit, Isabella. You were a lot tougher, and braver, than most people knew."

She'd ended up as an innkeeper, running Chapters and playing the role of a Southern lady. *But she never truly conformed,* I realized, remembering Scott's mention of cheetah-print leggings. She'd always retained her love of adventure.

My lips twitched into a wry smile as I acknowledged the truth—that trait was something I might have inherited, along with her house.

* * *

Ophelia and Bernadette were the first to arrive for my afternoon gathering. I greeted them on the front porch, where I'd arranged some folding chairs to complement the regular contingent of wooden rockers.

"I thought it would be nice to use the front porch today," I said, as I set a tray of snacks on a teak console table placed beneath the dining room windows.

"It is a little cooler out, which is a blessing." Ophelia adjusted the folds of her tulip-print skirt over her knees as she relaxed in one of the rockers.

Bernadette slouched against one of the porch-roof posts, her hand gripping the top rail of the balustrade. "I hear the police caught their killer last night, right here at Chapters."

"Yes. I'll fill in the details once everyone arrives." As I surveyed the porch, I noticed Ellen and Gavin strolling over from Ellen's front yard.

Bernadette's eyebrows drew together over her nose. "I see the mystery man's still here."

"He's Ellen's cousin," I said mildly.

"Don't believe it. Not a speck of resemblance between them, and there's just something . . ." Bernadette snapped her mouth shut as Gavin bounded up the porch steps. She gave him a mumbled *hello*, which was echoed, in much more gracious tones, by Ophelia.

"Good afternoon, ladies," Gavin said, his gaze lingering on Ophelia so long that Bernadette shot him a sharp glance.

"Yes, hello," Ellen said, as she joined us on the porch. "I know Julie and Scott are coming." She looked everyone over, her blue eyes bright. "Who else are we expecting?"

"Pete and Sandy, but I wouldn't be surprised if they're a little late." I unstacked some plastic cups and arranged them around a pitcher of ice water. "The café's open until two, and I'm sure they have a lot of clean-up after closing." I turned to face my guests. "Help yourselves to hors d'oeuvres and snacks. There's water on the table, but also wine, beer, and soft drinks in the cooler on the floor."

"A beer sounds good," Gavin, sliding past me to reach the cooler, cast me a searching glance. "Can I get you one, Charlotte?"

"Not a beer drinker," I confessed. "But I wouldn't mind some wine."

"I'd like a beer," Ellen said.

Gavin pulled a can of chardonnay from the cooler along with a bottle of beer and handed them to Ellen and me before grabbing a beer for himself. "Anyone else?" he asked. "There are some sodas, if you prefer that."

"Think I'll stick with water." Bernadette crossed to the table. "Better for my girlish figure," she added, fixing Gavin with a challenging stare. "What is it you do again, Mr. Howard? I can never remember."

"Gavin," he said, twisting the lid of the beer in one swift motion. "And I'm a freelance researcher."

"That pays well enough to live on these days?" she asked, as she poured water into one of the plastic cups. "You want water too, Fee?"

"No, I'll take wine," Ophelia said. "And Bernie, please stop badgering. Gavin isn't required to tell you the story of his life." She beamed as Gavin handed her one of the chilled cans of wine. "Don't pay her any mind. My sister is rather nosy, I'm afraid."

"It's all right." Gavin's smile brought color to Ophelia's cheeks. "I expect she's just protective of her family and friends. There's nothing wrong with that."

As he moved away from Ophelia, I studied Gavin for a moment, realizing once again how easily he could blend in with any crowd. *A seemingly ordinary man,* I thought, *but one involved in an extraordinary career. Which makes him interesting, if not a trifle disconcerting.*

Bernadette settled in the rocker next to her sister as Julie and Scott climbed the front porch steps and joined the party. They were followed by Sandy and Pete, who were still wearing their café uniforms—Dancing Dolphin logo T-shirts and khaki shorts.

A few minutes later, once all the guests had chosen their preferred drinks and some snacks and taken their seats, I crossed to the railing and turned to face the group. "I'm sure you're all anxious to hear what's going on with the Lisette Bradford case, which is one reason I wanted to bring everyone together today. So let me fill you in, direct from the authorities—I got a call from Detective Johnson this morning and she brought me up to date."

I shared the information the detective had provided, adding, "Amanda Nobel left this morning. Of course, she was cleared of any involvement, as was Roger Warren."

"I assume they're still holding Billy Bradford on the trespassing charge?" Scott asked.

"I didn't ask about that, but I assume so, although I guess he could've made bail. Obviously, given Harper Gregg's confession, he's no longer a murder suspect."

"To be honest, I feel a little sorry for the guy." Julie leaned against the arm Scott had draped over the back of her chair. "I know he behaved foolishly, but I think he really did love Lisette. I mean, that's why he was so determined to track down Roger when he thought Roger was the culprit."

"Stalking is a weird way to show love," Ellen said dryly before taking a swig of beer.

I eyed her, surprised at her choice of beverage. Which was silly, of course. Nothing Ellen did should surprise me anymore.

The conversation swirled around the topic of Harper's capture and confession for a few minutes, before drifting into a more general discussion of murder.

"I know we read stuff for the book club involving killing and other types of violence, but I never thought we'd see two murders in Beaufort in as many years," Sandy said.

"It isn't what you'd expect," Scott said. "Although the history of the region does include its fair share of death." He lifted his hand in a what-can-you-do gesture. "Wars, pirates, land disputes. It's not as if this area has always been the most peaceful place on Earth."

"I suppose that's true," Ellen said. "There's Fort Macon, for instance. It's seen more than one battle over the years."

Bernadette crossed her stocky legs, hiking up her plaid Bermuda shorts. "Isn't that like most places? Everyone chooses to think they're isolated from danger, but it isn't really true. Wherever you have people, power struggles, and passion . . ." She allowed this thought to hang in the air as she pushed off from the floor and sent her chair rocking.

"Oh dear, I don't know if I like that idea. I'd hate to think I'm constantly living in harm's way, especially in my own hometown," Ophelia said, punctuating her words with a dramatic shudder.

Gavin's gaze was focused on Ophelia. "I'm sure you aren't in any danger, Ms. Sandburg," he said.

"Are you?" Ellen, sitting on one side of him, while I sat on the other, muttered this under her breath.

"Yes," he replied, in a quiet voice only she and I could hear.

"Well, I say we propose a toast," Pete said, holding up his can of wine. "To no more murders in Beaufort."

Everyone lifted a bottle or can to that, with Sandy saying "Amen" after we all repeated the toast.

Ellen then cleverly directed the conversation elsewhere—to a lively lecture on the pirate history of the area, led by Scott. As the ensuing discussion wound down, Ophelia and Bernadette begged off, saying they needed to go home to start dinner. They were followed by Pete and Sandy, who confessed they were exhausted due to their busy day at the café.

Scott pulled a comical face as the Nelsons hurried off. "Looks like my erudition had the usual effect—chasing everyone away."

"I doubt that," Gavin said, as he rose to his feet. "In fact, I think I'm going to have to buy that book of yours."

"Just happen to stock it at my bookshop," Julie said, with a grin.

Gavin tapped his empty beer bottle against his palm. "Yes, but I'm afraid I'm leaving town tomorrow."

"I have a website." Julie dug into her small purse and pulled out a business card. "All the info's on here. You can order online, and I'll ship the book anywhere." She leapt out of her chair and crossed to him. "And if you want, I can keep your address on file for future orders." She cast me a swift glance.

"That might be a bit of a problem," Gavin said as he took the card.

Meeting Julie's mischievous gaze, I gave a little shake of my head. "He lives on his boat."

"Really? How exciting." Julie turned back to Scott. "Don't you think that sounds romantic, dear?"

"I think it sounds like someone who doesn't want to be tracked down," Scott said mildly. He gave Gavin a wink. "Hiding from the Feds or something? Or just escaping a few ex-wives?"

"Really, Scott." Julie placed her hands on her hips. "Not everyone appreciates your goofy sense of humor."

"It's fine." Gavin strolled over to the console table and set down his empty bottle. "I'm sure my lifestyle seems a little odd to most."

And they don't know the half of it, I thought, but said, "It's not for everyone, but if it suits you, I think that's fine."

Gavin looked me over. "Not something I'd expect you'd want, though."

I met his intent gaze with a lift of my chin. "I like having a home."

"Speaking of home," Scott said, standing to join Julie. "Perhaps we should be heading there, sweetheart? I have that fillet I was planning to grill for dinner."

"Ah, the grill master at work." I flashed Scott a smile before hugging Julie. "Run along, I'll give you a call soon."

"Maybe we can do lunch sometime this week? I recall you saying you don't have any guests," Julie said, as they crossed to the steps

"Maybe. The truth is, I'm thinking about heading out of town for a few days later this week. It's a good opportunity to visit my parents. Not sure of the timing yet. I'll let you know more when I finalize my plans."

Julie shot me a questioning look but turned aside without saying anything when Scott threw his arm around her shoulders and led her away from the porch.

"I should be going too," Ellen said as she watched Scott and Julie depart. "Shandy will need a walk soon. Thanks, Charlotte." She laid a hand on my arm for a moment. "Feel free to stop by soon so we can catch up on all the details concerning the murder investigation and . . . everything," she added, with a swift glance at Gavin. "You coming?"

"In a minute." Gavin pressed one palm against the top of the console table. "I just thought . . . Well, I wouldn't mind another beer, if it's okay with Charlotte."

"Alright. Come by when you're done." Ellen stared at him, her expression unreadable. "You told me earlier that you were going to spend the night on the boat, then leave in the morning. Which is fine, but I'd appreciate a more formal goodbye."

"At your command," Gavin said, giving her a sketchy salute.

Ellen pursed her lips. "I'm not your superior."

"Oh, I think you probably are," he replied, with a sardonic smile. "But yes, I promise to stop by your house before I head to the harbor."

Ellen sniffed and muttered something about *snippy youngsters* before turning to me with a brilliant smile. "See you soon, dear," she said.

She marched down the steps and over to her house, her head held high.

"So, off duty this week?" Gavin asked, as he fished another beer out of the cooler.

"For once. It doesn't happen often. Not in the summer months, anyway." I brushed my fingers through my hair, shoving it behind my ears. "Of course, I shouldn't be happy about that. I don't make any money when I don't have guests."

"But I suspect right now you don't mind." Gavin took a sip of the beer, his eyes focused on my face.

"I'm actually happy for the break. You have to admit, it's been a pretty crazy week."

"Hmm . . . Not that strange for me, but I suppose your life is usually less dramatic."

"Thankfully, yes." I walked over to the porch railing and stared out toward the street.

"You could use something to calm your nerves."

I turned to find Gavin standing right behind me. He must've set the bottle down, as his hands were empty.

I pressed my back into the rail as we made eye contact. Gavin's eyes were glittering with amusement and something else I couldn't name. *Or don't want to,* I thought, forcing myself to maintain a calm tone. "Such as?"

"Evening boat ride?"

"Excuse me?" There was no preventing the slight squeak raising my voice.

"I was thinking I should take the boat out this evening, just to check everything before I set out on a longer trip." Gavin moved in closer. "I wouldn't mind company."

"Before you sail off into the sunset?"

"Not really possible, unless I head to Panama, but metaphorically speaking"—Gavin pressed his palm against the side of my face—"yes."

I turned my head slightly, forcing him to drop his hand. "A short jaunt, just like the other day?"

"But without the annoying discussion of past transgressions and contract killers."

I looked back into his eyes. "Just a sail to enjoy the beauty of the sea and sky?"

"And the stars," he said, his smile brilliant as those heavenly bodies. "You should see the stars from the water, Charlotte. It's magical."

"In that case, I think I'll say yes." I straightened, pulling away from the railing to stand without support. "I could use a little magic in my life."

"Couldn't we all?" Gavin said.

I examined his face for a moment. "So I guess I'll see you later, at the boat."

"Seven o'clock. Don't be late," Gavin said, as he stepped back and walked over to the table to retrieve his beer.

"Would you sail off without me?" I asked, keeping my tone light.

Gavin smiled and saluted me with the brown bottle. "No. But why cut a fine evening short with avoidable delays?"

"Especially since it's your last night here," I said, growing bolder as this realization hit me. *Nothing to worry about,* I told myself. *There won't be any complications. He'll be far away tomorrow.* "You'll be gone after that."

But Gavin's next words sent my thoughts spiraling again. *Not necessarily,* I admitted, *in a bad way.*

"For now," he said. "But I do know how to find my way back."

Acknowledgments

I offer my sincere thanks to—

My wonderful agent, Frances Black of Literary Counsel.

My talented and supportive editor, Faith Black Ross at Crooked Lane Books.

The entire team at Crooked Lane Books, especially: Matt Martz, Jenny Chen, Melissa Rechter, and Madeline Rathle.

Cover designer Ben Perini.

My critique partners and fellow authors, Richard Taylor Pearson and Lindsey Duga.

All of the bloggers, podcasters, Youtubers, and reviewers who have mentioned, reviewed, and boosted my books.

The bookstores and libraries who have acquired, stocked, and promoted my books.

My husband Kevin, my son, Thomas, my mom, and the rest of my family.

My friends, including the online writers' community.

My readers, who make all the work worthwhile.